Mercury in Retrograde

Also by Paula Froelich

It! Nine Secrets of the Rich and Famous That'll Take You to the Top

Mercury in Retrograde

A NOVEL

PAULA FROELICH

ATRIA BOOKS
New York London Toronto Sydney
S

ATRIA BOOKS
A Division of Simon & Schuster, Inc.
1230 Avenue of the Americas
New York, NY 10020

This book is a work of fiction. Names, characters, places, and incidents either are products of the author's imagination or are used fictitiously. Any resemblance to actual events or locales or persons, living or dead, is entirely coincidental.

First Atria Books hardcover edition June 2009

ATRIA BOOKS and colophon are trademarks of Simon & Schuster, Inc.

For information about special discounts for bulk purchases, please contact Simon & Schuster Special Sales at 1-866-506-1949 or business@simonandschuster.com.

The Simon & Schuster Speakers Bureau can bring authors to your live event. For more information or to book an event contact the Simon & Schuster Speakers Bureau at 866-248-3049 or visit our website at www.simonspeakers.com.

Designed by Nancy Singer

Manufactured in the United States of America

10 9 8 7 6 5 4 3 2

Library of Congress Cataloging-in-Publication Data

Froelich, Paula.
Mercury in retrograde : a novel / by Paula Froelich.—1st Atria Books hardcover ed.
p. cm.
1. Women—Fiction. 2. SoHo (New York, N.Y.)—Fiction. 3. Chick lit.
I. Title.
PS3606.R583M47 2009
813'.6—dc22 2009010414

ISBN 978-1-4165-9893-0
ISBN 978-1-4391-0182-7 (ebook)

Mercury in Retrograde

Introduction

When Mercury spins directly between the Earth and the Sun—a condition that astrologers call "Mercury in retrograde"—it appears to the untrained eye looking through a telescope to be hurtling backward. But, in fact, it's moving at the same pace it always does, approximately three times faster than Earth. It's just your perspective that shifts, in the same odd way it changes when the car next to you on the freeway seems to be moving backward as you inch up beside it. And there's the disconcerting feeling that what you think you're experiencing isn't reflective of reality. As even the lowliest $3.99-a-minute fortune teller will inform you, Mercury in retrograde means one thing: if something can go wrong, it will.

Basically, shit just happens.

1

SCORPIO:

With Mercury falling into a particularly difficult retrograde, the best advice for you is to JUST STAY HOME. All communications with senior management are fraught with difficulty, and it is best to keep your own counsel.

Penelope Mercury hadn't meant to quit her job without another one waiting in the wings.

In fact, she hadn't meant to quit at all.

Nor had she meant to set the back photo studio on fire.

And it was a complete accident that she had thrown up all over her boss.

But, well, she had.

That Wednesday started off pretty much like every other day for Penelope, with a harsh six a.m. wakeup call from the notoriously indecisive morning news editor of the *New York Telegraph,* Dan Martman, aka "Martman," who suffered from a severe Napoleonic complex. ("Both 'complex one,' teeny tiny height, and the more nefarious 'complex two,' teeny tiny penis," Penelope had once told her best friend Neal DuBoix. "He's not only short, but Farrah in Business slept with him once and said he's *really* edited for length, you know . . . down there . . .")

Not surprisingly, Martman made up for his indecisiveness and famous shortcomings in volume and ferocity. "Mercury!" he screamed down the early morning line, jolting Penelope out of a deep sleep. "Some asshole got into a fight with his girlfriend and threw her cat out of her fourteenth-floor apartment window in Evergreen Gardens, you know, in the Soundview section of the Bronx. Get the girlfriend, get a picture of the dead cat when it was still an alive cat, and interview the neighbors! Go! Go! Go!"

"Do we have her address?" Penelope asked, grabbing for her bedside notepad and pen as Martman rambled off the number and street of the unfortunate cat lady. "And is she gonna let me in or is this a blind drop-in?" Her nose was running. She leaned over and peeked out of the window. The sky was a heavy, unfortunate color of gray and snow covered the ground. She quickly added, "I'm still kind of sick from doorstepping in Queens during last week's blizzard and today doesn't look like it's gonna be much better."

One of the more unattractive aspects of being a general assignment reporter or "G.A.R." (an acronym pronounced similarly to the sound one made when sent out on assignment to some hellhole)—besides the low pay—was that the GAR spent much of her (its) professional life "doorstepping." This meant standing outside someone's home who may have had something newsworthy (read: terrible) happen to them, waiting for him or her to come in or out so as to grab a quote or a picture, while evading fists, snarling dogs, and curses and simultaneously trying to jam one's foot in the door before it closed and locked indefinitely. Doorstepping could take hours and you couldn't even move from the spot to go to the bathroom, because if you missed your target and God forbid someone from the *Post* or the *Daily News* got them instead of you, your ass was Martman grass.

"Who fucking cares if there's a storm? It's your goddamn job!" Martman yelled into the phone.

Before Martman could hang up on her or work himself into more of a lather, Penelope tried to ask him about the court reporting position that had just opened up, the one she had volubly coveted for five years.

"Well, okay, but did you make a decision on Kershank's job? You said I was the frontrun—"

"Just get the goddamn story!" Martman screamed, cutting her off before hanging up.

Sammy Kershank had given notice a month earlier to go work for *Newsweek*, leaving his job as a Manhattan court reporter tantalizingly open. Penelope, who'd been slaving away under Martman's iron fist, proving herself as a GAR, had been eyeing the position since she'd started at the *Telegraph* seven years earlier.

Penelope sighed. She wanted that job more than anything she'd ever wanted in her life. She pushed play on her CD alarm clock that was shoved into the corner of her bed (alongside her makeshift "desk area" of notebooks, pens, and tissues). "*She works hard for the money,*" Donna Summer belted out, "*so hard for it honey, so you better treat her right—alright!*"

You tell 'em, Donna. Penelope smiled as she hacked out a cough, giving Ms. Summer a mental high five as she threw her slightly yellowed down comforter off and blew her nose in one of the tissues that was tucked in beside the alarm clock.

Penelope had moved to New York in 2002 after four years of struggling through a journalism major at Ohio State University (academia was never her thing), not too far from her hometown of Cincinnati, brimming with dreams of a Pulitzer and all the usual excitement of a recent New York transplant.

She found the tiny three-room rent-stabilized apartment at 198 Sullivan Street between Prince and Houston in the hip area of Soho by calling a number on the front of the building that had read, "Apartments: No Fee." The fourth-floor walk-up was only a thousand dollars a month. More accustomed to Ohio real estate prices, Penelope didn't realize it was a steal. ("I always thought that for a grand a month I'd get a terrace or at least a real bathroom," she'd said to Neal, who'd responded, "Dorothy, you're not in Ohio anymore").

It turned out to be so cheap for New York because the bedroom was small enough that it could fit only a full-sized bed and a dresser—which she'd fortuitously found on the street corner two weeks after she'd moved in. Despite having a few water stains on the top, it was a beautiful cherry wood and worked perfectly. The kitchen sink in the tiny room that held a half-stove and a fridge doubled as the bathroom sink, as the bathroom was actually a series of two closets on either side of the living room—one of which hid a toilet, and the other disguised a shower.

The living room was a misnomer. It was ten feet by ten feet and didn't leave very much room to live in at all. But Penelope had managed to squeeze in a small futon from IKEA (prized for its ability to deconstruct and get through the door more than for any other reason), a glass coffee table, and a small cozy chair that looked like a faux-leather La-Z-Boy but didn't lounge back. On the bright side, coffee drips on pleather could be wiped away like nothing ever happened.

"It used to be an old tenement building, and no one was supposed to have their own bathroom," the old man who was to become her landlord said. "So we made do. But it's got its original tin ceilings and hardwood floors. Don't eat too much in here, though. There are rats in the walls we've been trying to exterminate for years."

Penelope took the apartment immediately, despite the palpable presence of rats and absence of terrace, more out of necessity than anything else, and set about getting a reporting job. After a brief and unhappy internship at a financial weekly that lasted the duration of a single issue, she met someone who knew someone who got her a job as a copy kid at the *New York Telegraph,* a tabloid with headlines like "Kabloomie!" (about American troops bombing poppy fields in Afghanistan) or "I-say-ah You're Fired!" (about Isaiah Thomas being dismissed from the Knicks after losing a sexual harassment case against a coworker he'd continually referred to as a "bitch").

Two years later Penelope was promoted from copy kid—where basic duties included getting coffee for any editor who felt thirsty and lazy (basically, all of them), collecting packages from the messenger center, running errands, and sorting mail—to general assignment reporter. She was a great GAR. She'd go anywhere, do anything, ask the most ridiculous questions, and could gain almost anyone's trust.

The job had also helped decorate her apartment for free and thus, seven years later, reflected her many travels throughout the boroughs of New York. Above her bed was a large Jackson Pollock–esque drip oil painting that Sherry, the homeless woman/artist who'd rescued a dog from certain death off the subway tracks in Chelsea during rush hour ("Bum Ride!" page 12, lead story, September 18, 2002), had pulled from her shopping cart and given to Penelope after Penelope had taken her to lunch during their interview. In the living room there was a small wooden chair in the corner with an embroidered seat cushion that Mrs. Blackstone, who ran a thrift shop in Crown Heights that had been burgled ("Burglar Breaks in Looking for a Steal," page 21, bottom story, April 7, 2005), had sold her at a steep discount. Penelope had received the 1940s Formica kitchen table gratis from the Grubmans, a Coney Island carnie couple—she was the bearded lady, he was the escape artist—who were cleaning out their storage closet as Penelope interviewed them about Mrs. Grubman's beard catching on fire during an unfortunate incident with the flame swallower ("Beard Burn!" page 19, right-hand column, July 25, 2004). And all over the walls and fridge were other collected artwork and personal treasures that Penelope had picked up while on various assignments: a Ghanaian bust from Harlem, an Indian painting of the goddess Shiva she'd gotten during a story in Bellerose, Queens, a watercolor of Athens from Astoria, a tiny Torah from Borough Park, and a kitschy set of Russian nesting dolls she'd gotten as a gift from Olga, a Russian escort from Brighton Beach, after Penelope had convinced the *Telegraph* to pay Olga's bail during the 2006 Russian hooker crackdown in exchange for an exclusive interview ("Mayor Rages: No More Russkie Rent Girls!" the entire front page or "The Wood" as it was known at the paper, February 10, 2006). She'd also given Olga the number of a nearby shelter and a women's support group, but figured Olga probably wouldn't use either.

Besides artwork and furniture, she'd also picked up her best, and pretty much only, friend. She'd met Neal, a chic interior decorator for the city's elite, during a stakeout four years earlier. She doorstepped him during a thunderstorm after his ex-boyfriend, Bernard Bertrand, a dog groomer who'd owned a store called Doggy 'Do and Pussies Too! attempted to burn down the Madison Avenue apartment of Nan Thrice, Neal's society queen client, after Neal broke up with him. The society queen's social standing made her interesting to the paper, but Penelope knew nothing about her. After five hours of sitting on his stoop in the rain, chain smoking under a flimsy black umbrella, Neal had taken pity on her, invited her inside, and given her an exclusive interview. She'd been his "little work in progress" ever since.

His other pet project was a society girl named Lena Lippencrass, and from the stories Neal always told about Lena, she sounded like she could be even more of a project than Penelope. Neal called her "Lipstick Carcrash," for reasons he refused to tell Penelope but which she assumed were due to Lipstick's glamorous job at the fashion magazine *Y* and her unfortunate habit of colliding with any kind of obstacle, be it a step, an errant tree limb, or a man.

"I've seen the entire world by subway," Penelope told Neal. After seven years at the *Telegraph*, she figured she knew one person from almost every community on every block in New York and had probably written about them.

But all the really good, juicy stories were uncovered in the court system. Penelope had refused offers of other beats in hopes of being available once her dream job opened up. She didn't want to get sidetracked. Two years earlier she'd even turned down the transport beat, despite the minor pay increase.

"It would be a lateral move that would take me out of the running for courts forever," Penelope explained to Neal. "The transport guys never advance in the paper. Lou Francis was on it for six years and had a heart attack, Kwani Hadebe was so bored with that beat he *chose* to go back to copyediting, and the only person who went anywhere semi-interesting after working transport was Christine Pride—who left for WKBC to do their traffic updates. She's now known as the 'Car Cutie.'"

The hierarchy at the *Telegraph* was complicated. If you took the right job, you moved up within the paper. If you took the wrong job, you were condemned to that desk forever. Penelope preferred to stay in the GAR pool and still be considered than to sell herself short for an extra five thousand dollars a year, even if that extra five grand would've meant she could stop working the ten hours of overtime a week that ensured Penelope could pay her rent, and maybe have a semblance of a social life.

But holding out for so long was proving to be a tricky game. It was an unwritten rule at the *Telegraph* that if you were in one position for more than five years, you were considered a "lifer" in that specific job. And Penelope, whose five-year clock was ticking, did not want to be a GAR lifer. GAR lifers eventually become "rewrites"—rewriting wire copy and putting in random phone calls to back up the work of the street GARs. While the workload was easier and the chance of being fired without a lawsuit was slim to none, GAR lifers' careers were DOA—no chance of promotion or pay hike. Penelope called them "floaters"—a term she also used to refer to the little bits of poop that refused to flush in the toilet. ("No matter what they do—or don't do—they just keep popping back up.") Penelope lived in terror of a potential GAR-to-floater career trajectory.

So when Kershank gave notice, Penelope began lobbying like her life depended on it for his position, working overtime and even when sick. She'd started dropping by Martman's desk every day at least twice, showering him with compliments ("You look so great today, Martman, did you get a haircut?" "Is that a new cologne? It's amazing"), and peppering him with her knowledge of the court system, picked up from years of watching Court TV and *Law & Order.*

Martman, a man who was more susceptible to flattery than any actual display of court knowledge, seemed open to the idea of Penelope replacing Kershank and just last week said, "You're the front-runner! Now get to Coney Island and get me that midget and his mermaid lover. Now!"

Penelope groaned. It was too early and cold for the Bronx, but she consoled herself with the thought that it was only for a day or two more. She lumbered out of bed to the kitchen sink, where she brushed her teeth and washed her face. She noted her exhausted, disheveled image in the mirror, but decided to take a shower later and put on her "doorstepping" armor. First, long underwear (top and bottom) then a pair of jeans, a T-shirt, and a long-sleeved crewneck sweater, which she layered under a turtleneck sweater and a cardigan. After lacing up her hiking boots, she donned her long pink puffer coat, which Neal had begged her for years to ditch, that made her look like a small pink Michelin man. "Helloooo, gorgeous!" Penelope said to her reflection in the mirror.

Penelope rolled her long, dark blond curly hair into a bun and made a futile attempt to tame the frizzes that were creating a halo around her head. *Good enough!* she thought and danced over to the CD/radio alarm clock, cutting off Donna Summer at *"Lookin' for some hot stuff baby this evenin', I need some hot stuff baby toniiiight!"*

She grabbed her hefty reporter's bag—which carried a notebook, several chewed-up pens, an extra sweater, her purse, and a stick of deodorant—and shut off the apartment lights before making her way out onto Sullivan Street.

The weather had been forecasted as fifteen degrees with a winter storm on the way, but with the wind chill it felt at least twenty degrees colder, and the mixture of snow and sleet blowing perpendicularly into her face made it worse. Shivering, Penelope fought her way against the wind up Sixth Avenue to the West Fourth Street subway station four blocks away. After slipping twice on the stairs leading down to the trains, she finally made it onto the platform and hopped on the A train heading for one of the high-rise buildings in the Evergreen Gardens projects—which was neither green nor surrounded by gardens.

LIBRA:

Mercury, the cosmic trickster, is about to play havoc on your life. Shun making important decisions during this time as some crucial piece of information, or component, has gone astray or awry.

• • •

Fifteen blocks and about twenty worlds away, in a duplex garden apartment in a brownstone on West Twelfth Street, Lena "Lipstick" Lippencrass's alarm clock went off at exactly 7:25 a.m.

Lena yawned, waking from her Ambien-induced slumber with the cool cucumber slices that she had gingerly put on her eyes the night before still in place. She stretched and, slapping off the alarm, dropped the cucumber slices into the Hermés ashtray wedged in between the clock and the crystal block lamp on her nightstand, which also concealed Lipstick's personal items: pens, hair ties, her prescription stash of Ambien, Xanax in a pillbox shaped like a Fabergé egg ("so Kate Moss"), Klonopin—for dire occasions—and the new diet pills Dr. Sachs on East Eighty-fourth had started prescribing to the social set ("They're amazing!" said Lena's mother, Lana Lippencrass. "I lost twenty pounds in two weeks—at that rate you can be practically Somalian by the Met Gala, darling!").

Lipstick fumbled around to the right side of the bed to what looked like the other nightstand's twin but was really a cleverly designed mini fridge that held small bottles of Poland Spring water and more cucumber slices in a bowl of water—freshly cut by Gloria, the maid, who came every Tuesday and Thursday. Opening the fridge, Lipstick grabbed a bottle of water and downed it. Dehydration was a killer.

It was pitch black in her room, thanks to the double-weight drapes that concealed the entire glass wall to the left of the bed, which led to her Parisian-style garden, with the exception of the faint glow from her laptop lying on the pillow next to her head. It was in that exact spot where her ex, Thad Newton III, had laid his disheveled blond, genetically blessed head comfortably for two years until Lipstick saw a photo of him—posted on the socialite gossip website, Socialstatus.com—drunkenly tongue-wrestling with her nemesis, Bitsy Farmdale. She'd dismissed him instantly after seeing that distressing Web post eight months ago, and the right side of the bed had been empty of human content ever since.

While she had dated Thad for two years, Lipstick had known him for almost a decade. And it was because of him that she'd been given her unusual moniker by her dearest friend, Neal, whose father Dennis had been close friends with Lipstick's father, Martin, since their Harvard days.

Lipstick had been on summer break between her freshman and sophomore years at Princeton and had just gotten her driver's license at the ripe old age of twenty. She'd been driving Neal out to the Hamptons in her mother's BMW, where they'd planned to spend the weekend dining at Sant Ambroeus, playing tennis and going to cocktail parties. Lipstick was, in particular, excited about Nelly Hooper's beach barbecue later that evening where she was hoping to see Thad Newton III, whom she'd spent the previous weekend flirting with.

"He's already called twice to make sure I'm coming!" Lipstick said gleefully, not paying particular attention to the road. "But I think Bitsy may have gotten her claws into him first."

"Now, who is he again?" Neal asked, buckling his seat belt as Lipstick veered onto the shoulder of the Long Island Expressway for a moment before correcting the wheel. "Didn't he come from Rhode Island?"

"He's perfect," Lipstick said, taking Exit 70 to get to Montauk Highway. "He's a banker at J.P. Morgan, lives on the Upper East Side—west of Park Avenue—went to Dartmouth, his family owns the biggest house in Newport and a cottage in Provence, and he's texting me! Can you believe it?"

"He almost sounds like your father. I'm sure your mother is excited," Neal said, smirking.

"Excited? Why do you think she let me drive her car out? I told her all about him and said the only way we'd make it to

Nelly's in time was to drive—otherwise we'd be on the Jitney with the rest of the serfs." Lipstick licked her lips. They were dry. "Neal honey, will you pass me my lipstick? I need to refresh."

Neal reached back behind the driver's seat and grabbed Lipstick's Gucci tote. Rummaging through it he found her Revlon Super Lustrous Lipstick and quipped, "Slumming it with Revlon, huh? What happened to the MAC Viva Glam I gave you?"

Ignoring him, Lipstick grabbed the makeup and, disregarding traffic, artfully reapplied the color to her lips while looking in the rearview mirror. All would have been fine had that damn curve in Route 27—which Lipstick swore she knew by heart—not appeared out of nowhere. As she was putting on her final touches to her bottom lip, the BMW ran off the road into the guardrail, and Lipstick's lipstick smeared across her face, a graphic war wound. It was truly a Lipstick Carcrash—a name Neal had lovingly called her ever since, but which Lipstick had forbade him to tell anyone else the provenance of.

Neal, laughing hysterically, had pulled some facial cleansing cloths from her purse and cleaned Lipstick up enough that she looked almost normal. Meanwhile, the damage to the car was fairly superficial and Lipstick still made it to Nelly's just in time to see Thad whisper sweet nothings in Bitsy's ear.

Lipstick hadn't seen Thad for several years after that incident until she ran into him at the American Museum of Natural History's winter gala. By then Bitsy was out of the picture and Lipstick was back in for the next two years.

"I should have paid more attention," Lipstick later grumbled to Neal. "The universe was trying to warn me off him the first time around."

Lipstick opened her laptop, and the screen immediately went from the hazy blue of sleep mode to Socialstatus.com, which she'd been reading prior to falling asleep. The main page was a scroll of photos and captions—the one she'd been obsessed with the night before was a picture of Bitsy with Thad at the Newton family's New Year's Eve gala in Rhode Island. Lipstick clicked on the photo (caption: "Cutest Power Couple Ever???") to read the comments, from the supportive ("Bitsy is the new Aerin Lauder. All class and beauty") to the snide ("If she wants a ring so badly, she should have taken note of Mrs. Newton's dress code for the evening: Rhode Island preppy, not New York formal") to the outright nasty ("Someone should tell Bitsy Thad likes bank accounts, not women. Rhode Island is scruffy old money—but it hasn't appreciated well. He's only with her because LL dumped him. And LL's daddy is worth more—*definitely* the BBD: Bigger Better Deal between those two").

Lipstick always felt dirty after reading the website, which was run by two mean queens in San Francisco, but over the years it had come to rule young New York society. Everybody liked to see pictures of themselves, and unlike the society magazines, *Avenue, Quest,* or *Town & Country,* viewers could comment on the photos and spill gossip, however nasty or untrue it was. And best of all—the young up-and-coming socialites could rank themselves, creating a tangible popularity game, keeping them forever—no matter how old—in high school.

Lipstick took a deep breath and clicked refresh on the website to see that week's results: Bitsy Farmdale was first. Lipstick was sixth.

Disappointed, Lipstick shut the laptop, sighed, and took one last cuddle underneath her thousand-count Frette sheets before hopping out of the king-sized bed she'd specially ordered from the Four Seasons Hotel. She ambled across the white Persian carpet covering the ebonized fishbone floors and, opening the drapes, momentarily blinded herself with the light. She stumbled backward into one of the two nailhead chairs that framed the fireplace, stubbing her toe.

Beyond the nailhead chairs was the creamy limestone bathroom, complete with a "rain room" shower with two oversized ceiling nozzles, a limestone bench, and steam capability. There was also a large egg-shaped limestone tub and a double sink along a mirrored wall.

Not bad, Lipstick, in red Juicy sweatpants and a tank top, thought, eyeing her image in the mirror. Despite eating shellfish last night, her eyes weren't as puffy as she'd thought they'd be. Best of all, her ass didn't seem to have been affected by the dinner with her *Y* magazine coworkers during which she had succumbed to all five courses at Daniel and endured their uncomfortable stares and whispers for the entire meal. "You're really going to chub out this time," Muffie Dinklage, the senior fashion editor, whispered to Lipstick over her soufflé.

But that hadn't happened. Yet. She wasn't exactly thin, per se, but Lipstick was an Amazonian blue blood. She wasn't fat, just big boned, and being five feet, ten inches—over six feet in heels—didn't help. But she did try to stay in shape by dabbling with Pilates or Cardio Funk—whatever was in that particular month—and made it to Sally Brindle's yoga workshop on Broome Street in Soho at least once a week. Lipstick loved Sally, who was not just a yoga teacher, but had, over the years, become a friend and she showed Lipstick how to help maintain her body without starving herself. Had Lipstick devoted her life to the method study of anorexia like some of her Spence schoolmates, she could have modeled. Lipstick was classically beautiful with big brown eyes and full lips. Her prominent nose fit her face and hadn't been chopped down by Dr. Dan Baker, as had the noses of most of the socialites she knew. Her sandy brown hair fell below her shoulder blades in a long, layered Gisele Bundchen way that was artfully streaked blond by Rita Starnella of the Warren Tricomi Salon every month.

Not that her father, Martin Lippencrass, or her mother, Lana, who was the current president of the Daughters of the

American Revolution, would have let her model. "Just look at those tacky Hearsts." Lana had gasped upon picking up *Harper's Bazaar* one day and seeing Lydia Hearst—the strawberry-blond publicity-seeking granddaughter of William Randolph Hearst—on the cover. "Have they no shame? Her grandfather is rolling in his grave right now. She's not even doing it for charity!" Besides, Lipstick wouldn't have been able to do it anyway. An innate insecurity and inability to sit still would have stopped any modeling career in its tracks. In all of the Lippencrass family photos, Lipstick's shoulders were slightly hunched to cover up her height, and she was always biting her lip or the inside of her cheek when she should have been smiling.

Lipstick glanced at her watch. She needed to get going. Today was meeting day.

After her shower Lipstick went into the walk-in closet, a former third bedroom that now housed her clothing collection. It was packed with the thousands of dresses, skirts, jeans, pants, blouses, purses, and shoes Lipstick had lovingly compiled over the years. Behind the door hung a Polaroid camera and a quilted bulletin board covered with photos of Lipstick in various outfits. Every Thursday at noon sharp, Jack Marshall, the imposing owner/editor/publisher of *Y* magazine, held an editorial meeting—insisting his staff forgo lunch, which he felt helped them lose extra weight (and, according to Jack, *everyone* could stand to get rid of a few pounds)—and God help you if you were dressed in something twice, or worse, something he despised. Last week, the Polaroid showed she'd worn a black Comme des Garcons dress with Manolo heels and a red Versace purse to the meeting. In the margin of the Polaroid was a note saying, "J hates red purse. Ditch." The offending bag was now in the back of the closet with last season's Prada.

After racing through several clothing racks and shoe shelves, Lipstick finally chose a pair of black wool Gucci pants, a brown

Gucci sweater, a cream Calvin Klein blouse, a pair of black patent leather Dolce & Gabbana heels, and a Marc Jacobs patent leather satchel.

She snapped a quick Polaroid of her outfit in the bathroom mirror, ran out of the apartment, and caught a cab to the offices of *Y* magazine.

> **SCORPIO:**
> Mercury wreaks havoc with your senses . . . and sinuses. All business should be put on hold as nothing is bound to get done anyway.

Round about that time, at approximately 8:30 a.m., Penelope popped out of the subway onto the Bronx streets like a large, layered, pink jack-in-the-box. Sweating from the heat of the subway and the effort of dragging her bag up three flights of stairs, the second she hit the fresh, subzero air above ground, she felt a chill as her perspiration began to freeze. For a quick, hot second, she wished she had taken her father's advice to become a certified public accountant.

Her morning soundtrack was still playing in her head, tunes now courtesy of Foreigner. "*You're as cold as ice, you're willing to sacrifice our loooove . . .*"

By the time she reached the building—a particularly rundown high-rise in a sea of structures that had all seen better days—the weather improbably managed to get worse ("*You want paradise, but someday you'll pay the price, I knoooow . . .*"). And no one seemed to be home in apartment 14B, much to her dismay.

This is not a good sign. But I'll be in courts soon. In a nice, dry courtroom, miles away from Martman and paragraphs away from the front page . . . I'll wait out that cat woman if it takes me all day. I'll even interview the dead cat if I have to . . .

The wind whipped up the clouds and, as Penelope shivered under the minuscule concrete canopy of the high-rise waiting for the dead cat lady to emerge from her apartment or even answer her buzzer, sleet continued to blow sideways, straight into her face.

Across the street, in the cozy confines of his once silvery blue but now fully rusted 1989 Honda Civic, was Bert Salvino, the staff photographer who'd been sent to meet her and get pictures of the former cat owner or any neighbors who would talk about how wonderful the dead cat was or how horrible the now ex-boyfriend was. Bert, a forty-two-year-old with a greasily sparse comb-over who smelled like he hadn't bathed since 1996, was sitting in his aesthetically crappy but warm and dry hatchback. The car only had one seat—the driver's seat. Bert hated everyone—especially "dickhead reporters"—so much that he'd ripped out all of the other seats so that he, legally, wouldn't be able to chauffeur anyone else, anywhere, ever.

Bert was always sent as a last resort. His refusal to get out of his car meant that he almost always missed the shot—and when he did get it, it was inevitably blurry. He should have been fired, but he was on disability. After 9/11, which Bert and every other photographer and reporter at the paper had been sent to cover, Bert had claimed that he'd tripped over a part of the fallen towers, busting his knee. Six years later he was still complaining and filing for disability every few months, despite perfect X-rays and several newsroom eyewitness accounts that he had never actually gotten closer to Ground Zero than Canal Street, about fifteen blocks north of where the twin towers had once stood.

When she saw Bert's car parked in front of the high-rise, Penelope called Martman to question the paper's choice of photographer for the day, enraging him even further. "Listen, I can't stand the guy either, but you try and fire a disabled guy—I'd have a lawsuit on my ass in a second," Martman screamed. "And besides, he's all we got—there was a triple homicide in Midtown, so stop bitching and get me that fucking cat lady!"

Two hours and three inches of snow later, there was still no sign of life from the building and no one in 14B was answering the buzzer, which Penelope had been dutifully pressing with one frozen finger every five minutes, conserving body heat and warmth by only moving her arm from the elbow, like a garden gnome with one working finger.

At 10:35 a.m., just as a thin layer of ice was forming on the outside of Penelope's coat and she was morphing from small Michelin man to large strawberry Sno-Cone, Martman called again.

Penelope couldn't feel her frostbitten fingers but somehow fished her phone out of her coat pocket and pushed talk.

"Mercury!" said Martman. "Cat lady is in Queens! Get there now!"

"B-b-but," Penelope protested, "I h-h-have b-b-been here f-f-for two hours already—"

"Mercury, stop complaining! It was a cock-up on our end. Just get me the cat lady! Now!" And after rattling off the new address in rapid-fire, Martman hung up on her.

A near-frozen Penelope waddled over to Bert's Honda and knocked on the windshield.

Bert, reclining in the Civic in a summery outfit of T-shirt and jeans, topped only by a thin, zip-up fleece jacket, leaned over and grudgingly rolled the street-side window down an inch. He was on the phone and ignored her. Penelope was mesmerized by the heat emanating from the inch of open window. It was smelly heat, but it was still heat. She stuck her fingers on the rim of the pane to try and get any part of her body warm as she leaned in to shout through the open slot.

"B-b-bert," Penelope stammered, "w-w-e have t-t-to go to Queens—"

"Yeah, I know," Bert said as he hung up his phone, "just got the call. See you there." And with that, he rolled up the window, put the Honda in drive, and peeled off.

"I hope you b-b-break down on the T-t-triboro Bridge!" Penelope screamed after the disappearing car, before picking up her bag and trudging back to the subway.

Penelope's cough had worsened, and she began to wonder if she might have pneumonia. *I should have just taken a sick day,* Penelope thought. *I'm going to end up on a stretcher in Saint Vincent's.* She popped her last two Advil in the train station, got on the A train going downtown, and at Forty-second Street switched to the 7, the local to Queens.

> **SAGITTARIUS:**
> As Mercury swings around, get ready to deal with things you have put off in the past. It will not be pleasant, but necessary.

As Penelope made her way to Queens, Dana Gluck, who, up until that very moment, was well on her way to making her monthly quota in billable hours as a junior partner at Struck, Struck & Kornberg, was forced to unbutton the skirt of her favorite Armani suit, thanks to the twenty pounds she'd put on virtually overnight. To make matters worse, an hour into her fifteen-hour workday, Merck & Co., Inc., her biggest client—worth more than ten million dollars in annual revenues to her firm—informed her that it had been poached by the wily rival law firm, Krath & McGowan. And then, just as Dana was contemplating what diet plan she would utilize for lunch, the phone rang.

"Dana, are you sitting down?" said Ruth Gluck.

"Yeah, Mom." Dana sighed. "What's up?"

"I just ran into Noah's mother at Kroger."

"Oh, great. How is she?"

"She's pregnant."

"Huh? She's like seventy!"

"No. *She* is."

Dana's face went numb and her hand fell from her ear, dropping the phone onto the desk with a clatter. Something started buzzing loudly in her ears, and she could feel the bile rise from her stomach. Evya. That bitch. The mere suggestion of her ex-husband's new wife knocked the wind out of Dana.

"Dana? Dana? Hello? Dana?" her mom's voice squawked through the other end of the line.

Dana ran out of her office so fast she knocked her assistant down and barely made it into a stall in the Struck, Struck & Kornberg bathroom, where she sat on the toilet seat with her head in her hands, tears silently splashing onto her two-inch black patent leather Manolo Blahnik pumps.

SCORPIO:
All methods of communication will be flawed, giving rise to personal misunderstandings.

An hour later Penelope exited the subway in Long Island City. The second she hit fresh air—and cell service—her phone beeped, full of messages. The first was from her mother. "Penelope, it's your mother . . . you haven't called me or your father back in a *week*. We are concerned. I mean, we could be *dead,* or *dying* and how would you know? You wouldn't! We'd just be here, in Ohio, decomposing . . ." Penelope sighed and pressed delete.

The next message was also from her mother. "And another thing. Are you dating anyone? You're not getting any younger you know—you're twenty-eight! Did you get the article I sent you on harvesting your eggs? You should think about freezing . . ."

Again, Penelope pressed delete. She was freezing enough out in the street, and dating had never been easy for her. Since she'd been in New York, she hadn't had much free time and the few men she'd dated had hardly been memorable. Last year she'd even tried Match.com, which had introduced her to Tony, a balding energy trader who had an annoying penchant for high-fiving everyone within earshot every time he made what he thought was an interesting comment ("Yo, that dude looks like a lady—high five!" or "Duke guys do it best—high five!"). After high-fiving a guy, he would usually follow it up with a belly bump, a move Penelope referred to as the "sumo."

Their first date had been woeful, but Penelope had decided to give Tony another chance as he'd promised he'd take her to Da Silvano, a trendy and pricey restaurant by her house that she couldn't afford. He'd lied. Instead, Tony had taken her to a sports bar in Midtown to watch the Yankees beat the Red Sox, where he'd gotten so excited, he'd not only high-fived her ("Yeah! Yankees rule! High five!") he'd sumoed her and Penelope flew halfway across the room and landed on her ass ("It's not even post-season!" Penelope said as nearby bar patrons helped her to her feet). She'd called it quits after that, fearing permanent sumo-inflicted damage.

The last three calls were from Martman: "Mercury! Abort cat lady mission, she already talked to the *Daily News* and the *Post.* We need you down on Wall Street—some asshole's been selling World Trade Center rubble for five dollars a pop, like it's the Berlin Wall or something."

Next message: "Mercury? Mercury? Helloooo . . ."

Final message: "Mercury! Where the fuck are you? I've been trying to call you for an hour now. This is not funny! Get over to Wall Street *now*!"

Penelope sighed. If she'd felt any better she might have called Martman back and possibly demanded to use one of her three personal or ten vacation days. But two things held her back. First, a minor case of Stockholm syndrome, whereby she had grown accustomed to the abuse flung at her and instead of loathing her tormentor, was willing to jump through flaming hoops of fire to try to please him. And second, she really needed to impress him right now in order to secure Kershank's job. Otherwise, she was doomed.

Still huddling away from the driving snow in a doorway in Queens, Penelope spied Ahmad Musharif's corner bodega shining like a friendly beacon in the blizzard and ran for it. Ahmad's bodega was right by the main subway line in Long Island City, a hub to the rest of Queens, and she visited every couple of months. She entered the store and waved to Ahmad before searching for tissues, a bottle of water, and some Tylenol for the fever. As Penelope dialed Martman back, an overwhelming sense of Sisyphean dread enveloped her. *What's next?* Penelope thought. *Staten Island?*

"Mercury! Jesus Christ! Where the fuck have you been?" Martman bellowed when he answered. "The Daily Snooze and the *Post* got the cat lady in Brooklyn, the World Trade Center asshole has already been processed at central booking, and half the city is being shut down due to this storm and you go missing for hours. What the hell is going on? Where are you—Bert's been back in the office for half an hour!"

"I'b id Queens." Penelope sniffed. "Where you told be to go."

"Over an hour ago!" Martman shrieked.

"I was on the subway," Penelope said while digging through her tote bag to pay Ahmad for her stash of medicinal relief. "I couldn't get here eddy faster. Bert wouldn't let be id his car."

"What the fuck are you saying? I can't even understand you!" Martman said.

"Sorry. I'b sick again," Penelope said, sneezing.

"Well, just get back here! We need you in the office now!"

"Okay," Penelope said, wiping her nose on her jacket sleeve. "But I bay habe to leabe early cuz I don't feel so well."

"I had five people call out sick. You want Kershank's job, then you'll leave when your shift is over; now get in here!" Martman hung up.

Penelope sighed and dropped the phone from her ear, hanging her head like a sad, sick pink snowman.

"Madame Penelope," Ahmad said from behind the counter, "you do not look so good. You should not be out in this weather. Perhaps you should go home. How is your mother?"

"Thangs." Penelope sniffled before opening the water bottle and downing the two Tylenol from the paper pocket. "She's ogay . . . I'll fill you in lader, but I hab to go bag to the office now. By boss is a liddle crazy."

"Yes, yes," Ahmad said, nodding his head. "I could hear him from here. He does not sound like a stable man. You should not listen to him. Every time you come in here he is yelling at you over the phone."

"That's what eberybody says," Penelope said, forcing a laugh. She picked up her bag and, swinging it back onto her shoulder, took a deep breath and said somewhat cheerily, "But I'm gedding a promotion to Manhattan court reporter, so it's ogay!"

"Oh, congratulations!" Ahmad said, handing her a small Pakistani flag from the register. "Take this for good luck!"

"Thangs, Ahmad!" Penelope said, shoving the flag in her pocket, "hab a good day. I'll still come visit you when I'm working in courts!" She opened the door which, when she let go too soon, swung back and hit her with gale force smack in the forehead, but thankfully she was just numb enough not to feel it.

2

LIBRA:

Curb your self-indulgence. Take a philosophical tact to tasks at hand.

By noon, as Penelope was desperately trying to get back to the *Telegraph* on West Fifty-seventh Street and Dana was trying not to dissolve into a hysterical mess at work, Lipstick was safely ensconced in *Y*'s weekly editorial meeting in the gleaming white lacquer conference room on the thirty-sixth floor of 535 Madison Avenue. Jack Marshall, the revered editor of *Y*, wearing his new Prada chaps paired with a frilly pirate shirt ("So Galliano," Muffie whispered admiringly), and ankle boots, clapped his hands together and announced: "Everyone. I have succeeded in getting *Y* pulled from the shelves of Walmart, Kroger, and all those other nasty Midwestern places and thus, I think we are finally going to be able to keep our rate base down to forty-five thousand. Which is our *target* as an *elite* fashion magazine. Not any less, not any more. Do you *understand*? We at *Y* are about *quality* not quantity—never forget that! So stop using Gap shirts in our fashion spreads, Muffie. I don't care who they have guest-designing at that hellhole. It is still a Gap shirt!"

Lipstick giggled to Muffie: "Forty-five thousand rate base! *Y*'s subtitle should just be, 'Keep your grubby little hands off our gorgeous magazine!'"

"I don't see anything wrong with that, Lena," Muffie snapped back in a whisper. "Jack is a genius. He knows everything about fashion and our world. You should pay more attention to what he says."

Jack had moved on by then to critique Ashley Winksdale, the beauty editor, whose mother was an Italian princess and father ran the collateralized loan option business for Goldman Sachs. "Darling, you are behind the times!" Jack told her. "Gwyneth has been using snake venom on her face for a *year* now—an entire year! Do you *want* us to look foolish? Everyone knows the big thing now is pig embryo cream—it clears up those horrible lines within days. Not to be harsh, my dear, but you should look into it . . . and not just for the magazine. You're not the pedophile's dream you used to be, you know." Ashley, who swayed and nervously sat on her hands during the tirade, looked like a small child being berated. The fact that Ashley, who wore her straight, dark brown hair in a neat bob with bobby pins holding back her bangs, was only five foot one and insisted on dressing in wool jumpers with white shirts that had rounded collars and puffed sleeves only added to the effect.

After dissecting Ashley, Jack moved his implacable eye counterclockwise around the table to Dean McDonal, the dapper British lord/health editor ("Seriously, another spread on the abs diet thing? I know you're dating that author, but this is ridiculous!"), Sarah VanDart, the wife of an internet entrepreneur/articles editor ("We need to beef up coverage of the San Francisco scene. Can't your husband do anything? Isn't he in charge of the Google or something like that?"), Pansy Bainbridge, whose family had come over on the Mayflower and who was currently *Y*'s managing editor ("The expenses here are out of control. Daily trips to Swifty's are not considered source meetings"), Summer Holstein, Jack's goddaughter/photo editor ("Genius job, darling. But perhaps next time you could pick a cover photo that didn't look like a Sears ad?"), and so on down the line. With each critique, the target's face would freeze in a mask of terror, relaxing only when Jack would move on to focus his laserlike disappointment on the next victim.

"The net worth of this room alone could pay off the debt of not only Africa but Southeast Asia," Lipstick whispered to Muffie, who flipped back her long, pin-straight black hair, sniffed, and said, "Well, that is only *two* small countries, dear. It's not like we work at *Vogue* where they actually pay people." *Y* was not for the under-trust-funded. It was more like a glamorous hobby with benefits: parties, power, and a minor paycheck. At least, that was how Martin Lippencrass, whose patience with his daughter seemed to be waning by the day, viewed it. Upset that he had raised what he liked to call "a trifle" (on a good day) or a "succubus on my wallet" (on a bad), he'd been repeatedly trying to get Lipstick on the phone for over a month, "to discuss your cash flow"—calls she'd been artfully dodging.

As for her actual income, Lipstick wasn't sure how much she actually made. Seven years ago, when she started as a junior society correspondent right out of Princeton at the age of twenty-one, she thought she recalled something like the figure of twenty thousand dollars being bandied about. Now that she was the senior society editor, in charge of all the coverage of any social event anywhere in New York City, she assumed she must have gotten a raise or three, but she had never really paid attention during the meetings about money. As a good aristocrat, money talk always made her uncomfortable. It was gauche. And because her paychecks went straight to her father's accountant, she wasn't quite sure what her actual earned monthly income was. Either way, it was a small drop in the large bucket. Martin

Lippencrass's net worth, according to the annual *Forbes* billionaires issue, hovered around $3.5 billion. Although he'd always sniff and say, upon reading the issue, "That is incorrect."

"Lena!" Jack, whose tirade had finally come full circle around the table, barked.

Lipstick jumped. "Yes?"

"Your coverage of the Whitney Gala and the fall season was superb. But May is going to be tough. It will be war. It seems Nan Thrice's botched face-lift has finally healed and she has come out of hiding. She is chairing the American Ballet Ball *and* the Burkhas for Bahrain gala."

"Bahrain?" Lipstick said. "Why does Bahrain need a charity ball?"

"Do you know how many inappropriately dressed indentured servants there are in Bahrain that need our help?" Jack said. "That, and Nan's niece is dating the prince of Bahrain. Either way. Nan is out and about and back leading the circuit, and Elsie Courter is *pissed*. Elsie has now announced she will chair *three* galas to Nan's two, making the total number of events on the society calendar leading up to and including the ultimate society and fashion event, the Met Gala, in May—which, as you know, is *the* month of black-tie balls—well, that and November, but who's there yet?—a whopping twenty-five black-tie galas. And that's not even counting the smaller functions, which seem to have multiplied like herpes in a Mexican brothel. I hope you are prepared. This is our biggest season yet, and we can't have what happened last year, can we?"

The year before, Lipstick had fallen in love with a beautiful Karl Lagerfeld frock and made the mistake of wearing it to—gasp!—two events, and posing for pictures—horrors!—at both events. The pictures were posted on society websites like Socialstatus.com, and printed in Y, to her supreme embarrassment. And then there was that horrid picture of Lipstick lying flat on her stomach in the Lagerfeld dress at the Cancer Society Benefit after she'd tripped on the hem—or Bitsy Farmdale's carefully placed foot, depending on whom you asked. The photo appeared in the *Telegraph* under the headline: "Recycled Social Carpet." Jack was mortified when he found out one of his employees had made such a "plebian" gaffe and had fumed, "Never—*never*—be caught dead in the same dress twice. *Especially* if you've been photographed. Sometimes I feel as if I'm teaching society standards to a pimply faced teen in Junior Cotillion!"

Back at the meeting, Jack continued, "So, get a good night's sleep for the next few months because come May, you belong to charity!"

Jack took the business very seriously. He lived, breathed, and slept *Y* and considered the social pages, which covered every move and every dress that the women of the world's upper crust made and wore, second only to the fashion. His commitment to fashion and the figures that ruled that world was legendary, and his schedule was regimented to fit that universe. Labor Day was referred to as "that three-day weekend before New York Fashion Week," the Fourth of July was "Parisian couture week," and Christmas and New Year's Eve were simply called "Saint Barth's." If world politicians were outside of the fashion circle, they didn't count. When President Ford—whose wife was "no Jackie Kennedy"—died, Jack sniffed and said, "Bad suits." But fashion figures were an entirely different matter. When Gianni Versace was murdered, Jack's hysteria—and insistence that he heard about it even as Andrew Cunanan's gun was still smoking on the Miami street—earned him the title the Gianni Death Caller.

The title had stuck, not that Jack minded. He was the first person at Y, and thus New York, to learn that Gianni Versace had been shot—despite claims to the contrary that *Vogue* editrix Anna Wintour was the first call on the tipster's phone list ("Fuck *Vogue*," Jack had sneered to Lipstick, "cow pies in Arkansas relate to *Vogue*! Only the true fashion believers get, and I mean really *get,* us").

Several years ago, on Black Tuesday, as it was now known in the office, everyone immediately knew something was wrong. From outside his centrally located Jeffrey Bilhuber–decorated glass office, everyone could see and hear when Jack had suddenly stood up, knocking his Philippe Starck chair over, and shrieked into the phone: "GIANNI! GIAAAAANI!" before collapsing on his desk in a faint.

Jack's two assistants, the Hoover twins, tall blond former Abercrombie & Fitch models, ran in to help him. Several minutes later, after Jack, through ashen lips and rolled-back eyes, had managed to eke out: "Gianni . . . shot . . . . dead . . ." they ran out of the office hysterically crying, pulling at their hair and screaming the news to everyone in 535 Madison like fey Gucci-clad town barkers.

"It was amazing," Lipstick had told Neal once over dinner, eating a forbidden breadstick—"Carbs equal cellulite," was Jack's favorite mantra—"They all fell to pieces. Muffie was hyperventilating for days, Jack had fainting spells for almost a year, and the Hoover twins had to take a week at Calvin Klein's castle in Southampton to get over it. I can't believe we put out a magazine that month. They still mention it in hushed tones and every year wear all black on that day. Well, Muffie wears vintage Versace—but only the stuff designed by Gianni, not that trashy sister."

"Darling," Neal cooed, "for our crowd you can forget September eleventh, Gianni Versace's death—Armageddon!"

After the meeting ended, an hour and a half later, and all of the editors were filing out of the conference room, Lipstick grabbed Ashley and whispered, "I'm taking the afternoon off to do a little B&B—Bergdorf and Barneys. I like to call it 'working in the field.' You wanna come?"

"Sure," Ashley said, "I have to see if Bergdorf is stocking that pig product anyway. Or if they even know about it. Sometimes I think Jack makes stuff up just to screw with me."

"That," Lipstick said with a laugh, "would be *shocking*!"

> **SAGITTARIUS:**
> By putting off what you should have done earlier, you will feel the weight of the burden tenfold. You didn't trust yourself to begin with and listened to what others told you was the right thing to do and it's boomeranged.

It took Dana a little more than half an hour of yogic breathing to calm herself down to the point she could leave the bathroom stall. It took another ten minutes to wash her face, straighten her hair, and finally return to her office.

Once safely inside her glass walls, she pressed her intercom and instructed her secretary, "Hold my calls for the rest of the day, and if you wouldn't mind, could you have the janitors bring up a large garbage bin, please? I have some cleaning to do."

Dana sat back in her ergonomic swivel chair and sighed. She would have to face the drawers.

Her office was sparse, containing only her chair, a dark appropriately legal desk, and two other reception chairs for clients or underlings who needed to be grilled. Other than that, there was nothing but a corporate-approved print on the far wall above the oak-paneled, legal-sized drawers that held all sorts of items, including the one thing she'd been dreading most: her past.

Dana took a deep breath and opened the bottom drawer that had been closed under lock and key for some time and stared at the pictures and mementos that had once lined her desk and decorated her walls. It was time to let them go.

Just a little over a year ago Dana's full name was Dana Gluck

Glickman, and she was happily married—or so she thought—to Noah Glickman, a nice Jewish boy she had met five years earlier while waiting in line to see the Klimt exhibit at the Neue Galerie.

Dana, who'd graduated from Columbia Law School at twenty-four, had just been made a permanent associate at Struck, Struck & Kornberg after toiling for two years as a first- and then second-year associate at the firm and was working 80-hour weeks. The hours were so rough that one colleague of Dana's had come home early one morning after putting in an ungodly 100-hour, seven-day workweek to a note from his wife of three years that read, "Dear Chris: Since we've been married I have seen you a cumulative total of four months, and that includes the few hours you spent sleeping and, incidentally, not fucking me. I've had it. Good-bye. Love, Trish."

But Dana didn't mind. She didn't miss having a social life, and was happy going to work every day. She loved being a corporate litigator, loved trying to get her clients out of trouble and arguing that while, yes, it was reprehensible that perhaps they had dumped millions of pounds of toxins into the Hudson River in the 1970s, there was no actual proof that said toxins were directly responsible for the high rate of breast cancer around the Catskill Region.

And so, five years ago, thanks to the long hours and the stress of making permanent associate, Dana had lost more than sixty pounds. To celebrate her new, svelte hourglass form, she'd splurged at the spring sales at Barneys and Bergdorf, incurring a year's worth of credit card debt. But it was worth it, she decided, after her latest purchases—a pair of three-inch Christian Louboutin shoes and a form-fitting Yves Saint Laurent dress that were 80 percent off—had helped catch Noah's eye.

He was behind her in line at the Neue Galerie on a warm, sunny March day. She noticed him only when he accidentally stepped on her heel as he surged forward with the crowd waiting to get into the new exhibit, breaking a blister she had gotten from the new pair of Louboutins ("I am suffering for glamour," Dana grumbled to her Nigerian coworker and friend, Ifoema Ndekwe).

"Ow!" Dana cried, but when she turned around, her annoyance dissipated. Behind her was the most beautiful man she had ever seen. He was six feet four with black hair, black eyes, tan skin, and a chiseled face, and was dressed like he'd stepped out of a Brooks Brothers catalogue.

"I'm so sorry," the man said. "Are you okay?"

"Oh, um . . . it's okay, I don't need my heel anyway," Dana said with a little laugh.

"You must let me buy you a coffee afterward to make up for this."

Coffee lasted three days.

Dana knew from the moment their first three-day date ended that Noah Glickman was the one. He was Jewish *and* he was from Cleveland.

It turned out that Noah had even graduated from the same high school as Dana, albeit seven years earlier than she. After graduating Harvard summa cum laude he came to New York City to fulfill his capitalistic dream of owning his own apartment and house in East Hampton by the age of thirty-two. He had succeeded at both.

Ostensibly, Noah was a girl's dream come true. A handsome, wealthy investment banker for the tony firm Lazarus & Co., he lived in the penthouse duplex in a brownstone on the Upper West Side that had two decks and a wood-burning fireplace. He was funny and charming and seemed to adore Dana. But there were drawbacks. Noah was extremely competitive. What made him so successful at work made him annoying to Dana's friends. He swam, ran, biked, hiked—he loved almost anything that could be timed and thereby quantitatively prove he was better than everybody else. When Dana met Noah, he was thirty-four, had never been married, and was looking to settle down, if only because "all the guys at the firm are married and you can't get ahead if you're not married to a wife that will schmooze the other wives. Besides, I'm thirty-four. I should have kids soon." Dana had laughed that off. Her friends had not.

After two years of dating, Noah, an avid outdoorsman, took Dana—who hated any travel that didn't involve a made bed—on a camping trip to Maine in mid May. Dana, trying to be the perfect girlfriend, mustered up some fake enthusiasm and said, "Of course I'll go hiking in Maine. It sounds like so much . . . fun."

When she told Ifoema she and Noah were going on a hiking trip, Ifoema started laughing.

"What?" Dana said. "What's so funny? Lots of people go hiking!"

"Yeah." Ifoema snorted. "But you don't. Bring a video camera—I'm *dying* to see the outtakes. Nader once tried to get me to do something like that. I told him to stuff it." Nader was Ifoema's sweet but mostly silent husband, who was also from Nigeria.

"Seriously," Dana said. "I think he might propose this weekend. I will walk to Maine if I have to." By that time she'd been waiting for a proposal for months—ever since Noah slipped a cigar band around her ring finger one night when he picked her up from a work function at 55 Wall Street, cinched it till it fit, and then slipped it back into his pocket. "He was fitting my finger!" she said over the phone to Ifoema later that night.

"Great," Ifoema mumbled, still pissed that Noah had refused to pay his portion of the bar tab a week earlier as "you bet me I couldn't drink that Long Island Iced Tea in one gulp. I did it—you pay!"

And so Dana had gone to hike Acadia National Park during what would later go down as the nastiest weekend in May Maine had ever had.

On the way up to Maine in Noah's Range Rover, Dana put on a CD her yogi friend Sally Brindle made her for the trip, which started off with the Lemonheads singing, "*I lied about being the outdoor type*," and ended with David Allen Coe's "Jack Daniels If You Please."

Noah didn't see the humor or irony in it and opted to listen to Green Day instead.

It snowed the first night they set up camp in Acadia National Park and sleeted the second. Just as Dana, who by that time was coming down with the flu, had given up hope that this was *the* weekend and was just trying to catch up with Noah. As she trudged up yet another mountainside and turned the ridge, she saw Noah, kneeling in the frozen mud.

"Oh baby!" Dana cried, "Are you okay? Are you hurt? Can I help you?"

Noah was fine. And so was the three-carat cushion-cut diamond he slipped on her finger moments later.

A week later, Dana moved out of her Murray Hill apartment and into Noah's penthouse. A year later they got married under a chuppah in her parents' backyard and, after going to Tahiti on their honeymoon, set about finishing another item on Noah's to-do list: trying for a baby.

SCORPIO:

During a retrograde, do not seek promotion or try to change positions. It will only backfire.

Penelope rubbed the lump on her forehead as the West Fifty-seventh Street *Telegraph* elevator chugged its way to the third floor, its old brown carpeting curling up from the corners. The corklike ceiling panels had brown water stains, and the faux-wooden walls were covered with graffiti that read like a nerdy bathroom wall: "Martman deserves a Donkey Punch!" "For a good time call 917-678-4763 (Martman's home number)," and "Don't hate the player, hate the editor"—all next to a metal sign that read: "Security Camera Is On. Defacing Elevators Is Punishable by Law." The security camera's lens had been covered by a wad of gum for the past two years.

The elevator came to a stop, the doors opened, and Penelope stepped out into her own personal Fallujah. The noise was almost deafening. It was lunchtime for the 150 reporters and editors and so, in addition to the constant ringing of phones, the screaming for "copy!" and the news blaring from five television sets hanging over the main news edit desks, there was an undercurrent of munching and the crackling of fast-food wrappers.

The newsroom was an open floor plan of cubicles radiating from their focal point: Martman's desk. To the left of the Martman's desk was the photo editor's area where four or five people scoured the wires and photo sites and sifted through the staff photographers' snaps, looking for the best pictures of the day. Beyond the photo desk sat the pampered feature writers, whose luxury mystified Penelope. There were the movie reviewers ("They get paid to see movies all day! Do you think they get free popcorn too?"), the fashion girls ("How do they afford a Fendi bag on a *Telegraph* salary? And why do they always look immaculate?"), the nightlife reviewers ("Now *they* are smart—they figured out how to eat and drink for free for a living"), and the staff writers who sat in glass offices behind big desks all day in the warm office, making up trends ("Dating Disasters: Avoidable?" "Cork Wedgies Are the New Flats!" or Penelope's personal favorite, "Nudist Colonies: Worth the Embarrassment?"). Features was a Babel of disparate exceptions to traditional newspaper frugality.

Beyond Babel was Siberia, which housed the sports, business, and op-ed sections. Penelope had only been there once, when she was a copy kid and had been forced to deliver a package to the football correspondent, who'd been watching porn-ball—a triple-X-rated football video (which he swore was instrumental to his story of the day) that involved female "football players" and a very well-endowed coach. Penelope had never gone back.

Penelope preferred to stay in the comfortable confines of her turf, which lay to the right of the main edit desks. The newsroom buzzed with reporters, tapping away and yelling into phones, "No, you did not say he was a transvestite! I have it right here in my notes that he was a drag queen" or "Hello, this is Billy Winters, I'm looking for Mr. Shapiro . . . Yes, it seems your son jumped off the Fifty-fourth floor today in his building, can you comment?"

The light khaki walls and the black–and–shit-brown-striped carpeting had been installed to cover up treadmarks but failed to do so—particularly in the area around Penelope's cubicle, which she shared with Thatcher.

The six-by-twelve-foot cubicle, had no walls in between the two desks but there was a clear line of trash, newspapers, and Philly beef and Swiss sandwich wrappers from the deli next door, demarcating Thatcher's territory.

Thatcher was a middle-aged lummox who'd been hired from the *Daily News* a year earlier as a GAR lifer. He was also Martman's cousin and an unapologetic slob. His desk smelled like the Fresh Kills Landfill in Staten Island (where Penelope had once been sent to cover a story about a proposed condo development on the stinkiest property in New York City), thanks to his regular intake of three and a half Philly beef and Swiss sandwiches per diem, and his habit of throwing the final, uneaten half in the general direction of the garbage can underneath his desk. The bits that didn't make it in the can had fermented long ago.

Penelope's desk, by contrast, was starkly empty. There was the ancient computer, a couple of notepads, a few pens, and a picture of her and Neal at Coney Island from the summer before. Penelope needed the space on her desk not only for the mountain of clothes that she shed upon entering the office but, more important, for her oscillating fan, which she positioned so that it would blow the stench emanating from Thatcher's side of the mess away from her.

"Hey, Thatcher," Penelope said, her nose running and forehead throbbing, as she waddled up to her desk.

"Mmmhglmmph bethg," Thatcher muffled through his full mouth.

"Can'd udderstand you." Penelope sniffled, blowing her nose. Again. "Just swallow and thed tell be."

Thatcher swallowed, belched, and said, "Martman wants to meet with us."

"Okay. Whad for?" Penelope asked, unwinding her scarf, stepping out of her pink puffer jacket, and peeling off her hat.

Thatcher dropped his sub, staring at Penelope's head. "Holy shit! What happened to your head? It's all blown up like a big red balloon."

"Thangs." Penelope snuffled, rubbing the area around the bump.

"Yourfsmweatingsmpgh," Thatcher, who had gone back to eating his sub, said with his mouth full.

"Whad?" said Penelope, who began to feel very hot—boiling, really. She took off her cardigan, turtleneck, sweater, and T-shirt, piling them on the metal file drawers behind her computer, leaving only her floral-print long underwear shirt on.

Thatcher swallowed. "You're sweating like a pig."

"Loog who's talkig." Penelope laughed before digging her Marlboro Lights out of her bag and going around the corner to the rarely used back photo studio to smoke an illicit cigarette.

The photo studio was a tiny room hidden in the bowels of the newsroom that was used by several reporters as the illegal smoking shack—hence the yellowed walls that had once been the same light khaki as the newsroom. It was repainted every year but reacquired its sickly shade of yellow in a matter of weeks. Lately management had taken notice after one of the features girls (the self-designated "health reporter") complained about the smoke, and so big signs had popped up all over the door that read, NO SMOKING! SMOKE IN HERE AND YOU WILL BE FINED 10 HOURS OF OVERTIME, and GO OUTSIDE, IDIOTS!

"Too tired and cold to go back outside," Penelope rationalized to herself, ignoring the signs. "Besides, no one ever comes by here. They won't care." She slipped into the yellow room and lit up.

Feeling light-headed—whether it was from the fever or the cigarette, she wasn't sure—Penelope sat down in one of the two industrial metal chairs in the studio and took another drag off the cigarette just as she heard Martman's voice, which could travel through walls. "Mercury! Mercury! Where the fuck are you?"

A wave of nausea swept over her.

Penelope thought about whether she hated Martman and took another puff. He was promoting her, so she supposed he wasn't all bad.

She hoisted herself out of the chair, ground the lit end of her cigarette into the sole of her shoe, threw it in the overflowing trash bin by the door, not noticing that the butt, which had landed on top of a pile of old newsprint, was still lit.

LIBRA:

Bad omens don't always have to be in the obvious form of a black cat. Sometimes they can be blond.

• • •

Lipstick and Ashley finally made it to the Chanel department on the fifth floor of Bergdorf Goodman to shop for seasonal ball gowns. "The most magical place on earth," Lipstick said, sighing.

"I knew Jack made that stuff up about a pig-embryo cream," Ashley said, grouchy after having spent a fruitless thirty minutes scouring the basement beauty department in search of the fabricated product. "Now he's going to make me go to some chemist and have them do something with pig embryos just so he won't be called out as a liar. Maybe he'll just forget about it."

"Probably," Lipstick said, as a sequined dress caught her eye. "Ooooh," she cooed, "look at this one."

"It's only $7,500," Ashley said. She picked up a black-and-white taffeta number with Swarovski crystals detailing the bodice. "And look at this one. It's kind of flappery."

"Oh, that's cute," Lipstick said. "Hold on to it—I'll try it on too."

The girls moved through several departments, picking up dresses and tossing them back ("too slutty," "too old lady," "too *too*"), until Lipstick had five dresses she wanted to try on—two Pradas, one Alessandro Dell'Aqua, and two Chanels. She was about to go into a dressing room when she saw they'd come up right behind Bitsy Farmdale, Lipstick's social frenemy.

"You know, Ashley," Lipstick said, nervously, eyeing Bitsy, "I don't need to try these on. Let's just go pay for them."

"I'm not in a rush," Ashley said, twirling her hair.

"Well, I can always return them, and it's for work. I'm sure Daddy will take it off on taxes," Lipstick said, turning around just in time to come face-to-face with Bitsy.

"Lena," Bitsy said. Dressed in a white tank, a pink Chanel jacket, and tight pencil-cut dark jeans, Bitsy was a rail-thin blond whose shoulder-length hair was done up in bizarre corkscrew curls like an old Shirley Temple movie and pinned back with shiny gold barrettes that matched her jewelry. "So good to see you. You didn't show up to Margaret's bridal shower last week—we were worried about you."

"Sorry, I meant to call," Lipstick said, a little flustered.

"Well," Bitsy said, "you should call her. She's *very* hurt. I think you should mention it in *Y* to make it up to her."

"Of course! It's already in for the next issue," Lipstick said.

"What do you have there?" Bitsy asked.

"What?" Lipstick said.

"Those dresses," Bitsy said, pointing to the two Lipstick had in her arms and the three Ashley had in hers. Bitsy ignored Ashley, as she had ever since Ashley left her job at La Prairie and could therefore no longer send her free face cream worth thousands of dollars ("The second I became useless to her I became a nameless remora," Ashley said to Lipstick one day. "So, what's the bad news?" Lipstick asked).

"I'm just stocking up for the May season."

"Off the rack?" Bitsy sneered. "I'm surprised. Shocked, really."

"Well, I have some lovely couture and vintage dresses at home," Lipstick said.

"Of course you do. Just be careful. If you buy off the rack, someone could show up wearing the same dress as you. And *that* would be even more of a disaster than the time you wore that Lagerfeld dress to two events and then tripped and fell in front of everyone." Bitsy smirked as her phone started ringing. "Oops! It's Thad, have to go." Lipstick flinched at the sound of her ex-boyfriend's name. Enjoying the look of pain on Lipstick's face, Bitsy continued, "So nice seeing you, Lena, and"— waving a hand in Ashley's direction—"you."

"Okay, what was that about?" Ashley said, as Bitsy disappeared into the Chloé boutique at the other end of the floor. "You are way cooler than her and have an actual paying job with a magazine she kills herself to get into. You should be making her squirm, not the other way around. Not to mention she *stole* your ex-boyfriend!"

"Thanks for the reminder—I forgot about that," Lipstick said, making her way toward a cash register. "Ever since that sleepover in the seventh grade when Bitsy and her friends locked me out on her mother's balcony on the sixty-fifth floor and said they 'lost me' until the next morning, it was kind of game over. It was some sort of power play, and she won. It's been like that for years."

"That's ridiculous! Who wasn't a bitch in middle school?" Ashley said.

"I know, but Bitsy acts like she needs to put me in my place on a regular basis. I know it sucks, but that's the way it is."

"Why do you even put up with Bitsy and her friends? They're truly horrible. I mean, they all act like they're thirteen. Like *Mean Girls* is on repeat in their heads. I can't believe she ignores me. My mother's family used to rule Italy, for chrissake!"

"I've known her since I was two," Lipstick said, piling her dresses on the counter. "Her parents are friends with my parents and we were debutantes together. I have to be careful. She pretty much rules our world. If I piss her off, she could make things very difficult for me."

"*You* could make things difficult for *her,*" Ashley said as they waited for the salesgirl to tally up the five dresses Lipstick was buying. "What if you stopped writing about her? You'd cut off her oxygen supply. And see how long Thad stays with her if he thought she had no juice!"

"She'd still find a way to get in the magazine—through Jack or

Muffie." Lipstick sighed. "Either way, that's just how it is. There's a social pecking order, and she's the reigning queen of the under-thirty crowd. I don't really care, it's just part of my job. It's not like I actually hang out with her or the other Bitsies . . . much."

"The total is $35,572, miss," the saleslady cut in.

Lipstick rummaged in her tote and pulled out a black American Express card. "Here you go," she said, handing it to the saleslady. "So anyway, do you want to go to Barneys? Maybe they've heard of that cream there."

"Nah," Ashley said. "I'll just call it a day. Arthur is getting home early, and I think he may want to have sex." Arthur Winksdale was Ashley's husband of two years. Every other Friday he came home early from his job as an accountant to have sex, despite his wife's obvious lack of interest. "I mean, I know some people like it, but it's just so . . . messy," Ashley said.

"Miss," the saleslady cut in again.

"Yes?" Lipstick asked.

"The card's been declined. Do you have another one, perhaps?"

"That's impossible," Lipstick said, "it's a *black* card. They don't get declined. Can you call, please? It's probably the strip. I always forget to put it back in my wallet, and it gets all scratched up."

As the saleslady picked up the phone, Lipstick looked up and went pale.

"What's wrong?" Ashley said. "You look sick."

"It's Bitsy," Lipstick whispered through clenched teeth, making sure her mouth didn't move. "She's over there, behind that rack of Prada skirts. I think she heard my card get declined."

"Don't be silly," Ashley said. "She's on the phone and too self-centered to notice anything but her own reflection."

"Okay, maybe you're ri—"

"Miss," the saleslady cut in again. "They say your card's been deactivated."

"Shhhh!" Lipstick hissed. "Okay, okay, try this card." She pulled out a Visa.

Two cards later, it was clear that for some reason all of Lipstick's credit cards had been canceled, and Bitsy, who was off the phone by now, was walking toward them.

"Oh my God," Lipstick cried. "Put them on hold—I'll be back tomorrow to pick them up. Don't do anything with those dresses!"

"Everything okay, Lena?" Bitsy purred.

"Fine, Bitsy—I'm just not sure about the dresses," Lipstick said. "I think you may be right after all. Buying off the rack may be too risky."

"It always is," Bitsy agreed, giving Lipstick a little smirk.

Lipstick grabbed Ashley and the two ran out of the store.

SAGITTARIUS:

Trying to fit your round self into a square hole hurts—and never works. Your blind optimism on a certain matter led you astray.

The garbage bin had finally been brought to her office, and Dana was slowly sifting through the remnants of her former life. During her divorce, she hadn't wanted to throw things like wedding albums, anniversary pictures, vacation snaps, and love notes out, but she'd also not wanted them in her new home, so her back office drawer had acted like a perverse storage bin. She didn't tell many people what she'd undergone, but most of her coworkers surmised something had happened when she sent around an office email saying, "Henceforth I would like to be referred to, professionally and personally, as Dana Gluck."

A Tiffany-framed picture of her and Noah smiling happily into the camera made her tear up. Outwardly their relationship seemed so much like a cheesy Disney fairy tale that she often ignored signs of trouble that popped up every now and then. Noah, who was very supportive of her job at first, had a sudden about-face and pressured her to quit to focus on getting pregnant. Dana was okay with the pregnant part—she'd always wanted children—but she'd never wanted to be a housewife.

"You're never around," he told her. "I like to have my wife here when I come home."

"I'm here four out of five weeknights," Dana had countered. "I even got them to let me work from the apartment after five p.m., but Wednesdays are the big work nights and I have to stay until eight. I'm sorry."

"It's not like we need the money," Noah said sulkily. "I make enough to support a family of ten. Not that we even have kids yet. Maybe something's wrong with you. We had sex three times last week and you're not pregnant."

"It's not about the money," Dana had answered. "I love my job. And believe me, without it, I'd be a mess. You wouldn't want to come home to a bored mess every day, would you? And it's not my fault I'm not pregnant. I want a baby as much, if not more, than you!"

To make up for not being a housewife, Dana started getting up an hour earlier than usual, putting on a pot of coffee and making Noah breakfast (an egg-white omelet and seven-grain toast).

For their first anniversary Noah got Dana a mini-dachshund puppy—which she promptly named Karl Gluck-Glickman—and said, "Until you can get pregnant with a real baby, this will have to do." The subtle dig was hurtful, but Dana loved Karl, not just because he had been a gift but because Karl developed an instant dislike to almost everyone but Dana. He didn't even like Noah. She should have known.

Another source of tension was her weight. That first year of marriage she'd put on a few pounds, like so many other women do at that one-year mark, and started losing her permanent battle with the bulge. Not a lot, only twenty pounds, but enough to go up several pants sizes. "The lettuce diet was wearing thin, and besides, everyone gains weight the first year of marriage. It's normal! And Noah said he didn't care how I looked," Dana told her yoga teacher and friend, Sally Brindle, one day after yoga class as she ate her second chocolate croissant during Sunday brunch at Le Pain Quotidien in Tribeca.

"Yeah, right. See how long that lasts," Sally said. She had seen her fair share of clients deal with men and weight issues in the past.

"Getting plump," Noah would comment, which always made Dana blush. She would laugh it off and comment on his growing gut, but she ran to Sally's yoga studio the next morning after she'd made him breakfast and before heading to the office. In addition to yoga, she started attending Weight Watchers every Tuesday evening to shed the pounds that offended Noah so much.

Six months before they split up, Noah started nudging Dana out of the house on weekends, claiming, "I need my alone time, and you need to go to Weight Watchers."

"Weight Watchers is on Tuesdays, and you don't have to shove me out of my own house every night!" Dana shot back. "You say you want me home, so I'm home. Now you want me to leave?"

"You were so hot when we first met."

"I was borderline anorexic."

"Exactly."

"I think I still look hot."

"Suit yourself."

LIBRA:
Pay attention to dark omens, especially ones from your past.

In the cab downtown Ashley looked at Lipstick, who was sweating despite the freezing temperatures outside.

"You okay?"

"Yeah, thanks," Lipstick said, slumped in the seat of the cab. "Bitsy just freaks me out."

"No, I mean, are you okay—what's with the credit cards being declined?"

"Oh, Mommy probably lost her purse again and canceled all the cards. She always forgets to tell them to only cancel *her* cards—and not mine as well. No big deal. I'll just call her when I get home. But what a time to cancel! This will be all over the Upper East Side by dinnertime. Bitsy has a bigger mouth than the East River. I'm mortified."

"Forget her," Ashley said as the cab passed under the shadow of the Empire State Building.

"Yeah, I guess you're right. Besides, she's still mad that Cavalli gave me first look at his line last year, before her. Even if it was skanky."

But the unsettling feeling in Lipstick's stomach wouldn't go away.

Any run-in with Bitsy was a bad run-in. Not only was Bitsy pure spite, but it reminded Lipstick of Thad, whom her parents, she was convinced, had liked even more than their own flesh and blood daughter. Lana Lippencrass, who was as devoted to the website Socialstatus.com as Lipstick—if not more—was furious that Lipstick had dumped Thad and that he was now dating Bitsy. As if somehow, despite her breeding and pedigree, something was so wrong with her daughter—and therefore her—that someone from the Newton family would choose a Farmdale over a Lippencrass.

Lipstick's father, Martin, was irked as well. Thad's parents had sponsored his membership to the ever-exclusive Southridge Golf Club in the Hamptons, and when Lipstick dumped Thad, his parents dumped Martin.

The whole encounter with Bitsy brought back bad feelings for Lipstick, which she normally didn't like to think about *at all*, thank you very much. A black cat had crossed her path and she felt uneasy, as if it were an omen of doom.

3

SCORPIO:

Sudden and disturbing speech outbursts could affect your professional life and a collision with Capricorn will cause you to examine your internal side. Literally.

As she approached Martman's office, Penelope could see Thatcher inside, slumped over in a chair opposite Martman's desk, his flannel shirt lifted up. He was inspecting the contents of his belly button.

"Mercury, take a seat," Martman said as he shut his office door, pointing to the free chair next to Thatcher. Martman sat in the Posturepedic chair he had special-ordered a year ago to remedy his sciatica. Behind his desk the walls were covered in front-page *Telegraph* exclusives that had all been meticulously framed and lovingly hung by Martman's loyal secretary, Rosario, who guarded the three-by-four-foot area outside Martman's office like a rabid pit bull. On top of Martman's oak desk, which wrapped around the entire back half of the office, was his collection of beer steins that he swore he'd collected from around the world, but which looked suspiciously like the Global Beer Stein

Collection in the Franklin Mint ads in the back of the *National Enquirer.*

"Now," Martman said, clearing his throat, "I brought you two in here because you've both asked me about Kershank's job."

Both? Penelope thought. T*hatcher wants Kershank's job? He never said anything, he doesn't do anything, and there is no deli by the courthouse that serves Philly beef and Swiss sandwiches.*

"Mercury," Martman said, leaning back in his chair, with his hands together as if in prayer and the tips of his fingers tapping against his mouth. "You're a great city reporter and are semidependable—which is more than I can say about ninety percent of the rest of the newsroom."

"Semi? But—" Penelope stammered.

"Now hold on there, cowgirl. I'm not done," Martman said, resting his hands palms down on the desk in front of him and staring closely at her. "I value your work. Thatcher, you too. You're great at rewrite. Your desk smells and you look like hell, but I'm a man of my word."

Man of his word? A warning bell rang through the layers of fuzziness in Penelope's head. *When did that happen? And word for what?*

"I promised you this job when I hired you away from the *Daily News* last year," Martman said, looking at Thatcher. "I also remember telling my mother, your aunt, something to that effect as well. Which is why, after long deliberations, I've decided to let you cover Manhattan courts. Mercury, the next opening is yours."

"Whad?" Penelope cried, leaping out of her chair. "Thad's insane. You told be *I* was the front-rudder—"

"Sit down, Mercury," Martman said, standing up.

"Doh! Doh way . . . Thatcher? He doesn't eben *do* eddythig!"

Thatcher looked up and said, "Dude—not cool. Did you drink like a gallon of Hatorade all day?"

"You habn't eben *seen* be all day," Penelope yelled back, "because I'be been out freezing id the snow od a wild goose chase for doh dood reason!"

What came next happened in a kind of slow motion Penelope had previously assumed occurred only in Michael Bay movies or *The A-Team* reruns.

Martman kept talking. ". . . an important asset to the *Telegraph* . . . blah blah blah . . . a real star . . . blah blah blah . . . Thatcher . . . seniority . . . blah blah blah . . . he threatened to call my mother who's a real bitch if he didn't get the job . . . blah blah . . . You can be in the office more and do rewrite . . ." but Penelope couldn't follow what he was saying due to a strange buzzing in her ears.

The buzzing reached a crescendo as Martman was extolling the virtues of doorstepping, and Penelope became increasingly dizzy as her forehead started throbbing anew. "I deed to sit down," she said—which, in the arduous trek from her brain to her mouth, was retranslated and somehow came out as, "Fug you, I quit."

Martman cut off his speech midsentence.

Oops, Penelope thought as her eyes crossed and she swayed with nausea.

Her boss's face turned an alarming shade of purple.

She tried to walk to a chair as Martman blocked her path. He started screaming incoherently, spittle flying everywhere. "Fuck you? Fuck me? No way, sister, fuck *you*! . . . Blah blah . . . Fuck that! . . . Blah blah . . . fucking fired . . . get the fuck out . . . blah blah blah . . ."

It was then that Thatcher sniffed the air and said, "Hey, you guys smell smoke?"

A fire alarm suddenly went off and someone yelled, "The photo studio's on fire!"

Smoke poured from the end of the office where the smoking studio was and the sprinkler system was triggered, spraying a light rain all over the office.

Martman, still berating Penelope, was screaming with renewed vigor as droves of editors and reporters got up and ran for the fire exits.

Penelope wiped Martman's spittle off her face and, trying to push past him out of his office, mumbled, "Martman, move," as a tidal wave of her vomit erupted out of her mouth, covering him.

Martman froze as the remnants of the leftover lo mein Penelope had consumed the night before slid down his face and spackled his dark gray Men's Wearhouse suit. He uttered a high, girlish screech and, shoving her out of the way, ran for the men's room.

As he disappeared around the bend, Penelope had her last semicoherent thought of the day: *Get out now.*

LIBRA:

Mercury is focusing on your home and family issues, and the supply of your everyday needs . . .

Lipstick dropped Ashley off at her Gramercy Park town house and made it home as the winter sun disappeared early and the sky turned jet black. She walked up the stairs to the front door of the brownstone and straight back into her parlor floor apartment.

"Home," she said as she sighed and sank into the leather armchair in the front room. Lipstick loved this apartment—almost as much as she loved Lagerfeld. The two-bedroom, two-bathroom apartment was meticulously decorated by her favorite designer and friend, Neal DuBoix, who also designed the garden and the terrace off the kitchen at the back of the parlor floor. The first floor had dark brown floors, light gray walls, and brown and khaki furnishings. The small entryway held a petite black lacquer table, on which she always threw her keys, bag, and mail, and was next to the dark leather nailhead armchair that had come from her mother's grandfather's study. Above it hung an oil painting of her in Valentino couture as the debutante of the year, 1997, at the Le Bal Crillon des Debutantes in Paris. The portrait of her, two years later, at the New York debutante gala, The New York Infirmary Ball at the Waldorf Astoria, hung above the fireplace in the living room. She had again worn Valentino but lost out on Deb of the Year to Bitsy Farmdale, whose mother was rumored to have rigged the jury.

Lipstick's eyes shot open when she heard voices coming from her garden.

Oh, God, she thought. *What if somebody scaled the wall?* Her heart started racing, and she began to sweat. She could hear the banging of the garden doors downstairs. Someone was breaking into the apartment.

Lipstick grabbed her cell phone from her purse and keyed in 911. She tiptoed through the living room into the kitchen, took a large knife from the wooden knife block, and peered out of the glass doors leading down to the garden. She couldn't see anything, so she turned on the garden lights and stepped outside onto the terrace, her thumb hovering above the send button on her cell phone, which was set to call the police at a touch. She peered over the side of the railing and said, "Hellooooo . . ."

Looking back up at her were her parents.

"Lena, darling! You're home!" Lana cried, shivering in the cold in a thin baby-blue cashmere sweater set and tan wool pants. "We came out to check on the garden and the door locked behind us. Our coats and my purse are inside and everything. Thank God you're home and not out on one of your gallivants. We'd have died if we'd spent another minute out here!"

SAGITTARIUS:
Your oversights have led to a blindness that hid betrayal.

As Dana continued cleaning "the drawer," a photo fell out from a stack of papers. Dana picked it up and immediately the bile rose in her throat again. The photo of her, Noah, and his friend Bill—who was clinging onto the arm of a tall, gorgeous model—was almost too much for her.

Their marriage hadn't been going well, but nothing that Dana was too concerned about. Then one night, Noah didn't come home and didn't answer her many frenzied calls. All night. On her way to work the next day, Dana was getting on the southbound A train at Seventy-second Street and ran into Noah, getting off the train.

"It wasn't so much that Noah was getting *off* the train as I was getting *on* to go to work, it was that he was wearing the *same clothes from the night before,*" Dana slurred to Sally later, recalling her breakup in a drunken haze. "But *whatever*—I mean, it was *Noah*. He *said* he was helping his friend Bill move into a new apartment in Cobble Hill and then just crashed. I *swear,* it made sense! Bill is always asking for help with shit like that."

A week after Noah spent the night at Bill's, Dana found herself with a raging case of pubic lice. Semitraumatized after finding a tiny living thing residing below her underwear line, Dana called her mother who snapped, "You've got crabs. Are you having an affair on my darling son-in-law?"

When Dana confronted Noah, who had been suspiciously and discreetly scratching "down there" as well, about the invasion of the tiny bloodsucking pseudocrustaceans, he blamed Bill's most recent conquest: Evya, an Eastern European exchange student/model Bill met at Hunter College a month before in the psychology class for which he was a teacher's assistant.

"You know those Eastern European girls—they're all dirty and infect everything," Noah explained. "And crabs get everywhere."

It seemed logical enough and the tiny bloodsuckers were gone soon after, thanks to a bottle of RID and a fierce spring cleaning in late February, which Sally had helped with (Sally came dressed for nuclear winter, wearing a homemade hazmat suit and chanting, "Ooooom. Om. Ew. Oooom").

After that, Noah became . . . distracted. He spent much of his time furiously typing on his BlackBerry and came home from work even later than usual.

His newfound Crackberry addiction was so bad that during a dinner to celebrate their two-year anniversary at Nobu in Tribeca, Dana, not usually one to throw tantrums, threw her napkin down on the table. "Dammit!" she said. "If you are going to spend all night on that fucking BlackBerry, I may as well go home. What on God's green Earth is so important that you can sit here for an hour and ignore me on our anniversary?"

"Sorry, babe," Noah explained, looking sheepish. "It's Bill. He and Evya are having problems and I'm just trying to help them."

"What?" Dana asked, incredulous. "Crab girl? Bill is still with her? She cost us five hundred dollars in cleaning bills—and you're trying to help them stay together? You should help him by sending her a ticket back to Belarus!"

"You're right, babe, I'm sorry," Noah said and turned his BlackBerry off.

A week later, on a Thursday evening, Dana was putting on her mascara in the hall mirror in preparation for meeting Sally and some other friends at the Soho House to celebrate Sally's birthday and asked Noah if he wanted to come.

"I have to take a client out to dinner," he said. "See you at home later?" He kissed her on the cheek on her way out.

As she was walking to the corner of Seventy-fifth and Columbus to catch a cab downtown, Dana realized she'd forgotten the cupcakes she had bought Sally at the new Magnolia Bakery on Columbus and Seventieth. She was about a block away from her house nearing the corner of Seventy-fourth and Amsterdam, by the concrete playground, when she saw Noah, hunkered down against the wind in his shearling coat, a black scarf, and matching cashmere hat thirty feet in front of her.

I bet he's coming to meet me. God, he's great, Dana thought.

She was about to run up behind him and playfully slap his butt when Noah walked up to a tall, striking, black-haired model type waiting by the bus stop, put his arms around her, and, whispering, "Evya . . ." he gave the woman a long, deep kiss.

It turned out Noah had not been helping Bill, but rather, Evya—right into bed.

Dana stood there, frozen, feeling the blood rush from her face. She couldn't move for a good two minutes, long enough to watch Noah and Evya walk off, hand in hand, disappearing down West Seventy-fourth. When they were out of sight, Dana finally regained her senses enough to move and ran home sobbing across the playground. She called Sally—who made some excuses to her other friends at the Soho House, leaving a three-quarters-full bottle of wine, and came right over.

Noah didn't pick up the phone the twenty times Dana, imbued with the courage and hysteria that only a half bottle of Jack Daniels can give, tried calling. So, in a rage, she packed up all of his clothes, and Sally helped her carry them down the stairs to the vestibule by the trash on the first floor.

Sally was still there three hours later with a red, puffy-eyed and sniffling Dana when, from the window, they spied Noah coming back from his "business dinner." The friends sat on plastic garbage bags on the sofa (just in case Evya's crabs were back now that Noah was officially having an affair with her), waiting to confront him.

But Noah never came up, nor did he call. In the morning Dana went downstairs and saw that his bags were gone.

"He treated your two-year marriage like he'd treat a two-week hookup," Sally said months later. "What a sociopath."

LIBRA:
Your extravagance has led to unwanted attention, and the consequences will be severe.

"What are you guys doing out here?" Lena said, dropping the knife onto a patio chair. "You scared the hell out of me! I was about to call the cops."

"Don't talk to your mother that way," her father, dressed in his usual navy suit and tie, said, trudging up the steps with her mother and striding past Lipstick into the kitchen. "We were just checking on our investment."

"What?" Lipstick asked, coming in from the cold and locking the door behind her. "Your investment?"

"The apartment. It's ours, you know. We paid for it, and my name is on the deed, not yours."

"Oh, right," Lipstick sighed, rolling her eyes. Every couple of years her father got this way. Martin Lippencrass, the "King of Distressed Debt," according to *BusinessWeek,* was a self-made man, having "pulled myself up from my own bootstraps and got myself out of Brooklyn to the Upper East Side by my own wits." What Martin always edited out of the so-called rags-to-riches story was that while he did grow up in Brooklyn, it was in the upper-middle-class area of Brooklyn Heights, and when he went to Harvard, his parents had been able to pay for it.

"Lena, dear, we're worried about you," her mother, an older, more sophisticated version of her daughter, said, stroking Lipstick's hair.

"Why?" Lipstick asked, brushing aside her mother's hand. She sat down on one of the stools around the kitchen island while her parents remained standing. "I'm fine. Great, actually. Except for some reason my credit cards won't work. We have to sort that out."

"I'm glad you brought that up," Martin said.

"Me too—Bergdorf won't hold those dresses forever."

"What dresses?" Lana asked.

"Oh, Mommy, they are fabulous! There are two Chanels, one Allessandro Dell'Aqua and two Pradas. You'll love them!"

"Oh, that does sound nice—are they formal or casual?"

"Formal! Nan Thrice is out of intensive care and the May gala season is in hyperdrive."

"I'd heard that—"

"Enough!" Martin said, slamming his fist on the kitchen counter. "We are not here to talk dresses that I am expected to pay for."

Lipstick and Lana stopped talking and looked down at the floor like chastened children.

"Well, then, what are we here to discuss?" Lipstick asked. "And what are you doing snooping around my apartment while I'm not home? That's not cool."

"It's actually our apartment, dear," Lana said. "Although you insisted on getting an apartment down here—and without a doorman, I might add—we did pay for it."

"I know," Lipstick said, "you keep reminding me."

"Lena, your cousin Max has decided to come home," Martin said. "And we've decided to let him stay at the apartment."

Lipstick's twenty-four-year-old cousin Max—who'd been practically adopted by Lana since his mother, Lana's sister, died five years earlier due to complications that arose after an experimental cosmetic procedure involving fat transfers had gone awry—considered himself something of a modern-day Vasco da Gama with a touch of Mother Teresa. After four years at Brown, he decided to trek the Himalayas and spent a year in the Annapurna base camp "communing" with Sherpas and various monks. Max left Shangri-la after a physical altercation with some local Gurkhas for a two-year stint at the Peace Corps camp in Namibia, teaching locals English. "I already *have* money, Lena, thanks to the family," he told Lipstick. "I need to use my life to do good and explore."

It seemed he was finally ready to come home.

"Oh! That's great!" Lipstick said, clapping her hands. "Maxie's back! He can have the second bedroom."

"Well, actually, no." Martin said. "We've decided to give him the *entire* apartment. He's bringing some of the local African children he taught with him to study actual Americans—he calls it 'complete culture consumption' or something like that—and they'll need the whole place. You'll have to vacate, I'm afraid."

4

SCORPIO:

Differences of opinion may come up, especially between family members.

An hour later Penelope was back home but Neal hadn't returned her "urgent! SOS!" messages yet.

Omigod, omigod omigod, omigod, thought Penelope as she climbed the three flights to her apartment in shock and opened the gray metal front door.

Penelope made a beeline for the freezer, where she took out a bag of frozen peas to put on the angry red throbbing lump that was growing like a horn out of her forehead and attached it to her head via a black elastic headband. She then flung herself fully clothed onto the bed facedown and moaned, "Isshhhhhtar-rrrrr."

The box-office bomb had, over the years, become a euphemism Penelope used to describe anything akin to hell. Penelope's mother, Susan Rosenzweig Mercury, had a lifelong crush on both Dustin Hoffman and Warren Beatty and, in 1987, had been thrilled when the planets finally aligned to put her two dreamboats into the same big-screen comedy. While the critics had rightfully railed against the flick—which posed the affable odd couple as bickering lounge singers "hilariously getting caught up in a CIA drama on their way to the Ishtar Hilton"—Susan loved it with such fervor she'd insisted Penelope watch the dreaded flick with her at least once a month on their aging Betamax player for all of 1988. The movie left such an impression on Penelope that she'd since used the film's title as an adjective to describe the worst horrors imaginable. And now was very Ishtar.

Ishy ishy ISHTAR! she thought. *You have no job. Not only did you not get the promotion, you got fired. Or did you quit? I think you quit first. It sounds better, either way.*

But, oh no, you couldn't just stop there, could you? You lit the Telegraph *on fire. And threw up on your boss. To top it all off, you'll probably die from pneumonia by morning, looking like the demon in* Hellboy.

Five minutes of self-pitying cow moans later, Penelope rolled over and blindly fished her phone out of the pink puffer coat's pocket and, as she usually did in times of unexpected distress, called her mother.

"Are you *nuts*?" Susan cried after Penelope blubbered out the details of her horrific day. "Rule number one—*one*!—and this is important: never, *ever* quit a job without having another one! How are you going to pay the rent?"

Penelope's mother loved rules almost as much as she loved the movie *Ishtar*. Rules made her life orderly. And there were a lot of them, a side effect of being a primary-school teacher who was inexplicably still married to someone with whom she had almost nothing in common, namely Penelope's born-again, slightly paranoid, right-wing father, Jim Mercury. She felt rules provided stability to a world she often found dangerous and disappointing. They were her safety blanket.

Susan Mercury also liked to number the rules to give them added authority. When Penelope was a child, there were the obvious rules: "Rule Number 4: no cursing at your mother—I don't care what you say to your sister or your father but do *not* curse at me or I will smack that ass," "Rule Number 15: No TV until after dinner—*M*A*S*H* or *Taxi.* Not both—TV rots your mind!" and "Rule Number 32: All boogers go in the *trash can*!" (as opposed to "booger alley," which Penelope and her older sister Nicole had created in the space between their twin beds in the shared room). Later came rules like "Rule Number 214: Never date a man who is mean to the waiters, because that's how he will eventually treat you," "Rule Number 237: Never date a man with a van—only thieves and rapists drive vans!" and "Rule Number 112: Whoever makes dinner doesn't have to do the dishes—so start washing or you're grounded."

Back on the phone, Penelope, still sniffling and in full-blown flu mode, said hopefully, "Well, baybe you could load be sub bunny?"

It was a futile question.

"Penelope, even if we did have the money, you know damn well I wouldn't give it to you. Rule Number 21: We'll never give you a cent, but there's always a plane ticket home so you will never be homeless. Would you like a plane ticket home?"

"Doh," Penelope said, "I'd like sub bunny."

"You know your father and I don't have any money," Susan snapped, "especially since he joined that new church last month that insists on tithing—*tithing*!—as if, on your father's university salary and my teaching pay, we can afford to give ten percent to anything . . . Jim, stop that! Take that Jesus statue away, it's freaking me out!"

"Oh, ogay," Penelope mumbled. "Thangs eddyway."

"Now, you go back in there tomorrow and beg for that job back!" Susan ordered her.

Susan, unlike Penelope, had a fatalistic view of life and always chose the safer option when coming to a fork in the road. Even if the safer option was illogical or inane and made her miserable. Like her marriage.

Susan, a tiny Jewish woman from Queens, resembled Rhea Perlman from the '90s sitcom *Cheers*. Jim was a six-foot-three, Catholic-turned-Protestant blond redneck with a comb-over from Butler County, Kentucky. The two met on a blind date during both of their saner days at the University of Illinois at Urbana-Champaign and had been together ever since, despite Jim's being born again several times after the marriage and Susan's voting for Carter—twice. They had not really spoken *to* each other (as opposed to speaking *at* each other) since a fight in 1982, when, as Joe Cocker and Jennifer Warnes were warbling "(Love Lifts Us) Up Where We Belong" over the radio, Susan called Jim a Nazi for voting for "that damned actor" again ("*Love lifts us up where we belooong . . .*") and Jim called Susan a "pink-blooded commie" for her Dukakis vote ("*Where the eeeeagles cry—on a mountain hiiiigh . . .*"). But neither believed in divorce and so they stuck together through the years in an uneasy partnership based on that one belief they still had in common.

And they wonder why I can't find a date. Ha! As if I'd had a normal relationship to learn from . . .

Penelope's father had started to yell in the background, "Jesus loves a working woman, Pax Christi, baby!" followed by her mother's, "Jim, shut up and get rid of that goddamn Falwell poster!" when Penelope decided it was time to end the conversation.

As her parents continued to bicker, Penelope said, "Well, ogay, I'b goig dow, byeeeee!" and hung up the phone, sighed, and blew her nose.

After padding into the tiny kitchen to down three Sudafed, a mug of TheraFlu, and two Tylenol PMs, she passed out cold for twenty-four hours with the bag of defrosting peas strapped to her head and her pink puffer coat still on and the small green Pakistani flag Ahmad had given her earlier that day for good luck poking out of the pocket.

LIBRA:
You may need to downsize.

It wasn't going much better for Lipstick. Her parents had threatened to cut her off before, but this time was . . . different. Like they were serious. Martin was insisting she move out and work at his company. And he wasn't budging an inch.

"But that's not fair! It's *my* apartment!" Lipstick cried in desperation.

"Our apartment, actually, dear," Lana said.

"Whatever! That's ridiculous!"

"What's ridiculous is that at the ripe old age of twenty-seven you're wasting your life," Martin said. "Last month I got a credit card bill from you for fifty thousand dollars, which seems to be the norm these days. I indulged you and your mother during that damned debutante phase—but, young lady, I didn't pay full-price for Princeton for nothing! You studied art history yet you work at that . . . that *fashion* magazine?"

"I like it," Lipstick said, picking at her split ends.

"You may *like* it. But how is it making you a fully fledged member of society? It pays you a meager annual salary—which you spend in a month. It would be different if it were *Forbes,* or the *Wall Street Journal.* We humored you while you dated the Newton boy. Granted, his family has no money, well not like *our* money, but they have a name and a family crest dating back to Napoleon. Since then, well, you seem to have lost direction. I had higher hopes for you."

"Mom! Can you help me out here?" Lipstick cried.

Lana looked away. "I'm sorry Lena, I have to agree with your father on this one. Did you know Jonathan Framberg is now a partner in his father's law firm? Wasn't he in your class?"

"Lena," Martin continued, "we are giving you two months to clear out and come home. I want you under my eye. You can come work at my company in the real world. I'll show you the ropes—it'll be just like old times. You'll love it! And you'll be making your own money."

"But I don't want to!" Lipstick said, starting to cry.

"Well, you either come home and work with me—and I will turn your credit cards back on—or you're on your own. See if you can live on forty thousand dollars a year instead of forty thousand dollars a month."

Lipstick, wiping her eyes on her sleeve—ruining her blouse, she was sure—was quiet for a minute.

"Well?" Martin asked, walking over to the hall closet and handing Lana her coat and purse before putting on his cashmere overcoat.

"Oh, honey, this is so exciting!" Lana said, clapping her hands. "We'll have so much fun! The house has been so empty since you left."

"I'll call the movers tomorrow," Martin said, putting an arm around his wife and leading her toward the door.

"No, wait," Lipstick said, sniffling.

"What?" Martin asked, turning around.

"*I'll* call the movers."

"Taking responsibility for your own actions already—see, Lana, I told you she just needed to be shaken up a bit!" Martin nodded with approval toward his wife.

"No," Lipstick said, raising her head and shaking with fury. "I'll call the movers and move to my own place. I'm not coming home, and I'm certainly not working for you!"

5

SAGITTARIUS:

The time of hibernation in your private sector is coming to a close.

Dana's divorce was spiteful and became even more so as—even though Dana had done nothing wrong and had even tried to excel as the perfect working wife—Noah refused to talk to her directly.

"I just can't believe he hasn't called or texted or anything," Dana told Sally, despondent.

"Well, if he does," Sally said, putting her hand on Dana's, "you'll just tell him to go back to hell or Cleveland, or wherever it is that he came from."

"Two years! Two fucking years! I was married to the guy—and nothing!" Dana said, starting to cry.

"He might *not* call," Sally said.

And he didn't. Instead, Dana negotiated herself a good deal—in which she'd kept Karl, received a small cash settlement, and gotten a legal commitment from him to pay for her new apartment for the next ten years, which, at four thousand dollars a month plus utilities, worked out to close to $700,000 tax free. She'd fallen in love with the penthouse loft at 198 Sullivan Street the second she'd seen it.

Dana had chosen Soho as it was far, far away from the Upper West Side and Noah. Plus, Sally had once told her, "If you're going to be single in New York, Soho is the place to be. Lots of eye candy and plenty of bars to find a one-night stand in!" It was a funny building on a funny street. The tourist throngs that filled Soho from West Broadway for six blocks east to Broadway didn't come to that block, which, had Dana decided to renounce Judaism and become a Catholic, would've been perfect as it was bookended by Saint Anthony's convent on Prince Street and the church on Sullivan. In between, she counted two coffee shops, two dry cleaners, three restaurants, a meat store, a cheese store, and a knitting shop that Dana never set foot in. (People who knitted were to be avoided at all costs. For a capitalist like Dana, she just couldn't deal with the organic, Zen crowd that did things like Knit Nights. And worse, they were usually vegan, which was taking things a step too far, in her mind.) And best of all, there was a bar that quietly stayed open late so that when she walked Karl at night, there was always a smoker or two out to ensure her safety.

The building itself was a five-story, four-window-wide, walk-up tenement building that made Dana feel right at home thanks to a mosaic of the Jewish star in the foyer.

"Most of these apartments are rent-controlled or rent-stabilized," Mr. Brillman, the landlord, had told Dana upon showing her the apartment. "Some people have been here for years, and when they move out, we do enough collateral renovations to charge more. Once the rent goes above two thousand dollars, all rent-stabilization laws are moot."

The apartment Dana was looking at was not rent-stabilized and was grandly referred to as the Penthouse, even thought it was a five-flight walk-up.

"I consolidated all four apartments on this floor into one for my wife," Brillman said, sighing, "but then she died and my knees are going . . ."

The apartment was an 1,800-square-foot loft, with a large bedroom space in the back against the four floor-to-ceiling windows that looked out over McDougal Street (the quiet side), an open kitchen in the middle, a (nonworking) fireplace and a decent-sized bathroom and the living area, whose windows peered out over Sullivan Street. Best of all, there was access to the roof, half of which Mr. Brillman had cordoned off for his (and now her) own private use.

"I'll take it," Dana said, figuring the five-flight walk every day would counteract her marriage thighs and complement her Weight Watchers fitness program. Before she moved in, she got a contractor to resand the blond wood floors, install hidden closets along one whole wall of the apartment, and put in new kitchen appliances as well as bathroom fixtures. She also hired a gardener to replant the roof garden (her section of it) and got Mr. Brillman to sign an unheard-of ten-year lease.

Even though it was four thousand dollars a month, the apartment was still a coup; similar ones in the area were going for at least six thousand dollars, and Dana wanted to get as far away from the Upper West Side as possible.

"It's a whole 'nother country up there," Sally assured her. "You'll never see Noah or that slut ever again unless you want to." Dana didn't.

Six hours after hearing "Noah's Big News," Dana was almost finished cleaning out the drawer.

There was a knock at her office door. It was Ifoema.

"I'm getting a drink at O'Malley's if you want to come," Ifoema said kindly.

"No, I should get home," Dana said.

"You always go home," Ifoema answered. "And you look like you could use a drink."

Dana sighed. "Okay, you're right. Just give me a minute." It would mark the first time Dana had gone for an after-work drink in almost a year. She heaved herself off the floor and caught a look at herself in the full-length mirror behind her office closet door and froze.

"And here I am, single again after I thought I had found *the one,* forty-three pounds overweight, with my love handles hanging out over my skirt like muffin tops. I even own a small dog, who has tiny *Ralph Lauren* sweaters," Dana told Ifoema over vodka and diet cokes at O'Malley's on the corner. "I used to make fun of people like me—you know, 'Oh look at her, she's just trying to substitute a child with a dog, so pathetic,' 'Why bitch about weight—get on a treadmill' and 'How could you *not* know your husband was cheating on you? He stopped coming home and gave you crabs, for fuck's sake.' God totally got me."

"Well you *can* get on a treadmill and have a kid any time you want," Ifoema said.

"That's a load of crap, Ifoema," Dana said. "I've been on a treadmill my whole life, not to mention going up and down my five flights of stairs for a year, and still can't get rid of my thighs. And let's not talk about kids. . . ."

Dana was particularly sensitive about this subject. She grew up in an Orthodox Jewish family that hailed from Cleveland and Miami. She was raised in Cleveland by parents who were Orthodox, yet reformed enough to allow paper plates at Passover instead of having a separate set of china and who didn't believe in covering up the shoulders, hair, or ankles. Family was deemed a priority—but most important of all was growing the Jewish family tree. "Jews don't believe in heaven," Dana's mother explained to her when she was a child. "We believe in lineage. Your grandmother was only on this earth because of you, and her grandmother before that. We are the generations who went before us and are only here because of the generations that will go after us." Her earliest memory was of her mother buying her a doll and saying to her, "When you're a mother . . ."

Dana put her head in her hands and moaned, "I am from Cleveland, Ohio. I was supposed to be married by now with two kids and a good job but with a husband who had a better job so I didn't have to work if I didn't want to. And look at me! Nothing! No kids, a little fucking dog who has the entire Ralph Lauren doggie sweater and polo shirt collection to keep me company, and an ex-husband who cheated on me with a European exchange student slash model. It's so trite I could die."

"Evya did you a favor and got that cheating bastard off your hands," Ifoema said, trying to make Dana feel better. "You're the best lawyer I know, you made partner at the crazy young age of thirty, and maybe you just need to pick yourself up and get back out there. You're thirty-two now and when was the last time you went on a date?"

"I don't remember," Dana said.

"Okay," Ifoema tried again, "let me rephrase that. When was the last time you went out of your apartment and did *anything* . . . got a drink, had fun, went to dinner . . ."

"Ummm . . . tonight?" Dana mumbled. Ifoema rolled her eyes. "I went to a Weight Watchers meeting—"

"Exactly!" Ifoema said. "Why don't you, instead of staying home every night of every week, start going out again and put yourself out there. How are you supposed to meet anyone, much less a baby-daddy, in your apartment?"

"Where would I go?" Dana asked. "It's just so . . . daunting.

I feel like I gave it my best shot. I met the guy I was supposed to spend the rest of my life with, I got married, and, despite my every effort, he left me. What if it's meant to be?"

"That's bullshit," Ifoema said, slamming her fist on the table. "And I'm sick of hearing you say that. Noah was quite possibly one of the bigger assholes I have ever met and you fell in love with the image of a perfect husband, which he was *not*. Now, I have to go back upstairs and finish the Callahan brief, but next week, Nader and I are taking you out. Being a hermit doesn't suit you."

"Okay," Dana said, although she didn't look like it was okay.

"Say, next Tuesday?" Ifoema asked.

"Sure, whatever." Dana sighed, already knowing she had no intention of going, as that was Weight Watchers night.

Sure enough, the following week Dana bailed on Ifoema to attend Weight Watchers. At 8:00 p.m. that evening, elated that she'd lost two pounds, Dana walked into her apartment, tossed her briefcase, bursting with case files, behind the front door, took off her camel-colored Burberry overcoat, walked out of her four-inch black Manolos, unzipped the skirt of her black wool suit, and plopped down on her white sofa without bothering to take anything else off. Karl, who'd spent the day at Pup Culture, the doggie day care three blocks away, jumped on her lap.

"Hello, Mr. Kisses," she said and scratched his butt.

Karl got up, ran across the floor, and body slammed himself against the door, his signature *I have to pee* move.

"Okay, okay," Dana said. "I'll take you out."

Dana hauled herself off of the sofa and went looking in one of the hidden closets for her sneakers. *It shouldn't be this hard to find my shoes,* she thought. *It's not like I have any furniture to hide them behind.* When Dana moved in, she'd felt so burdened by life that she'd refused to clutter up her new apartment. She bought only a white sofa, a glass coffee table, a flat-screen TV, a small white kitchen table with one white chair, a white electronic scale she kept in front of the fridge, and a big white bed with a white nightstand. White made her feel clean.

Dana finally found the sneakers, which Karl had hidden under her bed, put them on, and, still in her work suit, took Karl out for a quick pee. On the way down the stairs, on the second-floor landing, she ran into what looked like a large, pink Michelin man (or in this case, woman). It was the girl from the fourth floor, wrapped in what looked like ten layers and a pink puffer coat.

"Oh, sorry," the girl said, barely looking up, as Karl started barking at her and tried to bite the edge of her coat.

"Karl!" Dana cried, yanking the snarling dog's leash, "stop that!" Turning to the girl, she said, "Sorry about that. He's a little . . . nuts."

"That's okay," the pink Michelin woman said. "No one likes this coat. Honestly, the way things are going, I'm surprised he didn't lunge at my throat."

"Bad day?"

"Try bad month."

"Yeah, I hear you," Dana said.

"Well, have a good night," the girl said, before trudging up one more flight.

SCORPIO:

As this is a sign that knows no boundaries in its explorations, this time can show you how to transcend your old self through taking a new look at your perceptions, opinions, and judgments concerning work. Be careful of latent stress, which could affect career opportunities and bring about financial shortcomings.

Penelope was tired. She'd been rejected for a position as staff writer for a women's magazine and then had to suffer through one more humiliating interview for another position that she didn't want but financially needed.

She'd found the listing for an associate editor at a little known plumbing trade publication called *Modern Faucets & Toilets* in the *New York Times*. Penelope had never really mastered how to wield a plunger, much less the intricacies of copper versus nickel piping, so the interview was awkward.

"Why do you want this job?" the managing editor asked.

"I need to pay my rent," Penelope answered, unable to summon the strength to lie. Granted, it would never have been her dream job, but her bank account was dipping into dangerously low territories and, according to the latest ATM statement, she had exactly $250 left before complete and utter *Ishtar* set in. She'd edit a cancer pamphlet if she had to, if only to pay next month's rent and not have to move back to Ohio.

All she wanted to do was eat her Chinese leftovers and go to bed. But Neal was coming over to cheer her up. *I'd better get my place somewhat cleaned up or Neal will freak,* she thought as she opened the door to her apartment.

It's amazing what depression can do to one's cleaning habits, she marveled to herself as she turned on the lights and took a good look around her apartment. Clothes were strewn everywhere and there was a week's worth of dishes in the sink.

Daily newspapers were piled high on the kitchen table. A pair of used underwear hung from the shower doorknob, and her bedroom looked like a bomb had gone off in a third-world market. Clothes spilled out from the closet, dresser, and bed, which hadn't been made for a month. Trinkets and knickknacks were all over the place, the newspapers she'd read in bed were on the floor, and the sheets on the bed itself were halfway off the mattress.

Neal was coming in twenty minutes, so she did what she could.

By 9:30, when she buzzed Neal up, Penelope, who moved her CD clock radio into the kitchen so she could rock out to her *Hair Metal Bands of the '80s* CD while she cleaned, had successfully thrown out all the old papers; relocated all the clothes from the living room, kitchen, and bathroom areas safely out of sight behind the bedroom door; and worked her way through the majority of the dirty dishes.

"Oh, Laverne!" Neal cried, upon entering and seeing the mountain of dripping dishes. Laverne was Neal's semi-psychotic Maltese poodle mix he was obsessed with—so much so that her visage was bedazzled on the black cashmere sweater he was wearing that night over a blue checked oxford and gray slacks. Laverne was trained when she wanted to be, but prone enough to grudge-pooping or biting that the cry "Oh, Laverne!" was commonplace, not just for when Laverne misbehaved, but for everyday shocking situations Neal encountered.

"Oh, pooky, this is nothing!" said Penelope, kissing Neal on the cheek while scrubbing a pot. "Done in a sec. Start drying, will you, so they don't fall over and break everywhere." Penelope stopped washing dishes to turn off the music and said, "Sorry 'bout the music. I was cleaning to it. And Poison drones out the construction during the day."

"What construction?" Neal asked as he grabbed a dishtowel and started drying the dishes.

"Mandonna moved out."

"Mandonna?"

"Yeah—you remember the Madonna-obsessed trannie next door who was always playing 'Holiday' till like four in the morning?"

"Oh, yes. She was . . . special."

"Well. She's gone. Said she'd found a cheaper place in West Chelsea by the bar where she does her cabaret act. I don't know if I believe her, though. I think she found some sugar she-male to move in with, but whatever. So they've been renovating it for the past couple weeks. Hopefully they'll be done soon; the work starts at eight a.m. and doesn't end till six. And now that I'm actually home to hear it, it drives me bazonkers."

"Has it been rented yet?" Neal asked as he wiped the last plate and put it in the cupboard.

"No, why? You redoing your apartment again and wanna slum it for a while? Come on, it'll be fun, I think they're installing an actual bathroom in there so it won't be too bad."

"No thank you," Neal said, uncorking a bottle of red wine and pouring Penelope a glass. "My Sutton Place apartment is just fine . . . but I do have this friend who needs a place. When will they be done?"

"My landlord said mid March. I better get a job soon, though, or he'll be renovating mine too."

"Not good, huh?" Neal asked gingerly, sipping his wine.

"The worst," Penelope said, plopping into the armchair and tearing up with self-pity. "I'm not exaggerating. In the past month I have been on nine job interviews. I have called in every contact I know, every news editor of every paper, and every managing editor of every magazine. No one is hiring. They either say they'll keep my résumé on file and they'll call if something comes up, or the honest ones just flat out tell me they're not interested. I got so desperate that today I went on an interview for something called *Modern Faucets & Toilets*. A *plumbing journal*! I fucking hate toilets! I still have nightmares about that bad drain clog last year. Believe me, it wasn't pretty . . ."

"What about one of those blogs?" Neal asked, deftly avoiding the details of Penelope's fecal clogging.

"Oh, please, don't even get me started on those things." Penelope sighed, taking another swig of wine for dramatic effect.

After Penelope had run through her contacts in traditional media, she'd tried websites and blogs. But she'd managed to quit/get herself fired at a particularly bad time of year. Most of the sites were fully staffed, and while some were hiring, they paid next to nothing.

"Let me get this straight," Penelope had said to one media

website owner during an interview. "You want me to blog for twelve hours a day, five days a week, and you'll only pay me ten dollars per post?"

"Minimum of ten posts a day—that's not bad," the owner, wearing a brand new gold Audemars Piguet watch and a perfectly tailored Armani suit, had said. "That's ten dollars an hour."

"Starbucks pays more," Penelope shot back, adding, "and they give lunch breaks and benefits."

The owner had blogged about her indignation after she'd left, noting "So-called 'mainstream media' reporters, like Penelope Mercury, have not a clue as to what life is like on the internet. Just because you used to get benefits, honey, doesn't mean you should expect them now. Your sense of entitlement and lack of work ethics are jaw-dropping. Especially since you burned down your last place of employment." That was pretty much it for Penelope's online interviews.

"A job is a job, babe," Neal said, topping off Penelope's wine glass.

"I know," Penelope said, taking a sip. "That's why I went to the interview. You'd think that seven years at the *Telegraph,* five as an actual reporter, would count for something."

"It's the time of year," Neal said.

"I mean, what the fuck? What kind of an asshole was I in a previous life that I deserve this?" Penelope half-laughed and lit a cigarette.

"Oh, please. You're not some rabid dog on the street or Britney Spears. Mercury is in retrograde, darling; everything is a little haywire."

"Ha! So I was in retrograde. What does that mean anyway, and do you really believe that stuff?" Penelope said, puffing on her Marlboro Light and laying her head down on the couch.

"Of course I do!" Neal said. "And why are you smoking? Haven't you learned your lesson? You almost burned down the *Telegraph,* wasn't that a big enough sign for you to stop?"

"Please," Penelope said, taking a long drag, "I've got other battles to fight right now. And frankly, it's the only thing that's keeping me even a little bit sane these days. When I get a job, I'll stop."

This was a mantra she'd told herself for years: "When I (fill in the blank) I'll stop." Penelope had been smoking since she was thirteen years old ("Um, hello? I was raised in Ohio—what else was I supposed to do? Tip cows?"), and while she realized it made her clothes and breath smell, atrophied her lungs, and—thanks to stringent New York smoking laws—basically ostracized her from the community at large, Penelope still loved cigarettes. She would quit, one day, when she was locked in an asylum where she couldn't hurt anyone. But she was still young enough not have the smoker's face (criss-crossed wrinkles) and until then, "Forget it. I actually think that because no one does it anymore, it makes me a little punk rock," she rationalized.

"Have you thought about TV?" Neal asked, ignoring Penelope's smoking dissertation. "You'd make a great producer."

"I wouldn't mind going into TV," Penelope said. "At least it's still considered journalism—however loosely—and it'd be a paycheck. I'll do anything right now. Why?"

"Maybe I can help," Neal said. "You remember David?"

Neal had met David two months ago at the Tool Box, a gay bar off the still yet to be gentrified part of the Upper East Side. They'd both been ogling the same go-go dancer—whose G-stringed bottom was obscuring their view of each other—and when the dancer left the stage for a break, their eyes met. David, a thirty-year-old transplant from Venice Beach, California, was a short guy—only around five-feet-two-inches tall—with jet black hair, a chiseled face, blindingly white teeth, and bright green eyes. Neal was smitten.

They had been casually seeing each other ever since. Two nights before, David, the assistant to the station manager at NY Access, New York's *other* local cable channel, mentioned that there was a job opening.

"David said they were looking for an assistant producer at New York Access," Neal said. "I could get you an interview if you want. But I don't think they pay much."

"And the *Telegraph* did?" Penelope snorted. "I got my annual one-to-three percent 'cost of living' increase every year—*if* I was lucky—and that was it. For seven years! I don't care. I just need a job. Who do I call?"

"I'll sort it out tomorrow," Neal said, "but on one condition."

"What?"

"You let me do something about . . . this," he said, waving his hands in her general direction.

"What's wrong with me?"

"Everything."

"Oh, not that again."

"No, really," Neal said, "you can *not* be walking into job interviews with the pink Michelin coat looking like a nineteen-year-old homeless wonder and expect them to hire you. I have a plan."

"What is the plan and how much money does it involve?" Penelope asked as she took a final drag of her cigarette before stubbing it out.

"Nothing, it's free. You just have to call your landlord tomorrow and get my friend Lipstick that damn apartment across the hall for two thousand dollars a month or less."

"That socialite friend of yours? She'd want to live here?"

"It's a long story. How much do you pay for this . . . palace?"

"It started out at a thousand dollars a month. It's now twelve-hundred dollars, which isn't bad considering I've lived here seven years. But the new renovated apartments are going for fourteen hundred to sixteen hundred dollars. That's because they have real bathrooms built in, with a tub and everything."

"Doesn't matter, that's perfect," Neal said. "Lips needed to find an apartment yesterday. Anyway, she doesn't have room to move all of her stuff. I told her I would help store the majority of her furniture and clothes, but frankly, there's a lot of editing in that closet that needs to be done. She already has like five trash bags full of Dolce, Dior, and Gucci going to Housing Works, but I think that you, my dear, are a much better charitable cause. We'll call it an apartment finder's fee."

"Nice." Penelope sniffed, rolling her eyes, "I'm a charity case now."

"Never let pride get in the way of a good wardrobe," Neal shot back.

"If this girl has so much money and good stuff, why does she want to move in here? The only really nice place in the building is the penthouse upstairs, and that chubby chick with the dachshund that just tried to bite me already lives there. And I heard she signed like a gazillion-year lease."

"That would be too expensive for her anyway," Neal said. "The one-bedroom next door will be fine. It's a long story, P, and I told her I wouldn't get into it, but just do it for me, okay? I'll bring the clothes over tomorrow after you call David about that job and your landlord about the apartment. She's a bit bigger than you, but alterations are cheaper than a wardrobe."

"Sure," Penelope said. "Let's toast to my first Gucci, Pucci, and Toochi!" They clinked glasses.

"Now, darling," Neal said, "you look like you haven't had a decent meal in a week. Let's go to Raoul's for steak, my treat!"

The next day, after Penelope called Mr. Brillman and got him to promise her he wouldn't show the apartment to anyone until he'd talked to Neal and his friend Lipstick, Penelope dialed David about the job at NY Access.

"The opening is for an assistant producer," David told Penelope over the phone. "It's basically a fancy title for the get coffee/carry extraneous camera and lighting equipment, union rules be damned, fix the teleprompter, and all-round general errand girl. You're totally qualified—in fact, you're overqualified. My boss Marge usually likes to hire 'em fresh out of college because they're pretty dispensable. But on the bright side, there are always opportunities to advance because of the turnover."

"Whatever," Penelope said. "What's it pay?"

"Only forty thousand dollars."

"Same as the *Telegraph*. Fine."

"Okay, Marge said you can come in Monday at two p.m., but I have to warn you . . ."

"What?"

"She's . . . a little difficult."

"Like what?"

"Like fucking crazy."

"Please. My boss at the *Telegraph* could've used an enema in 1992."

The following Monday, Penelope, who spent an hour that morning fighting with her blow dryer to get her hair straight-ish for the interview, walked into the NY Access offices in the warehouse section of East Twenty-eighth Street at 1:55 p.m.—exactly five minutes before her meeting with Marge Green was to begin. The reception area of the station was a dull gray room—the kind of color that looked like it had once been white but over the decades turned permanently dusty—with a heavy, peeling, rust-colored door that presumably led to the inner sanctums of the TV station. The only decoration on the walls was a shabby banner that read: NY ACCESS—NEW YORK'S OTHER LOCAL CABLE STATION! below a picture of the evening news anchors: TRACE AND KANDACE, SERVING UP THE NEWS HOT, JUST THE WAY YOU LIKE IT! The room itself was empty except for a moth-eaten multicolored wool sofa, a rickety coffee table, and a desk that hid the receptionist—a tiny, ancient woman with short gray hair, thick black Coke-bottle glasses, and a large hearing aid in her left ear. She was sitting on a small swivel chair and wearing a fuchsia muumuu with a name tag that read GLADYS, and barked "Yes?" after Penelope peered over the top of the desk to see if anyone was actually there.

"I'm here to see Marge Green." Penelope said. She was dressed in a tailored hand-me-down dark wool Armani suit and a gray cashmere overcoat from Neal's friend. Neal had come over several days before—"with just enough time for you to get alterations done before your big interview!"—armed with three huge bags stuffed full of designer clothes and at least two usable interview suits. "You look like you mugged Nan Thrice," Penelope said. The two had sorted out which clothes were best for Penelope, which pieces should be altered first, and which didn't have to be altered at all, and in the process cleaned out the majority of her old closet. The pink puffer was the first item to be tossed.

"What?!" the geriatric receptionist snapped.

"Marge Green—"

"Yes, she works here!"

"I know. I have an appointment to see her."

"Name!"

"Penelope Mercury."

"What?"

"Penelope—"

"Speak up!"

"PENELOPE MERCURY!"

"Sit!"

Two seconds later, Gladys barked into the phone, "Pamela Minklestein to see Marge!"

Penelope sat on the edge of the "vintage" wool sofa. She didn't want to stain the new-ish suit, and the couch looked like it had the recent remains of someone's lunch on it.

Twenty-five minutes later, as Penelope's eyes started to glaze over, Gladys called, "Through the green door, down the hall to the left."

Penelope collected her purse (a black Coach bag—also donated from Neal's friend) and, clutching her résumé, walked through the rust-colored door and down a long hallway that opened up into a large room with cubicles on the left (*Newsrooms are always the same,* Penelope thought) and a studio on the right. At the end of the cubicles was a stand-alone area where David was dressed smartly in what looked like a very expensive suit (*How can he afford that?* Penelope wondered. *It must be a knock-off*). He was seated behind a desk that guarded an office with a black door that was open. To the left of the door was a placard that read: "Marge Green. Station Manager."

Penelope rushed over to David, gushing, "Hiii!" before she looked around and said, "What happened here?" There were pockmarked holes in the wall behind David's head—as if someone had been hammering at the walls haphazardly as David sat there, leaving only his body outline intact.

"Don't ask," David said and sighed before calling into the office, "Marge, Penelope Mercury is here to see you."

Penelope could hear a woman talking loudly into a phone.

"Marge! Penelope Mercury is here to see you!" David yelled when his first interruption received no response. Penelope could hear the woman tell the other person on the line, "One minute, I have a two o'clock appointment," before a voice boomed, "Bring her in!"

David pointed to the door and said, "*Entrez,* my dear. But don't say I didn't warn you."

Penelope slunk into Marge's office as Marge resumed her conversation with an underling on the other end of the line.

"We gotta sex up the show! Sex sells!" Marge, a petite blonde of a certain age who looked like she'd had her fair share of plastic surgery, yelled into the phone while banging her fist against her desk. "Sit down," she instructed Penelope, pointing at the hard wooden chair opposite her desk before talking back into the phone, "No, not you! Anyway, where was I . . ."

As Marge debated the merits of sexing up the afternoon broadcast, Penelope placed her résumé on Marge's desk, which was cluttered with papers, pens, several staplers, a rickety old computer, and various stress balls. Behind Marge the wall was plastered with framed awards, marking her various achievements over the years: "1999: Best Local Newscast Producer: ABC's Marge Green—*New York* magazine," "*Time Out:* 2001 Special Achievement Award to CBS's Marge Green," "1997: CNN Innovator of the Year," "NBC Salutes Marge Green for her Emmy-Winning Year, 1989," and so on.

There were awards from almost every station imaginable. Marge was like the garden weed of local news—she had popped up everywhere—but some of the older awards, which had been typed out on a typewriter instead of a computer, had their dates rubbed off.

"Marge doesn't want anyone knowing how old she really is," David later explained. "She thinks that if she rubs out the dates, no one will be able to prove she isn't—ahem—'fifty.'"

There were some filing cabinets behind Marge's desk, on top of which was an industrial-sized coffee machine, with a coffee pot that looked like it had a half cup of coffee left in it, several empty coffee mugs, and a jar of Coffee-Mate.

Marge, hyped up on more than five pots of Colombia's finest ground beans, slammed down the phone, picked up Penelope's résumé, and said, "So! Pamela!"

"Penelope."

"You want to work at New York Access?"

"Yes, I think it's a—"

"David!" Marge cut Penelope off.

"Yes," David answered.

"My coffee's low. Get in here and make me some more!"

"I will in a second—"

"Now!"

"I have to go to the bathroom."

Marge pursed her lips into a thin, white line, and a vein on her forehead bulged dangerously.

"You went to the bathroom yesterday!" Marge said before picking up one of the staplers on her desk, leaning to her right, and flinging it out the door in David's general direction. There was a thud and Penelope heard David scream, "Aaahhh! You bitch—you got me!" before Marge got up and slammed her office door shut. "You just can't find good help around here," she said to no one in particular.

"So, Polly," Marge said, sitting back down behind her desk and turning her full attention to Penelope, "as you can see, I am extremely competitive and dedicated to my work." She smoothed down the lapels of her hot pink suit ("She thinks pastels and bright colors make her look younger," David had warned Penelope). "I need someone who can match that dedication. Is that you?"

"Sure . . ." Penelope said, aware that Marge was glaring at her. A bead of sweat rolled down her back and, feeling her one and only job opportunity slip away, Penelope sat up very straight and said, "I mean, yes! Yes, it is me! I am dedicated—I'm dedication incarnate!"

"Great," Marge said, sitting back in her chair, dropping Penelope's résumé back on her desk and staring at the ceiling. "You start Monday." She picked up the phone and barked, "David!" and Penelope was escorted from the room.

"You got the job," David said. "That's great." He now wore a small Band-Aid on his forehead.

"What just happened?" Penelope said.

"You got the job, darling—no unemployment lines for you!" David said.

"But she didn't even ask me anything."

"She never asks."

"How does she know I'll do a good job?'

"Because there were no other applicants."

"Did she just throw a stapler at you?"

"Oh, please—she does that all the time. It's a little game we play. She throws, she hits, she buys me Prada. If she misses I get nothing, so even though she has a horrible aim, I suck it up, dive in, and take one for the closet every now and then. It's kind of like playing a fun game of dodgeball. Except I get to go shopping afterward!"

Outside the NY Access offices, Penelope checked her voice mail. Her mother had called, naturally. "Penelope, it's your mother. What are you doing about a job? What is going on? You haven't called in two days and your father is very upset. He can't understand why you didn't go back and beg your boss for your old job back. He started speaking in tongues again. It's driving me up a wall. He said he'd stop if you called. I think he's feeling neglected."

The other call was from Neal.

"Penelope," he cried, "Lips got the apartment! Thank you so much, my sweet. It means so much to me. You will love her, I promise. Drinks on me when she moves in and has her first housewarming party. Now, how'd the interview go? Call me back and fill me in on everything!"

7

LIBRA:

You'll get more insights into how you deal with loss and gain, defeat and victory, destruction and regeneration. This will help you move unencumbered into a greater, purer fulfillment, opening your future in some important life area. But keep an eye on your belongings. Theft is a problem during the tail end of Retrograde.

The first Monday in March marked not only Penelope's first day of work at NY Access, but Lipstick's Big Move into the newly renovated and tiny (by her standards) apartment on the fourth floor of 198 Sullivan Street.

It had been three and a half weeks since her parents had issued their ultimatum and Lipstick had not spoken to them since, despite her mother leaving several messages on her voice mail.

The first message Lana left Lipstick was the night after the disastrous day Lipstick referred to as "Bitsy's Birthday." "Darling," Lana's voice rang through, "I'm terribly sorry about Daddy last night, but you know, it's for the best. I know you were trying to save face and seem brave, but I wanted to tell you that I'm so excited for you to come home. Daddy said you can even have the west wing of the East Hampton house all to yourself. I can't wait to see you; just let me know when to contact the movers!"

When Lipstick hadn't returned her call, Lana waited a week to record another message for her daughter.

"Darling, I haven't heard from you all week and I'm getting concerned," Lana cooed into the phone. "What am I supposed to tell the movers? Please call me back. I've had the geldings Barbuto and Barbetto moved from the Hamptons to the stables in Riverdale so we can do some riding on the weekends until summer. But I have to warn you, they make you suit the horse up yourself. It's awful. I almost fell off Barbetto yesterday when the saddle started sliding. Can you imagine? So embarrassing. The new housekeeper Rosanna comes to help me now. She has those strong, sturdy Guatemalan arms, you know."

After that, Lana waited another seven days to call her daughter after once again receiving radio silence.

"Darling, where have you been?" Lana asked, feigning ignorance. "I checked Socialstatus.com and saw the pictures of you at Annie Ratner's party so I know you're alive. I also saw that you are ranked just four short spots behind Bitsy for top young socialite. Good job, darling. She's a formidable opponent, you know. By the way, I haven't actually *heard* from you; I assume something is wrong with your phone? Frankly, I'm starting to get offended and Daddy is very upset. He's even suggested that perhaps you were serious when you said you weren't coming home. I told him not to be silly and took him to Scalinatella for dinner to calm him down. You know how much I hate that place: seventy-five dollars for a plate of pasta that just gives me wind."

During the time Lana was leaving Lipstick messages, Lipstick had been very busy. She and Neal had gone through her apartment, "editing," as Neal put it. He carted the majority of Lipstick's furnishings to a warehouse in Upper Manhattan, leaving Lipstick her bed, her armchair from the front hall, her debutante portraits and the Matisse, two coffee tables, a TV, and her stereo.

The hardest part of the edit had been whacking her closet down to a third of its original bulk and shoving the "keepers" into boxes for the move. Her ball gowns were stored in a large wardrobe box that Lipstick marked in thick, black indelible marker, "Do Not Touch," and for special effect, she'd drawn a crude image of a skull and bones with a dagger through the head.

The clothes she'd "left behind" ("So dramatic, Lips, you make it sound like you're in a Holocaust movie," Neal said) were either moved to storage or donated to Neal's friend Penelope. Anything that was left over, that was deemed not "classic," "just too dated," or "If I see you in that again I will burn it," went to a consignment store near Lipstick's new home in Soho. The resale store sent her checks totaling $3,500 from a stack of clothes that had cost at least $25,000. But money was money.

Barring selling off her entire wardrobe at a steep discount, there was always her salary, which was, in Lipstick's mind, negligible.

After she had a small, private word with the human resources department at Y, asking them to reroute her checks to a personal HSBC account as opposed to her father's business manager, she'd finally been able to sneak a peek at her biweekly earnings. And this is how Lipstick, the senior society editor at the exclusive fashion and society magazine Y, found out her annual wage was $43,500. After taxes she was left with $425 a week—or, roughly, lunch for four at Nello. Without tip.

In practical terms, it meant she could afford, at most, $1,400 a month for an apartment, which in Manhattan, would get her little more than a room and a toilet and allow her to live on water and grass—like the geldings, Barbuto and Barbetto.

Thankfully, her last monthly allowance deposit from her parents of ten thousand dollars had been made a week before their decree, so there was that.

But all in all, Lipstick was optimistic. She'd learned how to navigate the subway, taking the West Fourth Street stop to Thirty-fourth Street and walking from there, and was generally eager to be out on her own.

"Neal," she gushed one morning on her way to work. "It's amazing! There are so many people in New York! And so many different kinds—"

"Lips," Neal cut her off, "I love you but I don't have time for an 'I just found out New York City was a cultural melting pot' discussion. I have to be down in Tribeca in half an hour. The Madisons bought a loft for their son, who's being released early from Sing Sing next Monday for molesting their Westchester neighbor's daughter four years ago. I have to not only decorate the damn thing in a week, but inform the neighbors, discreetly of course, that he's on some sort of sex predator list. They're paying me extra for that."

The date before the move, Lipstick informed Muffie and Jack via email that she'd be taking some personal days for the next forty-eight hours and went home to meet Neal.

"You know, Neal," Lipstick said, sitting in her armchair in the middle of her empty living room, "I'm actually kind of excited. I feel like the weight of belongings is off me."

"Oh, Gandhi, do go on. Tell me more about how thrilled you are about being poor," Neal joked, while opening a closet door to ensure nothing had been left behind. "I'm just waiting for the day you want to shed the weight of belonging—as opposed to belongings."

"Hmm?" Lipstick asked, not paying attention. For a moment she truly was excited. Almost euphoric, as if, for the first time, she'd be out from under her parents' watchful eyes. She felt like a bird being set free from a cage, but moments later Lipstick's euphoria turned to fear and she started chewing her cuticles.

"Nothing, my dear. Now, are you sure you don't need me to help you move tomorrow?"

"Nope!" she said, with fake bravado even though her stomach was in knots and a small trickle of sweat—glisten, as she called it—ran down her back. "I'm on my own. I can do this. I know it. I can."

"That's right, Lips, convince yourself," Neal said, rubbing her back.

But by ten a.m., as the three large Russian moving men from FlatRate Movers—who'd sworn to her they would do the move for one thousand dollars—arrived in front of 198 Sullivan Street, Lipstick, in jeans, a cream Dolce cashmere sweater and an orange satin puffer vest with fur lining, was already exhausted and regretting that statement.

By 10:45, after she'd refused to fork over an additional thousand dollars in "tip money," the Russians split—claiming she'd never told them it was a fourth-floor walk-up and therefore she owed them an extra grand—leaving the fifteen boxes of clothes and shoes still out in front of 198's green door.

"But you can't just leave me here," Lipstick cried as Vlad started the moving van. "These boxes are full of Prada!"

Vlad, Dmitri, and Yergi ignored her plea, and Dmitri even tossed his cigarette butt out the window in her general direction as they pulled away.

At least they took the furniture up, Lipstick thought, trying to remain optimistic. But then she took a good look at the mountain of heavy boxes, stuffed so full they were bulging at their seams, and she felt momentarily overwhelmed.

Well, now you won't have to go to the gym or yoga for a week. Ass, be gone! she thought.

She grabbed the box nearest to her, lugged it to the front door, opened it, and pushed and pulled the box, which was a lot heavier than she'd thought it would be, up four flights of stairs.

By the time she'd finally negotiated the first box up the stairs and through the door of her new apartment, Lipstick's thighs were burning ("a good thing!"), she was sweating ("so gross") and her knee was beginning to swell under her jeans from tripping on the uneven stairs on the third flight ("ouch").

"One down, fourteen to go!" she told herself. But when Lipstick walked outside the building, something was wrong. There didn't seem to be as many boxes as there had been when she'd last seen them, and there was a guy with shoulder-length black hair squatting on the box farthest from the door right by the dry cleaners.

"Hey!" Lipstick said, a tone of alarm in her voice, "What are you doing? Don't sit on those—they're my clothes! And how come . . . wait a minute . . ." Lipstick counted the boxes. She recounted again. There were only twelve.

"Two of my boxes are missing!" she cried, running up to the man, who was looking at her with a mix of irritation and fascination, and poking a finger at him. "What did you do with them? I'm calling the police."

As Lipstick pulled her cell phone out from her back pocket, the guy, who looked to be in his thirties and would have been pretty cute except for paint smears on his hands and face, put his hand on Lipstick's arm and drawled, "Slow down, sister. I didn't take your boxes."

"Well, where are they?" Lipstick said, slapping her phone

shut and getting slightly hysterical, "They are full of—oh my God! Oh my God! Where are the dresses?"

The box that had been specially marked and packaged with her ball gowns was gone. "Thief!" Lipstick cried, shaking and pointing at the man. "Thief! Police! Someone arrest this man!"

"Now, just hold on," the man said, getting up from the box, "I didn't steal your damn boxes or dresses."

"Well then, where are they?" Lipstick demanded, starting to cry. "I move one fricking box and come down to two missing and you sitting on another . . . What am I supposed to think?"

"I was sitting here because I was watching it for you," the man said calmly. "I saw you fighting with the movers, went in to get a cup of coffee at Local, and when I came out, some guy was shoving two boxes into an unmarked van. When I yelled at him, he drove off. And so I've been sitting here, watching the rest of your boxes, waiting for you to come back down."

"Oh." Lipstick sniffed, wiping her tears on the sleeve of her sweater, "I'm . . . sorry. I guess I just . . . my dresses. They're all gone. I'm screwed! Did you get a license plate? Should we call the police? Can we catch him? How far do you think he got?"

"Dude, he's gone." The man sighed. "I'm sorry about your dresses, but let's focus on getting the rest of your stuff off the street."

"Huh?" Lipstick asked, her mind racing. *Dresses. Where are the dresses? Oh my God. Gala season starts in a week. What will I wear? What will I do? I have no dresses—Jack will kill me."*

Snapping his fingers in front of her zoned-out eyes, the man said, "Hello?"

"You're going to help me?" Lipstick mumbled. "I don't even know you . . . and why are you covered in paint?"

"I'm Zach. I live on the second floor, I have paint all over me because I'm an artist and yes, I'm going to help you. Now, open the front door, reach around behind the stairs for the door stopper, and prop open the door."

Lipstick did as she was told.

"Okay," she said, "now what?"

"Now move all the boxes into the building," Zach said, looking at her strangely. "Seriously, have you never moved before? Don't you know not to leave your stuff out on the street unguarded? Move everything inside and then shut the door so you can move the boxes into your apartment without it being stolen by some asshole on the street."

"Oh, okay," Lipstick said, grabbing a smaller box. "I'm not stupid, I swear. And no. I haven't moved before, and I wasn't supposed to be moving now."

It took Lipstick and Zach ten minutes to haul the remaining boxes into the front hallway of the apartment building. When they were done, Zach pulled out the stopper, shut the front door, and said, "You're on your own from here, doll." He started walking up the stairs.

"Huh?" Lipstick said, feeling her panic rise with every step he took. "Wait! You're leaving me? But I still have to get them up four more flights. . . ."

"Listen, princess, I may be an artist, but I still have shit to do," Zach said, scratching his head. "The last time I checked, I didn't work for a moving company. I have a show coming up and if I don't get this painting done by tomorrow and get it approved by the gallery, I won't be able to pay my rent. You're inside now; no one is going to steal your stuff. Besides," he added, looking at Lipstick's red, puffy face and laughing as he disappeared from view up the stairs, "you look like you're enjoying the exercise."

"Oh, yeah, right," Lipstick said, wiping off more sweat from her brow. "So much fun." Did he just call her fat? "Well, thanks for everything," she said. "I appreciate the help! Oh, and um, how can I thank you?"

"No need," came Zach's voice, floating down from the third floor. She heard a door open and slam shut. The building was quiet again.

Five minutes later, in the calm of the lobby of 198 Sullivan—past the old Jewish star tiled on the foyer floor, in between the mounds of boxes piled at the foot of the stairwell and the mailboxes, which were above the overflowing trash cans where residents dropped their garbage before Stan the super took it out every Tuesday, Wednesday, and Friday—Lipstick felt herself slipping into hysteria.

Sitting down on the bottom stair, Lipstick looked, with the mania of a caged rat, from the boxes to the top of the stairs, to the mailboxes (number 10 had a new white label that read LIPNCRAFF), back to the boxes, to the trash, back again to the boxes. She felt like she was going to hyperventilate.

In a panic, Lipstick called Neal. When he picked up, she described the accounts of the day, then she began crying, tears running down her face, "My ball gowns for the gala season! All of them—gone! Jack is going to kill me! Everyone will find out what has happened—everyone will know I've been cut off and forced into disgrace. I'll be ruined socially! Bitsy will die of happiness—she'll post it all over that damn Socialstatus.com website. I'll be a laughing stock! I'll be fired and out of a job with no money and then I'll be evicted. . . . It'll be worse than that time in seventh grade when she locked me out on her balcony all night during the big sleepover."

"Lipstick," Neal said sharply, "get a hold of yourself. Don't be ridiculous. No one will find out unless you tell them, and that balcony thing happened years ago. The dresses are a problem, but I have an idea."

"You do?" Lipstick sniffled.

"Yes. I will come over in a couple of hours when I'm done with Nan's new terrace garden and elaborate."

"But I need help now," Lipstick wailed. "How am I supposed to move all these boxes?"

"You're going to move them by putting one foot in front of the other and drag them up the stairs like you did the first one." Neal sighed, "I'd come earlier but a girl's got to make a living, you know, and I do have a day job. You wanted to be on your own, so start taking responsibility for your stuff and for yourself. The way you're acting you'd think you were lost in the Gobi desert!"

"Oh," Lipstick, sitting upright, said, "right. Of course. I knew that."

"Well then, get a move on," Neal said, "and I'll see you soon," before hanging up.

Lipstick was disgusted at her own self-pity and she'd had enough of it. She would move the boxes and be done with it.

But moving the boxes was easier said than done. On Lipstick's sixth trip up the stairs, towing a huge box of what she assumed were shoes based on what sounded like four-inch heels rattling, Lipstick backed into someone on the top step just as she was about to hit the end of the fourth flight. Lipstick dropped the box and it fell down to the third floor and burst open, spilling eight-hundred-dollar Louboutins and Manolos everywhere.

"Dag!" said Lipstick, who rarely if ever cursed (too déclassé), stamping her foot. "Dag, dag, dagdagdag!"

"Oh, my gosh—I'm so sorry," said a sweet, familiar voice behind her. "Let me help you with that!"

Lipstick turned from the disaster scene to face Sally Brindle, her longtime yoga instructor and only friend besides Neal who was not a social or in "the crowd."

"Sally," Lipstick said, taken aback, "what're you doing here?"

"I could ask the same thing." Sally, dressed in white yoga

pants and a white down jacket ("white is very pure"), smiled. "What's with the box of shoes? How come you're not at Y today?"

"Um, erm," Lipstick mumbled, looking away and slowly backing down the stairs to the box of shoes. "Well, I . . . had a day off."

"Wait a minute, these are yours," Sally said, moving past Lipstick to pick up a pair of five-inch Louboutins with a corset-like lace-up on the heels. "I know this fuck-me footwear—they're the ones that scratched up my studio floor last year when you conveniently forgot to read the No Shoes signs that are up everywhere."

"Yeeees," Lipstick said, averting her eyes as she tried to shove the errant heels back into the busted box.

"Are you doing a shoot here for the magazine or something?" Sally asked.

"Not really," said Lipstick, feeling like a trapped rat.

"Well, then what?" Sally asked, as she placed the last pair of shoes inside the box. "It's not like you're moving in," she said, looking closely at Lipstick.

"Actually, um, haha . . . I am," Lipstick said, standing up straight and looking Sally squarely in the eye.

"Wait, really?" Sally said. "I was just joking. Why are you moving in? What happened to your beautiful place on West Twelfth? Is everything okay?"

"Help me with this box and I'll fill you in," Lipstick said.

Sally not only helped Lipstick carry the busted box into Lipstick's new home, she stayed to help move the rest. Lipstick then finally filled Sally in on the past month's debacles—only after, of course, Lipstick elicited a promise from Sally not to tell anyone of her plight, which Sally assured her was unnecessary. "Yoga teachers are like therapists—it goes against our ethics to blab. Besides, you've been a client and a pal for years. And I don't even know the Bitsies. They bring their bad karma to Rashad uptown."

"Wow," Sally said, sitting down on a kitchen chair surrounded by boxes and looking at Lipstick in disbelief after Lipstick had finally finished her tale of woe. "Wow. Wow."

"Yeah," Lipstick agreed. "So, here I am, at the ripe old age of twenty-seven, kicked out, basically disowned, for all I know. Weird, huh?"

"What does your mom say?" Sally asked. "Have you talked to your parents at all since this happened?"

"No," Lipstick said, looking away. "I'm too angry to talk to them yet . . . I just think that there was a better way to do this. As in, maybe they could've given me a warning or something. Isn't that the kind of thing you tell someone ahead of time, you know? Like, 'Hey honey—after the long talks amongst ourselves and with you—we have decided to cut off your cards, cash, and apartment'?"

"Maybe you should call them," Sally suggested.

"Later," Lipstick said. "I mean, they raised me to be like this. They were the ones who begged me to go to $10,000-a-seat galas and wear $6,000 dresses. In fact, Mother was distressed if my picture *wasn't* taken and put in the Styles section or on that stupid Socialstatus.com website. It made her look better to her friends. She treated me like some doll she could dress up and control. And Daddy always kind of liked the perks that came with everything, including my job that he now says he hates. He was happy Mother was happy and used my career for his own purposes too. I mean, how does he think he got his firm that great box for the playoffs? I had to put the box owner's wife in *Y* for two months straight for that. And believe me—it was *not* easy convincing Jack to do that. He kept calling her a Bravo reality slut who wanted to buy her way into society. Daddy now wants me to go into the family business—and all because they're bored at home and need some sort of distraction. It's all been so humiliating and stressful to realize I was just their puppet. To be honest, I have no idea what I'm going to do about anything."

"Sounds like you should come back to yoga," Sally said, offering Lipstick a tissue.

"I can't afford it anymore," Lipstick said, taking the tissue and blowing her nose. "Do you know *Y* pays me less than a first-year investment banker at my dad's firm? I've been there for seven years!"

"My treat," Sally said, rubbing Lipstick's back. "You've always been so supportive of me over the years, getting all your friends to come when I opened my own studio and then writing about it in *Y*. It's the least I could do."

"I can't," Lipstick said, "I can't face walking into a studio and having to see . . . well, anyone. I just can't. It's hard enough to go to work and work functions these days pretending everything is fine."

"Well," Sally said, slowly, "what if we did it in the building?"

"Here?"

"Yeah, here. I have a private client in the building, and frankly, she could use some company."

"So that's what you're doing here," Lipstick said. "Why is she getting yoga in the middle of the day? Doesn't she work?"

"She took the day off."

"Is she . . . normal?"

"No, silly," Sally laughed. "No one is! But she's fine. She's just been having a rough year. Anyway, I'm going back upstairs to ask her now."

SAGITTARIUS:
Forming harmonious, warm social friendships, possibly related to group activities within a club, can figure now.

Dana was just stripping off her yoga clothes when she heard a knock at the door and Sally's voice came floating through, "Dana? Sweetheart? Are you decent?"

Karl Gluck started foaming at the mouth and barking hysterically, as he did when anyone came to the door, and Dana pulled her yoga pants back on, sighed, and said, "Coming . . ." She was tired. It was like all the emotion of the past year had finally caught up to her. She'd called in sick for the first time ever and had had Sally come over for an emergency yoga session.

Dana opened the door and immediately knew Sally was up to something. She had this impish look on her face.

"Dana . . . honey. I have a proposition for you."

"Yeeees?" Dana asked, shooing Karl, in a full-blown barking orgy, away from the door.

"Honey, remember when we talked about you maybe starting to meet people again?"

"I can't go to classes in the studio yet." Dana sighed. "I just can't."

"No, no, of course not," Sally said, smiling. "But may I please, please, please bring someone to you? Now, before you say no, she just moved into the building and is a very good friend of mine who seems to have fallen on some hard times. She is a lovely girl—you will just die for her, I swear—and just needs a little help right now."

"Oh, I don't know," Dana said, feeling a bit put upon. She had never had anyone in her apartment except for Sally, and she wasn't sure she wanted to open up her haven to a stranger.

"It would be a huge favor to me," Sally said. "And to sweeten the pot, I'll cut my rate in half."

"This woman means that much to you?" Dana asked. Sally's home visits, at two hundred dollars a pop, were expensive.

"She does. I wouldn't have half my business if it weren't for her."

"Can we do it on a trial basis and see how it goes?" Dana asked, too tired to say no.

"Absolutely!"

"Fine. Tell her to come next Wednesday."

"You. Are. A. Doll!" Sally squealed and hugged Dana before rushing back downstairs.

> **LIBRA:**
> Every dark cloud has a silver lining. You may just have to sew it in yourself.

As Lipstick was attempting to open her boxes and put things away, Sally came running down the stairs and burst into her apartment. Kissing Lipstick on the cheek, Sally said, "It's all done! Dana says it's fine—she'd love to have you. She lives on the top floor and we meet every Wednesday evening at seven and Saturdays at two."

By 6:00 p.m., Lipstick had arranged the furniture and managed to assemble a sort of closet area in the bedroom by the time Neal came over with a bottle of wine and a large box.

"Darling, I'm confused," Neal said, putting the wine on the kitchen counter, placing the box on the floor, and taking off his black cashmere coat and Paul Smith scarf, "Why is the bed in the living room?"

"Well," Lipstick said, "the bedroom is supersmall and has only one tiny closet, so I decided to make the bedroom the closet, the living room the bedroom, and the kitchen the dining area. It's not like I'll ever have anyone over here anyway and fifteen boxes of clothes, ugh, make that thirteen, just won't fit in one tiny closet."

"Okay," Neal said, opening the wine, "That makes sense. Oh! Now, open your present I brought you," pointing toward the box by the sink.

"It's a little small to fit Bergdorf's fourth floor," Lipstick mused, tearing open the box.

"Hmmm," she said when she finally succeeded in ripping off the tape and looked inside. "A sewing machine."

"Voilà, my dear," Neal said, flourishing his hand. "Your solution!"

"But what am I supposed to do with this?" Lipstick said, looking at the machine as if it were an alien artifact.

"Lips, please don't be coy," Neal said, sitting down in the armchair Lipstick had placed in the kitchen. "Were you not the best seamstress in Ms. Frampton's etiquette classes?"

Lipstick shuddered.

Every afternoon of every second Saturday, from the time she was twelve until she graduated summa cum laude from The Spence School, she'd been forced to attend Ms. Frampton's School of Arts and Etiquette, where society's strict guidelines were drummed into her head: Use the right fork. Sit up straight. No borrowing dresses from designers, only buying. Absolutely, no cursing *under any circumstances*. Polite conversation is an art form, so practice. Sit with your legs closed, knees together, and with your left leg crossing your right leg at the ankle. Don't cross your thighs—you'll get spider veins. Never get up and dance at a party unless the hostess or someone higher in the social pecking order has done so first. At a dinner party, speak to the person on your right for the first course and switch to the person on your left for the second course—and after that you may leave your seat for a bathroom break, but not before.

In addition, she'd also learned how to "be a lady," and was taught how to sew, embroider, set the perfect table, and play a good—but not too good—game of tennis.

"Yes, but that was years ago," Lipstick moaned.

"Did you not make me the most beautiful slipcover, in under an hour, I might add, for the Ryans' sofa when their schnauzer shat on it right before the *Elle Decor* magazine shoot? And did you not say you secretly enjoyed sewing it?"

"Okay, sure, but what does this have to do with what I can wear to the gala season?" Lipstick asked.

"Oh my, it's going to be one of those spell-it-out-for-you days, isn't it?" Neal sighed. "Make. Your. Own. Dresses."

"Really? Me? From what?"

"Yes, silly, you. You always have to alter your clothes anyway and are constantly complaining about how boring everything looks off the racks—"

"Not Balenciaga or Dior!" Lipstick gasped as if she'd heard something libelous.

"Please. No one from *Y* can hear you—don't mock-shock me, Lips," Neal quipped. "Do it yourself. Isn't that your motto these days?"

"Yeeees," Lipstick said, rubbing her forehead again.

"So, use your old clothes. We may have edited, but there are still way too many in that closet-slash-bedroom, and it's not like you can wear the same thing twice after Jack sees it anyway. To borrow a line from Tim Gunn: 'Make it work.' And to help, I brought you some old *Vogue*s from the 1950s and '60s. Don't ruin them—they're classics from my personal library."

Lipstick, feeling overwhelmed, put her head down on the kitchen table and let out a sigh.

"It's okay," Neal said, "Let's look on the bright side—you have a fabulous new apartment in Soho, which is way cooler than the Village, darling. Think of it as grungetastic! You are the Marc Jacobs of *Y* right now, dear—young, hip, urban, and downtown—and a designer."

"Yeah," Lipstick said, sitting up straight in her chair, "Marc Jacobs." She instantly felt better.

"Now, let's order Chinese. Penelope told me about this fantastic delivery called Mama Buddha. She said to order her the spare ribs."

"Penelope?"

"Penelope, your new next-door neighbor who got you the apartment and whom I invited over. She should be here any minute now, probably dressed in something that used to be yours."

As if on cue, there was a knock on the door and Penelope's voice came floating through the cracks, "Neal? You there? It's me. . . ."

Neal opened Lipstick's door to reveal a slightly harried Penelope, dressed, sure enough, in one of Lipstick's hand-me-downs—a black Dolce & Gabbana sleeveless dress that clearly hadn't been tailored yet and hung on her in a baglike way, topped off with a yellow cashmere cardigan with pearl buttons. She'd tried to straighten her hair for her first day of work, but it was still slightly frizzy and a few loose strands had escaped her ponytail, giving Penelope a fried halo.

Neal enveloped Penelope in a hug, introduced her to Lipstick, and ordered Chinese food for the three of them while Lipstick, recognizing her dress and sweater, stifled a giggle. Penelope looked like a little girl playing dress up in her mother's clothes. Lipstick liked her immediately.

Penelope, exhausted, was more than keen to meet her new neighbor, the socialite who'd fallen on hard times that she'd heard so much about in the past year. But when she saw her, Penelope couldn't help but be irked by the fact that Lipstick had spent all day moving and still looked gorgeous. She was a tiny bit jealous of the other woman in Neal's life, especially one who seemed to have had so much handed to her. But then Penelope saw her eyes, which were still red from crying, and she felt a pang of guilt.

"Hey," Penelope mumbled, offering her hand, "nice to meet you. Thanks for all the clothes and stuff."

"Oh no," Lipstick said, grabbing her hand, "thank you for the apartment. You saved my life! And my dress looks better on you than it ever did on me."

"Ha!" Penelope said. "Now I know you're a liar—but I'll take what I can get!"

Just then the food arrived, and they all crowded around Lipstick's makeshift kitchen table.

"So, how's the new job?" Neal asked Penelope. "How's my David treating you?"

"Oh, man." Penelope sighed, tossing a masticated rib into the garbage bag. "I love David—he saved my butt like ten times today, but everybody else at New York Access is nuts. They're all sniffing some powerful glue."

"Oh, sounds fun!" Lipstick said, slurping her sesame noodles.

"Well. Not exactly," Penelope said, giving Lipstick and Neal an odd look.

SCORPIO:
Venus warms your privacy sector, and there can be very private love feelings and longings. But remember: In all areas, in order to move forward, you may have to take a step backward.

Penelope's job as an "assistant producer" was slightly more demeaning than she'd anticipated.

Penelope arrived for work at the NY Access newsroom on East Twenty-eighth Street a full fifteen minutes early. Once again, Gladys made her wait in the dingy reception area until David okayed her entry, and once again, Gladys called her Pamela.

"Penelope," David said when he saw her walk into the newsroom, "I'm so glad you actually showed up. Let me take you around and introduce you to people."

David guided her first to the "studio" area, which was divided into three sections: a sofa ("for interviews"), an anchor desk, and a green-screen area where the weather segment was done. It was all shiny and two dimensional in a way that television studios are, and while it may have looked authentic and homey through the distance of a TV screen, in person it looked cheap. Behind the IKEA sofa was a mock-up of Fifth Avenue so that when the cameras were on, it would look as if the studio were on the busy thoroughfare, in the heart of the city, rather than in the dingy warehouse district. The anchor "desk" was a shell of painted-over plywood, and there were signs that read NY ACCESS: #1 FOR NEWS! that could be rolled in or out of sight to add a three-dimensional aspect to any part of the set while reminding the viewers that they were, in fact, watching a high quality telecast.

Stepping over wires and dodging cameras, David took Penelope's arm and walked her over to the makeup room just as Marge's voice was heard ringing through the walls, "Coffee! David, where's my coffee?"

"Oh, blast that bitch." David sighed. "Penelope, wait right here; I'll be back in a second."

"Okay," Penelope said, taking a seat in the director's chair farthest from the door. "Take your time. I'm good."

Five minutes later, in walked the station's news anchor, Trace Howard. Penelope recognized him from his photo on the promotional poster by the front door where he stood with the station's other anchor, Kandace Karllsen, linking arms and smiling. Trace was a preternaturally tan sixty-two-year-old man with dyed, thinning hair on his head but a full *Magnum P.I.* mustache on his face and a new, young girlfriend every month or two.

He strutted into the makeup room, dropped his briefcase by the door, took one look at Penelope, and announced, "I am a powerful and attractive man!" before taking the seat next to hers and demanding, "Teeth whitening paste, please."

"Huh?" Penelope asked, jumping out of her chair.

"Teeth whitening paste, please," Trace said, staring straight ahead at himself in the mirror. "It's in the drawer. Hand it to me. Now."

"Oh, right. Gotcha," Penelope said and started sifting through several drawers until she found the required paste in the drawer by Trace's left knee.

As she was getting the paste out of the drawer, she felt his knee brush her ass.

"Hey!" Penelope exclaimed.

"Yes?" Trace asked, still staring at himself in the mirror. "My paste?"

She rolled her eyes but handed him the paste. Trace applied it to his teeth and, pulling his lips back into a skeletal grimace so the paste wouldn't be wiped off, barked, "Apply the tanning cream to my scalp!"

"Tanning cream?" Penelope asked, looking around the spare makeup room. A small, nervous-looking middle-aged woman with mousy brown hair dressed in an absurdly bright orange sherbet–colored suit outside the makeup room averted her eyes and pretended to be *very busy* as Trace, settling into his director's chair, leaned his head back and, still baring his cream-coated teeth, again demanded, "Tanning cream. Scalp. Now!" Turning toward the sherbet-colored suit, he ordered, "Berry! Get in here and show this girl how it's done!"

Berry, who turned out to be Trace's well-seasoned assistant, rushed over, grabbed a can of spray-on hair and some small rectangular sponges out of the drawer by Trace's right knee, and placed them in front of Trace. Berry whispered into Penelope's ear, "Spray it on him."

"What?" Penelope said. "Spray *hair* on him?" This was too much. Surely, she couldn't be serious? She was a fucking reporter, not a stylist—

"Shhh!" Berry, a nervous woman, said, not wanting to disturb Trace's concentration. "Yes. Spot spray, pat down, and repeat until he has a full head of hair. And hurry up!"

"Oh," Penelope said as the canister was thrust into one hand and a sponge in another. Apparently, Berry was serious. "Ew. Okay . . ."

Penelope picked up the "Can-O-Hair," walked around to face Trace's bald spots, which from a certain angle appeared to form a shape like Africa, picked one obvious expanse of hair-free scalp in the area that would have been Sudan or Egypt, and gingerly pressed the spray. A glob of dark brown, viscous fiber-like substance, the same color as Trace's dyed hair, shot out and sat on the spot like a small hair pyramid.

Penelope choked as some of the loose fiber in the air shot up her nose.

"Mmmph, bleargh," she said, gagging.

Trace's eyes popped open. "Well, pat it down, woman! I don't have all day."

"Okay," Penelope said, turning her face away and trying to breathe actual air. "Got it!" It was demeaning, but not as demeaning as going back to Cincinnati and living with her parents, so . . .

She grabbed a sponge and patted the "hair" down, fully covering the bald spots. "Not bad," she said, surveying her follicular artwork, "not bad."

After several applications of tanning cream, David finally came back from coffee duty and, ignoring Trace, loudly announced, "Penelope, scalp-covering duties are *not* in your job description—we have a makeup girl who comes in two times a week who takes care of that—and Trace is not supposed to wash it off every day unless it's summertime. He has shower caps." Turning toward Trace, David snapped, "Trace, that's enough. Marge wants you on set. Now," he said, turning back toward Penelope, "come with me and meet everyone else."

Guiding her by the elbow, David steered Penelope into the newsroom and toward the other main news anchor, Kandace Karllsen, a pie-faced, plump, bottle blond of Swedish descent who described herself as a "real, expressive" newswoman "with heart." This meant that when she talked she swished her hands in and out—using them as props to "drive her point home" while she fixated on "proper a-NUN-see-ay-SHUN"—and teared up during stories about puppies, babies, and firemen. In an attempt to make herself seem smarter than she actually was, she often made up words that sounded "bookschooled."

"Oh, Hel-LO," Kandace said looking Penelope up and down several times, taking in her Lipstick-donated outfit and black patent leather pumps from Candie's that Penelope had picked up at Macy's for thirty-five dollars on sale.

"A-DOR-able! Stick close to me (hand swish in) and you (hand swish out) will learn *irreduceible* amounts (hand swish in)."

Kandace came from CNN and was therefore, at least according to her, NY Access's "number one star," which didn't go over well with the station's other self-professed star, Trace Howard (he of the spray-painted bald spot). So Kandace and Trace ignored each other. Their egos were too big to acknowledge each other unless they absolutely had to. As Trace walked past Kandace, Penelope, and David, leaving the unmistakable smell of

Drakkar Noir wafting in the air, Kandace, who had celebrated her "annual thirty-fifth birthday" for the past nine years, said rather loudly to his back, "That man is just irretrievably jealous that I used to be the sole anchor for the two a.m. newscast on CNN for over five years."

Trace glowered, not breaking his stride. "That fat old meatball screwed the CNN bureau chief to get that job. And who watches at two a.m.? A mime outside of Yankee Stadium during the playoffs would get more viewers! Whereas, *I* am a powerful and attractive man!"

"And on with our tour!" David said, grabbing Penelope's arm and rushing her away from a boiling Kandace to introduce her to the rest of the newsroom. First up was Laura Lopez—nee Spincer—the tall, athletic-looking, blond-haired, blue-eyed "entertainment girl" who was actually thirty-six.

"She plays up the Hispanic last name," David whispered to Penelope as they approached Laura's desk, "despite not having any actual Hispanic lineage. She acquired her Latino last name through her ex-husband, a Puerto Rican tax inspector. They were only married for six months when Laura discovered his penchant for young African-American men. Ouch! I know, right? So, she kicked him out, but kept his last name as she feels it gives her 'a leg up in this cutthroat TV business.'"

Penelope and David, not noticing Laura listening to them, started to giggle.

"Fine, you go ahead and laugh now," Laura snapped while David rolled his eyes, "but by 2011, Hispanics will be the largest demographic in the U.S. and they are going to want to watch one of their own, Laura Lo-PEZ!"

Penelope eyed Laura's desk where she kept pictures of her idols—Natalie Morales, Geraldo Rivera, and Charo—framed in silver on her desk. She also had a "fame wall" to the left of her desk decorated with photos of her and the celebrities she had interviewed on junkets. There was a picture of Laura and Beth Blow—an unfortunate but appropriate last name as the twenty-one-year-old starlet of such movies as *Moodracer, 23 Ways to Die,* and *Muff* had been arrested with her mother last year in a Times Square hotel room doing lines of cocaine.

"She gets such a bad rap," Laura said, catching Penelope looking at the photo. "That Beth is just such a sweet, down-to-earth girl—and unlike the others her age, she can actually act. We're very close." There were also photos of Laura and the thrice-married action star, Snake Marlin ("Just a doll—a *real* gentleman," Laura cooed. "Is he grabbing your boob and flipping off the camera?" Penelope asked, peering closely at the picture, as David pinched her arm), and Laura and Ryan Jones, the manic-depressive comedic actor who had supposedly overcome a bad methamphetamine problem but nonetheless still tried to commit suicide two years ago ("So funny, not depressing at all!"), among dozens of others.

After fifteen more minutes of show and tell, David was finally able to drag Penelope away. "Be careful of the Lopez," he warned, "as long as she thinks you're useful and dispensable, she'll be friendly, but if she ever feels threatened, she'll turn on you in a second and eat you for lunch."

David then introduced her to the station's sportscaster, Mike "Heisman" Cutcher, nicknamed not after the trophy he certainly never won, but because during his sportscasts, he was famous for calling out good plays while pulling a "Heisman Pose"—putting one hand that cupped an invisible football by his ear, while his other arm stretched straight out in front of him—then shouting, "Hey-OH, *there's* the Heisman!" He used this signature move during any good play, even when it involved sports that were not football.

The next stop on David's Meet NY Access tour was near a lone cubicle in the back that was shrouded in darkness as several lights had blown out. There sat the weatherman, the mono-named "Storm." Storm usually kept to himself—and his weather charts, maps, and websites—in the far corner of the NY Access offices.

As Penelope and David walked by Storm's desk, David whispered to Penelope, "We don't really talk to Storm unless we actually have to. He listens to a *lot* of late-night talk radio." Storm's desk had a large picture of his idolized namesake, Strom Thurmond (his mother had been mildly dyslexic, which turned out to be a boon for his climate-centric career), and David warned her, "Stay away from him. He's liberal only with sharing his latest conspiracy theories—which usually have to do with government-controlled weather-bending machines and alien anal probes that most likely do not exist except in the far corners of Storm's mind."

"Or bedroom?" Penelope mused.

"Touché," David laughed.

Penelope was then introduced to Eric, the main cameraman, Stew, the sound guy, hordes of other assistant producers, and a particularly cute producer named Thomas, a tall man with sandy brown hair in a dark suit and glasses, who looked like a younger version of William Hurt in *Broadcast News*.

"So you're the new inmate," Thomas said, smiling. "David told me about you. Penelope Mercury, right? You came from the *Telegraph*."

"Um, yeah," Penelope said, a little flustered yet flattered.

"You did some really good street reporting over there. We picked up a lot of your stories. My favorite was the one about the guy in Queens who tried to get married to his dog. What was the headline again?"

"Bitchin' Bride," Penelope said, blushing. Nobody had ever mentioned specific stories she'd done before.

"Yes! Bitchin' Bride—absolutely genius! Whatever happened to him?"

"I think he's in Bellevue and the dog was put up for adoption."

"Right, well, it was good work. Glad to have you on board. I hope you'll stay longer than your predecessor." Turning to David, Thomas asked, "David, how long did the last one work here? One, two months?"

"Something like that," David said.

A voice called from the studio, "Thomas, we need you on set, now! Someone's walked off with the evening news placard."

"Well, it was nice meeting you," Penelope said, shaking his hand.

"You too," Thomas said, smiling again. "Stick around for a while. It's really not so bad."

"He's yummy," Penelope whispered to David as Thomas walked off to deal with the crisis on set.

"Don't get a crush just yet," David warned. "He's a great producer but keeps to himself. Never mixes work with pleasure."

"What's his story?" Penelope asked, even more interested now that Thomas was unattainable.

"Not sure, really," David said. "He's been here for like four years. Used to do documentaries in Pakistan or something intellectual like that. Not sure why he came back. Laura's been trying to open that trap door for years with no luck."

On the completion of David's tour, he whispered, "Trace is fine—just stay away from his hands, they're as bad as his knees. Kandace is a pain, but somewhat harmless. The others are okay. Well, not *okay,* but you know. Just keep your head down, do what they tell you to do, within reason of course, and above all, try and steer clear of Marge. She takes a little . . . getting used to. She's bipolar, but she's really not that bad. She's been around for years and this place is pretty much her last stop—and she knows it."

It was sage advice that Penelope took to heart, and that day she managed to stay out of Marge's way, busying herself with Trace's superficial demands and helping Eric set up the shots for the evening news, until just after the afternoon editorial meeting, in which everyone gathered in Marge's office to talk about stories for the evening news and feature segments.

Penelope, who'd been trying to find Trace another bottle of spray-on hair (he'd used up the last bottle while trying to fluff up a patch on his chest—he was wearing his shirt open by two buttons that day), was fifteen minutes late to the meeting. That was not a good thing.

"Polly," Marge said, as Penelope tried to sneak into the meeting, "since you obviously don't understand how important these meetings are and *clearly* need to learn this business from the ground up, you will stay after and do the Rolodex." A shudder ran through the office as Penelope's new coworkers eyed her sympathetically.

Marge's favorite punishment for office infractions was to have the offending party sit across from her at her desk and check every name, number, and address in her Rolodex, under her steely, watchful eye . . . starting with the Aarons. She would listen to the offender make the call say, "Excuse me, this is (fill in the blank) from Marge Gelb-Green's office at New York Access and I am just confirming your address and telephone number . . ." Marge would wait until the punishee had hung up (or more likely, been hung up on) and then say, "I didn't hear you get the maid's cell phone number! The maid has a cell phone! Call back!"

To make amends for her tardiness, Penelope had been forced to do the Rolodex for more than five hours and only reached the Davisons in Marge's long list of contacts by the time she was relieved for the day.

Back at Lipstick's apartment, Penelope was just finishing up the tale of her peculiar day when her cell phone rang.

"Oy." Penelope sighed. "My mom, I'll call her later. She probably wants to know if I'm out on the street yet."

Lipstick nodded. "Yeah. I'm still waiting for my parents to realize I meant it when I said I was living on my own. Although, I have to admit, I'm a little . . . terrified. This whole being-broke thing is scary."

"Ha," Penelope said, waving her hand in the air as if there were a fly. "Please, it's a piece of cake. I've been broke my whole life—and look at me! I'm fiiine," causing Neal to burst into laughter. Ignoring Neal, Penelope continued. "Just start taking the subway, don't shop, borrow office supplies like pens, and soap, and toilet paper, and get to know Sam the deli man and Maddie at the coffee shop next door, Local. They're both sympathetic food suppliers. Stick with me—you'll be a pro at brokeness by the end of the week!"

"Oh my, ladies," Neal snickered, "you two are priceless in your cluelessness. Penelope, perhaps you can give Lipstick some lessons on how to be poor, and Lipstick, perhaps you can warm up your sewing techniques by helping alter your old clothes for Penelope. Darling, this beautiful dress is at least two sizes too big."

"Hey, I think it looks *fabulous,*" Penelope said. "Lipstick, I'd be happy to help more, but can we talk later? I have to wake up early for the morning 'strategy' meeting, and if I'm late, I have to do the Rolodex. Again."

"Okay," Lipstick said, clearing the paper plates and throwing them into the trash. "But do you want to do yoga with me in this girl Dana's apartment on the top floor Wednesday night? My friend Sally Brindle invited me."

"Sally Brindle?" Penelope asked. "What is that? Some kind of riding gear?"

"No, silly." Lipstick laughed. "She's my yoga teacher. And she gives private lessons to Dana in the building, like, twice a week."

"So why does Dana want us there if she pays for private lessons?" Penelope asked, itching to light up a cigarette.

"Weeellll," Lipstick said, "I don't know if Dana so much wants us there as Sally does. Sally's a little worried about her. She apparently hasn't left the apartment for a year because she's depressed or something, and Sally thinks company would be good for her."

"Is she that woman with the wiener dog?" Penelope asked.

"I don't know," Lipstick said. "Sally didn't say anything about a dog, but please come; I don't know her and it could be awkward. And it's free!"

Penelope, concerned about Dana's supposed agoraphobia, said, "Is she some weird reclusive freak who's going to, like, start dressing like me and one day stealth-attack me with a stiletto, single-white-female style? I mean—seriously. From what I can tell, all she does is work fifteen hours a day and walk that crazy dog. I don't think she's ever come home drunk or said more than three words to anyone."

"Well, maybe?" Lipstick said.

"Okay," Penelope said, standing up and wiping her hands on her black dress. Lipstick winced. It was her old Dolce, after all. "Why not? I'm about as flexible as Rahm Emanuel but it could be fun—and 'free' is a broke girl's favorite word. Knock on my door Wednesday. I'll be home around six or seven."

Penelope kissed Neal and Lipstick good-bye and entered her apartment just as her phone rang. It was her mother. Again.

"Penelope, it's your mother," Susan Rosenzweig Mercury announced.

"I know, Ma," Penelope said. "Your name came up on my phone. Like it does *every* time you call."

"Don't be fresh!" Susan snapped. "So. How was your first day back at work? Did you apologize?"

"Ma." Penelope sighed. "I told you. I'm not working at the *Telegraph* anymore. I'm at a local cable channel."

"Oh!" Susan squealed. "TV, how glamorous—Jim! Jim, put that Bible down and get over here—*my* daughter's gonna be on TV!"

"Well, not quite," Penelope said, "I'm an assistant producer, which is basically a gofer."

"Penelope Mercury," Susan said. "Rule number thirty-seven, any job that pays is a good job. Did the check bounce? Do they beat you? What's the problem?"

"No, Ma, no problem . . . I was just trying to tell you how my first day we—," Penelope said, before her mother cut her off.

"Jim! Talk to *your* daughter. She's already complaining. This is your doing, you know. If you hadn't been so indecisive with the whole Jesus-versus-Jewish thing she'd be a doctor or a lawyer by now. You said you'd convert to Judaism for me. But did you? No!"

Penelope sat down on her living room sofa and turned her TV on mute, silently watching reruns of *The Dukes of Hazzard* on Country Music Television while her parents bickered. Bo was so much cuter than Luke. She couldn't believe she once thought Luke was the hottie. Maybe it was like *Star Wars*. Everyone always thought Luke Skywalker was the stud until they grew up and realized he was totally gay and that Han Solo was the hunkalicious one.

Penelope's thoughts were interrupted by her father.

"Penelope, it's your dad," Jim, who had finally succeeded in wresting the phone away from Susan, said. "Just wanna say, I love you, your mother loves you, and Jesus loves you. Now, what channel you on?"

"You can't watch me, Dad," Penelope said. "I work at a *local* cable access in New York and you live in Cincinnati, Ohio. And besides, I'm not on air, I'm an assistant producer."

"An assistant producer. Wow, that sounds neat. But be careful, those liberal TV folks will try and warp your mind. I'll pray for you," Jim said. "Jesus rules, baby!"

"Thanks, Dad—I'll keep that in mind," Penelope said, "Love you. Tell Ma I said 'bye."

As Jim and Susan were shouting their good-byes, Penelope hung up the phone and turned the volume on the TV up just as Bo and Luke Duke jumped in the General Lee for the thousandth time and fishtailed out of Uncle Jesse's farm.

SAGITTARIUS:
Inertia weighs in during Uranus's cycle, and you must pay extra attention to the scales.

Dana was mortified. How could she have gained five pounds? She had been sticking to the Weight Watchers diet, cheating only mildly, and doing her yoga group twice a week with the girls from her building for the last month. But when she stepped on the weigh-in scale before the Weight Watchers meeting in Tribeca, there it was in electronic numbers: 158. It would have been fine had she been five foot eleven inches instead of five foot four—or five foot four and pregnant. Alas, she was neither.

"The scales don't lie," the weigh-in nurse said when Dana suggested that perhaps she was mistaken.

May you burn in the seventh circle of Dante's hell with my legal brethren. "Yes, but do they negotiate?" Dana inquired politely.

The nurse gave her a blank stare. "Just kidding!" Dana said, but the nurse didn't laugh. Dana collected her things and went into the meeting and breathed a sigh of relief. They were all there.

And they were all still fatter than she had ever been. In order of fatness: Corynne, the airline check-in desk manager (five foot three, 175 pounds); Annie, the human resources director (five foot seven, 196 pounds); Helen the cashier (five foot five, 228 pounds); and Marjorie, the i-banker (five foot six, 301 pounds).

"Dana," Marjorie said, looking at her with annoyance, "why are you here?"

"I'm here because I'm fat," Dana said.

"You are not fat," Annie said. "I'm fat. Helen is fat; Corynne is fat. Marjorie, you're obese." Marjorie nodded gravely. "You, Dana," Annie continued, "are not fat. You are chubby."

"Well, I used to be fat," Dana said.

"And now you're not," Helen countered.

"I don't want to argue the issue," Dana said, pinching the roll of flesh hanging over her suit pants. "But may I present the evidence?"

"That's flab, but it ain't fat," Helen grumbled.

"Well, if it makes you feel better, I'm gaining. I'm five pounds more than I was last week. And I'm still thirty pounds over my target weight. And who are you all to be criticizing me? I was fat, then I wasn't, then I was fat again and lost it, and now I'm gaining again. This is supposed to be a support group!"

"Sorry, Dana," Marjorie said, "it's been a rough week for all of us. I got pushed out of all the photos from the Go Green event at work because the photographer said they didn't have a wide-angle lens."

"I put out the candy bowl by my desk and this bitch who sits next to me accused me of trying to make everyone in the office as fat I as I am," Annie said. "She called me the Candy Enabler."

"Well, my boss told me that if I gain any more weight I won't be able to fit in the uniform and they'll have to suspend me," Corynne said, nibbling on a low-calorie snack bar.

"I hooked up with a guy and when I took my shirt off he screamed, 'Flabulanche!' and laughed," Helen whispered, sitting on her hands and looking at an invisible spot on her lap.

"That's just actionable," Dana said. "Marjorie and Corynne, you two should file a harassment suit and Helen, you should've punched the guy. Let me know if you need help. But don't get angry with me for wanting to be skinny."

But the truth was, the girls had a point. As much as Dana hated to admit it, although she *had* gained weight, she knew she didn't need to be going to the meetings anymore. Dana, who'd gained forty pounds during the first year of her marriage, had begun them at Noah's insistence. So she'd gone to the meetings and lost some of the weight over a period of a year.

But then he'd left her for Evya and the weight had come back. Walking home after the meeting, Dana quietly admitted to herself that perhaps she didn't need the meetings—she needed a shrink. The meetings were basically Dana's sole social contact with the rest of the world outside of work. She had become a shut-in who was obsessed with her weight.

The only other people she had semiregular contact with were the (skinny) yoga girls, Penelope and Lipstick and sometimes their friend Neal who, upon setting foot in her loft for the first time, announced, "Oh! So chic! So fabulous! So . . . Philippe Starck!"

The group was a funny one. At first Dana had resented the intrusion, but after the second week, she looked forward to it.

She loved living vicariously through them.

Lipstick was a glamourous Barbie-like figure—if Barbie were almost six-feet-tall and semicracked out on Klonopins. She'd been cut off by her parents and was living her life like Kabuki theater, but was trying her best to keep up appearances—and always looked good doing it. Dana was also intrigued with Lipstick's side gig as a seamstress—who knew socialites could sew?—of which Dana was benefiting from as well. If Lipstick screwed up on sizing and constructed something too big, she'd sometimes give it to Dana—like the bias-cut dress she'd created from some cashmere sweaters last week. It didn't fit Lipstick properly so she had donated it to Dana, who loved it, even though she didn't have anywhere to wear it to.

Dana knew it was Lipstick's way of encouraging her to stop being a recluse. Every time she proffered something, Lipstick would say, "So, you know, if you'd like to come to dinner sometime, you can wear this," or "Hey, there's a big party for this new artist at the Deitch Gallery. You could wear that skirt I made." If something was too small, she'd give it to Penelope, who was always eager for more clothing—and invitations. "I'll go, sure!" Penelope would squeal eagerly when Lipstick asked her out somewhere. "What else do I have going on? Nothing, that's what! Count me in!"

Lipstick was one of those people who seemed to think more of others—and their opinions of her—than of herself. And it was funny to watch what seemed to be Lipstick's first experience with actually working. And working *hard*. Lipstick had established a routine: she went to her day job at Y, covered the events for the magazine in the evenings, and then late at night she came home to whip up another creation, sometimes staying up until the early hours of the morning. But, as Lipstick admitted to the girls, Neal was right: "I do love sewing. And there's something so satisfying about manual labor."

The only drawback was that it ravaged her hands. Lipstick had had a hard time readjusting to the needles, pins, and sewing machine and had taken to wearing small ladylike kid gloves at all times to cover up her battle-scarred fingers. Even during yoga. Lipstick removed her gloves during the third week at Penelope's insistence, and Dana gasped at Lipstick's once beautifully manicured fingers, with raw and angry-looking cuticles, covered in pinpricks and Band-Aids.

"Sewing is hazardous to one's facade," Lipstick shrugged as she put her gloves back on.

Then there was Penelope, who always looked like she had just escaped a close encounter with a twister. Which, in a way, was appropriate; her life seemed like a tornado. Dana always looked forward to hearing about Penelope's crazy new job at NY Access, which would have crippled lesser people with its daily humiliations. But Penelope had a strange optimism. While events didn't always seem to go her way, at least they were moving forward—or backward or sideways. Either way, they were still *moving*. Dana felt that just by being in her proximity, she too could pick up some momentum.

> **SCORPIO:**
> A very active and effective career phase has commenced, even if you don't recognize the opportunities presented to you.

And things were indeed happening to Penelope.

For starters, she was semipromoted. It wasn't a case of wowing anyone with her work ethic (which was fine), seeing an opening and going for it (she'd had enough of that), or impressing the powers that be with her amazing gofering/bald-spot-covering skills. It was more that she bothered to show up and, by virtue of that, found herself, as they say, "in the right place at the right time," even if she had to dodge Trace's hands and knees while doing so.

That morning, the entire staff of NY Access was crammed into Marge's office for a particularly hellish story meeting. Nobody dared move. The faces of the producers, crew, and talent wore a uniform look of sheer terror. Even the office cockroaches were in hiding.

Marge was on the warpath. Her fourth face-lift hadn't been as successful as she'd thought it would be, leaving her not "refreshed," as she had hoped, but instead, a little . . . tight. Her surgeon, the renowned Dr. Dick Barnes, MD, told her during her post-op checkup the day before, "It's the swelling, Marge. It *will* go down. It's just taking a little longer to heal this time. . . . Yes, I know Marge, I owe you a lot. . . . I have thanked you for your pieces on me and my work—which I assure you, is spectacular in this instance—many times. . . . But you have to understand . . . even though you tell people you're fifty, you're not. And the body takes more time to heal as it gets older."

"How dare you!" Marge had screeched as she stormed out of the office. "I'm forty-two!"

In addition to being terrified of looking like Barbara Walters in a wind tunnel (with what David had termed the Iraq look of constant shock and awe) for the rest of her life, Marge's meds weren't working as well. Apparently, if you take the Blues (Percocet), the Pinks (Klonopin), and the Greens (Valium) on a regular basis, their effectiveness wears off—a fact Marge had overlooked for the past nine years as she popped her handful of pills daily, in a combination and amount that would have long since killed individuals of lesser constitutions.

"It's like a big bowl of Good 'n Plentys at her house," David once mused to Penelope. "It's insane. You walk in her bedroom and there's a glass vase full of the pills, like a party bowl from the seventies. She says she likes the way the colors meld. They match her Beverly Hills Hotel–meets-rabid-birds-of-paradise décor."

This morning, having run out of all three color pills simultaneously, nothing was mollifying Marge's anger.

And corporate had called. The numbers were down.

"What? Doesn't *anyone* have *any* ideas?" she screeched, pounding her fist onto her desk, spilling her ninth cup of coffee. "What the *hell* do I *pay* you all for? Are you on strike? Did your paychecks bounce and I wasn't aware of it? Have you all been licking the lead paint off your walls? I want to hear some ideas here, people! Something *new* . . . something *fresh*! Start talking or someone's getting fired!"

A young, naïve assistant producer who had just been hired a week earlier raised her hand and said, "Um, excuse me, we could do an exposé on the fine dining establishments that have large rodent problems and multiple health violations—the latest restaurant health report just came out and—"

"God, that's so *boring* and *tired*!" Marge roared as the young woman's mouth slammed closed. "Channel Five did that *two years* ago. I mean, it's always okay to revisit, but that's something that should have been done three weeks ago—*before* the damned health report came out! What's your name?"

The woman, who was just out of college and had been hired for her inexperience and willingness to work for next to nothing, froze. "Kelly James, ma'am . . ."

The room went silent.

"Uh-oh," David murmured to Penelope, who was clutching a tray of office supplies Marge had asked for at the meeting's outset. "Mount Saint Marge is gonna blow."

Marge's new face went from red to purple, the vein in her forehead began to throb, and her eyes bulged like a rare Madagascar monkey. For a second it was almost peaceful—the calm before a hurricane.

And then the storm hit.

"Ma'am?!" Marge said, throwing a magazine that had been in front of her in Kelly's general direction. "Ma'am? Who do you think I am, Kelly James? A *geriatric*? Do you think I've lost my faculties and shit my Depends like someone's grandparents in a nursing home?!"

"I . . . I didn't mean anything by it—" Kelly said.

"Get . . . out . . . of . . . here," Marge seethed.

"But—" Kelly protested, her eyes watering.

"Now!"

Kelly (who ended up not being permanently banished due to a Blues-induced change of heart two hours later, but was forced to do the Rolodex for three days straight) burst into tears and fled the room, as Marge roared, "Who's next? Are you people *retarded*? Did a *short bus* drop you all off at work today? Give me ideas *now* . . . NOW!"

Terrified, the office crowd started shouting out ideas all at once. There was safety in numbers, and if several ideas were thrown at Marge, she would not be able to match an idea to one person, so the chances of another public humiliation were minimum.

"High-wire jobs—New York's most dangerous jobs—send someone up the Empire State Building in a window-washer rig!"

"Billionaire speed dating—why do rich guys need dates and who are the hookers who show up?"

"Heart-healthy meals—be a Calorie Commando!"

"Runway fashion—who really wears that shit?"

"Sexy Easter bunny outfits that will make your man hop into bed!"

"Wait!" Marge roared, slamming down her coffee cup so hard it chipped on the edge. "What was that about bunnies and sex?"

"Ah . . ." a voice in the back said, "it was, ah, sexy Easter outfits that will make your man hop into bed—you know, kind of like board shorts for guys—you can wear board shorts on land or in the ocean. Dual functions . . . a sexy bunny outfit that can be worn to hide eggs and host Easter parties but is hot enough to wear in the boudoir."

"Who said that?" Marge demanded.

The William Hurt look-alike raised his hand and said, "Me."

Penelope turned toward the voice. Her heart skipped a beat. He was hot supreme.

"ME? What kind of name is that?" Marge demanded.

"Fine, Marge, I will play your crazy game. I, Thomas Howard, had the hot bunny idea."

"How long have you worked here?"

"Four years, Marge, you know that. I've been producing the evening news for you for three years."

"Well, where the hell have you been hiding, Thomas Howard? That is the most genius idea I have heard all week! It's sexy—sex sells, people! *And* it has bunnies in it—people absolutely *adore* animals! Especially cute fuzzy ones! Fabulous! Where's Lopez?"

"Laura's out today," David piped up. "She's interviewing Sam Dwain for his new movie *Monster Men* at the Regency. The junket runs all day. She won't be back till late afternoon."

"Who the hell are we going to get on such short notice?" Marge roared. "You! Blondie!" She pointed at Penelope, who promptly dropped the tray of office supplies she was holding. "Get into makeup and put on something colorful! You're doing the hot bunny story. NOW!! But clean up that mess first. God! Can't we get any good help around here?"

And that is how Penelope ended up later that day at Walt's World of Curios, a "novelty" (read: sex) store on Seventh Avenue South and Charles Street, in the only "sexy bunny" outfit they could find—a skintight fuzzy X-rated Bugs Bunny costume that smelled like someone had worn it before, with her "Smile, It's Monday!" grandma underwear peeking through the outfit's cutout crotch. The effect was more silly than sexy, but none of that mattered to Marge, who upon hearing a detailed description of the outfit barked, "Love it!" before slamming down the phone.

Standing in aisle four, Thomas got off the phone. "Marge wants to make the piece a feature, so we have to do some promos," he excitedly told Penelope, who was breaking out in a rash on her neck from the polyester suit that had a heart-shaped cutout to show bunny cleavage; large, oversized bunny paws and feet; as well as a hole for her face to stick through what would have been the costume's mouth, with two large rabbit teeth hanging menacingly just above her forehead, obstructing her view.

"Oh, God, no."

"Sorry, Marge said we had to."

"Are we shooting from inside the . . . Easter paradise?" Penelope asked, sweeping her large rabbit paw hand over a wall of shiny, pastel-colored "marital aids."

"No, there's a bakery with a good Easter display two blocks away. We can do it there."

"I have to go out in public like this?" Penelope moaned. "I can barely move with these feet. I had to do a weird fascist march just to get out of the changing room."

"Hey," Walt, the store's owner, said, "you only paid for an hour—take it wherever you want, but I want this back by five. Comic-Con is in town next week and this is one of the more popular outfits."

"Comic-Con?" Penelope asked.

"The comic book convention," Walt said, rolling his eyes.

Two minutes later, Penelope, in the smelly, nasty bunny suit, tripped down Seventh Avenue South with the crew to Maven's Bakery, which had Easter cakes in the window. Thanks to an unseasonable cold snap, it was freezing and the wind was tearing down the avenue, whipping up garbage and silt, making it hard for Penelope to fully open her eyes despite the bunny teeth blocking the wind.

"I feel like a camel in a freezing sandstorm," Penelope shivered as Eric and Stew set up the cameras for the shot. "A really hideous, promiscuous bunny-camel."

"Get into a sexy stance!" Thomas yelled through the wind at Penelope when they reached the bakery. "Make sure the egg cakes are in the shot!"

She put her hand on her hips, grinning madly while thrusting her chest out in her best manic mascot pose. "Um, okay . . . how's this?" Penelope—who'd never considered herself particularly sexy—asked.

"Well, how about something . . . sexier," Thomas suggested. "Lean against the glass and jut your hip out . . . yeah, yeah, that's it. Now put one hand up on the wall and one on your hip . . . yeah! Perfect!"

"I look like a bunny version of Jodie Foster in *Taxi Driver,*" Penelope said. "I could take a stand and say I'm not doing this. I used to be a respectable reporter, you know."

"Marge said she *really* wanted it," Thomas said. "I'll admit, it was a stupid idea, but Marge liked it and it will be both our asses if you walk out on the big shoot of the day. Besides, what else are you gonna do today—dodge Trace's clammy hands while you find more teeth whitening paste for him?"

Penelope backed down. "Okay. You have a point. Besides, nobody watches NY Access anyway, right? But you'd better tell her I deserve a raise for this."

"Fine, fine, just pose . . . okay great . . . now look at the camera and say, 'This Easter, come hop into bed with New York Access!'"

A guy in a black town car rolled his window down and wolf-whistled at Penelope.

"Hey, thanks!" Penelope said, waving after the car. Looking toward Thomas, she said, "That's the first time I've been whistled at since, like, junior high."

"Let's go, Penelope," Thomas said. "Say the line and we're out." Several people stopped to stare at the shoot and the oddity in front of them, creating a small crowd.

"Um," Penelope said, feeling more than a little awkward and shy in front of an audience. "In front of all these people? Seriously?"

"Oh, come on. You look kind of cute, actually," Thomas said. "Just say it . . . they probably won't even run it!"

"I look cute? Really?" Penelope blushed. Maybe the bunny outfit wasn't *so* bad.

Cars honked their horns as they drove by and a man from a nearby scaffolding screamed, "Hey bunny babe, wanna find my Easter egg?"

"Ooooh, that's a good one," Thomas said. "We'll do that too!"

"Oh, no," Penelope said. "Fine, I'll say the first one—but I'm not saying the bad pick-up line. A bunny has got to have standards." She got herself back into the "sexy stance" on the bakery's glass window, positioned in between an egg cake and an Easter basket. As the wind howled in her face, she screeched, "This Easter come hop into bed with . . . Argh!"

Someone had tossed a half-eaten hot dog at her head from a passing car. The actual hot dog and bun had bounced off the top of the bunny face, but the condiments remained. Relish dripped down the bunny's buck teeth onto her face and Penelope suddenly contemplated going back to the *Telegraph*.

After Eric, the cameraman, helped her clean off, Penelope regained her composure, once again assumed the "sexy stance," and howled into the wind, "This Easter come hop into bed with New York Access!"

"Perfect!" Thomas said. "Now, let's do it again."

"Satan," Penelope said, shivering.

LIBRA:

Your work environment will change. Expect a sudden influx of creativity that will be noticed—and envied—by all.

• • •

As Penelope was being tortured in the West Village, Lipstick was uptown covering a trunk show at Portia Vanderven's East Ninetieth Street townhouse with Ashley. Portia was a former model who, immediately after her 1999 wedding to Goldman Sachs managing director Ralph Vanderven, had set about sealing the deal by providing him with two adorable children, Maxwell and Harriet. The children, who spoke fluent Spanish and called their nanny, "Madre Marta," and Portia, "Madre Portia," were the light of her life and "so precious, no diamond could compare to them." But even more important, Maxwell and Harriet provided physical assurance of a heftier divorce settlement should her husband Ralph ever leave her for the Russian rhythmic gymnast he was rumored to be seeing on the side.

Not that Portia was alone in her predicament. The ladies of the Upper East Side were all atwitter. Just a year ago there were several high-profile splits: the Kramers, the Gettys, the von Furstmergs. All of which had involved women from the same "Russian Invasion," one member of which was trying to coerce Ralph into international relations.

Portia was on red alert. News of Ralph's affair was all over town, whispered about over lunch at Fred's, the racks at Bendel's, and the bar at La Goulue. But Portia's options were limited. She wasn't going to leave him and hand over her husband, the private plane, the yacht, and the houses in the Hamptons and Palm Beach to some woman he'd happened to have met at the notorious hunting grounds of the *Bull & Bear* after work one day, and who'd been flexibly fucking him for just six months. That Russkie would have to work much harder than that. "You don't leave your husband over infidelity. That's ridiculous. Men aren't supposed to be monogamous—that's just a bourgeois lie that Americans made up. I'm more . . . European. Ralph and I have a partnership, a corporation. There's more to marriage then just romance and sex," Portia, momentarily letting her guard down, had told Lipstick over lunch a week earlier. "Besides, what would become of me if I did leave him? Or, God forbid, he left me? I'll tell you what—not much. There's not much of a market for a forty-two-year-old divorcée with two children who demands a certain lifestyle these days. He would remarry and that hooker would get the money and the name and I would be forgotten."

So to combat the anger, boredom, and frustration of having fulfilled all societal and connubial promises—and still be stuck in a semiloveless marriage that may or may not be torn asunder by a lithe and limber gymnast—Portia decided to do what several others in her situation had done: start a handbag/jewelry line, and then have a big party to celebrate it.

"It's shimple really," Portia, who was on her fifth Grey Goose gimlet by then, said to Lipstick. "I love handbagsh, I have about a *million* of them—and I obvioushly know fashion. I'm front row at Parish couture every year. Sho why not shtart my own very upshcale acceshories line?"

Lipstick noted the framed picture on one of the mantels of Portia with her good friend, socialite-turned-designer Tory Burch, whose eponymous line not only sold out at Saks Fifth Avenue but, thanks to several *Oprah* appearances, had sold out everywhere else as well. "Tory and her husband shplit—and she shtill got to keep her shocial shtanding," Portia slurred, picking up the picture and looking at it closely. "She's more entrenched than ever becaushe of that line. It *made* her. Shocially. Financially. I mean, she's *famous* now. She's got more money than her ex *and* she got to date Lanshe Armshtrong. That clothing line let her *be* the man and *get* the man."

"Okaaay, Portia," Lipstick said, taking the picture out of Portia's hands and breaking her trance. "Let's take a break from the drinks, just for a little bit, 'kay? Oh, look, Bethie and Birdie just arrived. . . ."

"Darling," Portia, looking Lipstick up and down with her gimlet-soaked eye, said in a loud, drunken voice before Lipstick could make a clean getaway, "*who* are you wearing?"

Just as Portia demanded to know about Lipstick's sartorial surprise, there was a lull in the room. All eyes turned toward Lipstick and on her latest creation: a crimson-red silk cocktail dress made from a Miu Miu dress and matching jacket she'd deconstructed and ripped apart at the seams a week earlier. It had a high collar that swept around the back of Lipstick's neck, draping on her shoulders and coming together in a low V. It was perfectly shaped, thanks to Lipstick's workmanship and the corset in the old Miu Miu dress that flared out to just above her knee—making it look like a Dior dress from the 1960s. Neal's old *Vogue*s had come in handy after all.

The eyes belonged to Ashley, Lipstick's coworker; the women who made up Bitsy Farmdale's posse, also known as The Bitsies: Peaches Swarovski, the crystal heiress; Gwendolyn "Gwynnie" Bacardi, the rum heiress; Mary MacDaniels (her father was a Scottish lord); Fernela Branca, who'd married into the family that created the liquor Fernet Branca; and Lulu Ward-Nass, of the textile monopoly. Thankfully, Bitsy herself had yet to show up. Also milling around was SueAnne Cavendish from Dolce & Gabbana, Ivanka Baer from *Vogue,* Marybelle Whitehead from *Glamour,* Susan Naim from *Harper's Bazaar,* Bethany Applewood, the head buyer for *Bergdorf,* and a host of other fashionistas. All looking at Lipstick's dress.

"It's beautiful," Susan gushed. "Where did you get it?"

"I didn't see that at any of the viewings last fashion week," Ivanka said. "Is it Prada?"

"No," Lipstick said evasively. "Just a dress I picked up in my travels."

"Figures," said Peaches. "Every time I see someone with a gorgeous creation, they never want to share the designer. Come on, Lena, it's not like we're all going to run out and buy the same dress. We just want to know where we can get it."

"Seriously, I'm not being a bitch," Lipstick said, "I got it in Paris last summer—"

"Oh, the French! They are just divine," Susan from *Harper's* sighed.

"You've been wearing a lot of this mysterious designer lately," Fernela said. "There was that blue gown you wore to the Alzheimer's benefit, the pantsuit at the Bahrain ball, the dress at the Tourrette's luncheon . . . you seem to have an awful lot of these clothes. Yet you won't share?"

"The designer is very . . . shy," Lipstick explained. "Although I'm sure she will be thrilled that you've been keeping tabs on all the clothes she's made for me."

"So! It's couture!" Lulu gasped. "I thought I knew all the couturiers in Paris. Who is she?"

"I . . . I can't say, sorry," Lipstick stammered. "I have to go, I'm expected at a dinner downtown in ten minutes."

"Why rush off? Bitsy will be here in a second," Lulu sniped. "She'll know who you're wearing. She knows everyone."

"Sorry, dinner plans, you know . . ." Lipstick gasped.

"Well, will you be wearing her to the Met next month?" Fernela asked, slyly. "Because as you know, you *have* to register the designer who is sitting at your table. And as I'm on the committee, I noticed you purchased your table months ago but never listed a designer."

"You'll see," Lipstick said, grabbing her coat and heading toward the door. "I don't have to register until two weeks before. So I guess you'll just have to wait."

Lipstick rushed outside into the freezing wind.

Ten minutes later Lipstick tried to navigate the whole "subway thing" at the East Ninety-sixth Street and Lexington station, but was having a hell of a time with her MetroCard. She swiped her card at the turnstile. It beeped and flashed, "Swipe Again at This Turnstile." After eight swipes, Lipstick got frustrated and went to another turnstile. When she swiped her card there it read, "JUST BEEN USED." She could hear the train rumbling its approach.

She ran up to the ticket booth. The station clerk ignored her.

"Excuse me, sir," Lipstick said, tapping on the glass. "Um, I swiped and swiped and it kept saying swipe again, but then I tried at another one and now it won't let me in! Help?"

The clerk, an ancient man of indeterminate age, didn't lift his eyes from the *New York Post* he was reading. "Should've kept swiping at the first turnstile, like it told ya."

"But I did and nothing was happening and now the train is here and I have to get home."

"Nothin' I can do. If it's a monthly or weekly card, you'll have to wait twenty minutes till you can go in again. I just can't bend the rules for everyone who wants to swipe their friends in."

"But I didn't swipe anyone in," Lipstick cried, frustrated, as she saw the train pull into the station. "Oh, darn. Forget it!" And, as the clerk kept reading, Lipstick did what she thought she would never do (besides riding the subway): something illegal. She jumped the turnstile and ran onto the train just as the doors were closing.

Trembling with excitement, Lipstick sat on the 4 express train to Union Square, where she transferred to the local and got out at Bleecker Street, wearing a huge grin on her face the whole way.

Later that night at yoga, Lipstick was still excited.

"You guys—you should have seen it!" she gushed to Penelope, Dana, and Sally during their sun salutations. "It was so cool, I was a *criminal*!"

"Okay, Jesse James," Penelope said, rolling her eyes and attempting to stand on one leg without falling. She liked Lipstick but thought that sometimes her "look at me having fun being poor" tales were annoying. "Take it easy there. I can't afford bail if you get caught, and I don't even want to think about what that damned society website that you're so obsessed with would say if there was a police report."

Over the past month or so, Penelope had had to face her snap judgments head on. Dana, whom she'd always thought was an aloof workaholic, *was* a workaholic, but was also very sweet. She'd let Penelope and Lipstick join her yoga class free of charge and was always there to offer advice if they needed it. Which they did. A lot.

But Penelope didn't understand Dana's depression. It had been, after all, a full year since her divorce. It was almost as if Dana were still trying to fit the image her jackass ex-husband had tried to stuff her into. The marriage was the one thing Dana, the ultimate type-A personality, had ever done that failed and, therefore, she couldn't get past it.

As for Lipstick, Penelope had expected Neal's friend to be an airheaded, cocaine-addicted snob—which, up until then, she'd assumed all socialites were. But she was fun and generous and didn't touch the Colombian marching powder. However, sometimes her tendency to treat being "poor" like a trip to Epcot Center was grating. After all, Lipstick wasn't really poor. Penelope and Lipstick were, according to national statistics, actually middle-class, although in New York, that placed them firmly in the lower middle-class section of society.

At that moment Lipstick leaned down to hug her head to her knees and came face-to-face with her burgeoning belly.

"Uch," she moaned, disgusted. "I hate Rachael Ray."

"Hello, non sequitur," Penelope said. "I'll admit—Rachael Ray's annoying but why you gotta hate?"

Lipstick sighed, standing up straight, while Sally began to meditate in the corner and Dana lay flat on her back.

"I've been trying to live on like twenty-five dollars a day. I took your advice, Penelope. I got a monthly MetroCard, stole toilet paper from my office, and I've been making my own breakfasts and meals on the weekends. So I started watching the Food Network while I sew, and Rachael Ray is always like, 'I do it cheap for the everyday family, blahblahblah. . . . Watch me travel on forty-five dollars a day, blahblahblah. . . .' And she lies! Lies! You just *can't* do New York on forty-five dollars a day. I think the Food Network producers must've slipped her some cash. And then I watched her cooking show and I gained ten pounds off of those damn 'sammies' and 'stoups.' That's it. I'm switching to Lean Cuisine and Martha Stewart."

"Well, you could always go to Weight Watchers," Dana said. "I . . . um. I went to a Weight Watchers meeting last night."

"Is that where you're always going on Tuesday nights?" Lipstick asked.

"Huh?" Penelope asked. "What do you need to go to Weight Watchers for? You're not that . . . heavy."

Well," Dana said, "I am a bit. And I was really fat once. I gained a lot of weight during my marriage and my husband used to make me go."

"And you were *sad* when you two divorced?" Penelope quipped.

"Hey, I lost the weight—and kept most of it off. Kind of."

"So why do you go back now?" Lipstick said.

"It's hard to explain," Dana said, lunging into a fantastic warrior pose.

"We're waiting," Penelope said.

"You guys are going to think I'm nuts," Dana said, holding her pose and staring straight ahead.

"News flash, we already do," Penelope said, trying to match Dana's pose, but wobbling. "But we're all nuts, so go on . . ."

"I can't stop going. It's like an addiction. For one hour every week I go to this church basement and I'm the skinny, pretty girl."

"That's sick," Penelope said.

"Yeah," Lipstick agreed, walking over to her purse and peeling open a low-calorie snack bar.

"Don't judge," Dana snapped, stepping back from her lunging pose. "You two aren't exactly role models for having your life together—Penelope is working as a gofer-slash-sex bunny after she got fired, threw up on her boss, and almost burned down the *Telegraph*."

"Hey," Penelope interjected, "It was just the one room."

"And you," Dana said, turning to Lipstick, "are consumed with worry that a bunch of idiots will find out that you're broke and even worse, can't afford a ten-thousand-dollar dress anymore. And you don't even know how to ride the subway, for chrissake. You've lived here your whole life."

"Well, some people just don't need the subway . . ." Lipstick said, looking down at her bare feet and dropping her snack bar.

"The point is, I'm trying to deal with my shit the best I can," Dana said. "And if Weight Watchers makes me feel better and helps me get up in the morning and get out the door, why judge? It's bad enough my ex is having a baby with that fucking Victoria's Secret model—the baby I should be having—without feeling like a loser from two people I barely even know except that we do yoga a few times a week."

Sally finally snapped out of her meditational state to murmur, "Amen."

"Sorry," Penelope mumbled.

"Yeah, me too," Lipstick said. "But I can't believe you want to get pregnant so badly. It freaks me out. My friend Elly Portman got pregnant last year and it did *not* go well."

"Oh, I know Elly," Sally said, doing a full backbend. "She used to do private sessions until she started Pilates."

"Wasn't she the socialite who ran over all those people in the Hamptons?" Penelope asked.

"*Accidentally.*" Lipstick exhaled, starting another sun salutation.

Elly Portman, a model-turned-PR powerhouse, was well known to almost everyone in New York as six years ago she'd "accidentally" backed her SUV into a crowd of people lining up outside Aero nightclub in Southampton at three in the morning. Elly had immediately been whisked away by friends, preventing the police from getting a Breathalyzer test, but not from charging her with leaving the scene of a crime. The story had made the front page of the *Telegraph,* the *Post,* and the *Daily News*—for six weeks.

Two months in prison, a year of community service, and more than three million dollars' worth of payouts to the victims later, Elly met the love of her life at a work function and, a little more than a year later, married him. Soon after she'd gotten pregnant and subsequently found out that during pregnancy, one couldn't use any recreational/prescription drugs, cigarettes, or other appetite suppressants. And oddly enough, people actually encouraged her to stuff her mouth full of food. For the first time in her tiny, anorexic life, Elly Portman could eat whatever she wanted, whenever she wanted—and not be judged.

Sadly, for Elly, she went a little overboard.

"You guys, it was terrifying," Lipstick said, breathing into a downward dog. "She gained over ninety pounds."

"That *is* a lot." Dana sighed, matching Lipstick's pose.

"She was only eighty-five pounds to start with," Lipstick said.

"Oh, I remember that," Penelope said, trying in vain to stand on one foot. "The *Telegraph* ran a picture of her eight months pregnant and called her 'Jabba the Portman.'"

"She got so fat she broke her foot—just by walking on it!" Lipstick cried.

"Oh, come on," Dana said, "that's ridiculous. Nobody gets that fat."

"Elly did," Lipstick said. "Now everyone gets a gestational carrier, which is the hot new thing. Muffie at work had one and raves about her. She got the biological baby without the fat, stretch marks, or morning sickness. And don't even get me started on the actual birth. Ew."

"Well, I'm not going to get that fat!" Dana shot back. Fat and babies were clearly her particular sore spots. During Dana's divorce last year, which scandalized the Lubovitch section of her Miami family (thankfully, it was a small section from her Aunt Nedda's side and everyone knew Aunt Nedda was nuts), someone had anonymously sent her a copy of a new book, *It's Too Late: The Myth of Female Fertility and the Lies of Fertility Treatments.* Even worse, the package was postmarked from the saner climes of Cleveland (as opposed to the Lubovitch Miami).

The book, which caused a national outrage, was about how women need to "focus on finding a man like you find a job because your eggs are dying every day—and after thirty-five it's just not viable to have children naturally!"—at least according to the author, Dr. Julia Jacobson, MD, PhD. "Women need to tell their bosses in their twenties, 'Hey, I need to leave early and date. It's important to me! I want to have a family!' Because if you don't, you'll be forty with no children. People think they can just get in vitro at any age, like going to McDonald's. Well, in vitro is expensive and doesn't always work." What Dr. Julia didn't say was that at the ripe old age of fifty-two she conceived through fertility treatments with her fourth husband, a steel magnate from Dallas.

"Now that's called going out of your way to seal the deal," Penelope mused.

During the year that Dana tried to conceive with Noah, it hadn't happened as easily as she thought it would and Dr. Julia infuriated—and terrified—her. She felt as if her inability to have kids had contributed to the downfall of marriage and that when she couldn't conceive he'd found a younger, hotter someone who could. An embittered and frightened Dana now wondered if she was going to be "Aunt Dana" for the rest of her life.

"Take time off to date? I'm a lawyer! What would I tell the client?" Dana fumed. "'Sorry—can't go to court for you today because I have to go on a date with this guy I don't know because he may be the one and my eggs are dying as I speak?' I'd be fired!"

"Isn't the point moot anyway?" Sally asked. "Dana, you aren't actively doing anything to find a live sperm donor and won't leave the house once you come home from work except apparently for a Weight Watchers meeting. Unless you're planning on going it alone and getting in vitro, the outlook is grim, babe."

"I'm working on it!" Dana said. "I'm going to go out . . . soon."

"Actually, I may need you to come out next month," Lipstick said from the lotus position. "I need a date to the Met gala. I'm wearing my biggest creation and need some moral support. It's *the* event of the season and everyone is photographed and judged according to what they're wearing. And I can't go with any of the socials or someone from work because they'll just ask about my dress. The fifth degree I got at Portia's today almost broke me."

"I'll think about it," Dana said.

"No, say you'll go," Lipstick pleaded. "Please. I need you. I'll be with you the whole night; I won't leave your side and it will be fabulous, I swear!"

"And even if it's not—who cares?" Penelope said. "It'll be funny. Besides, I can't go. That's sweeps week for the cable news divisions, and I've been warned about the fifteen-hour work days."

"I wasn't even your first choice?" Dana said.

"Dana," Sally said while executing a perfect headstand, "just do it. Consider it better therapy than a Weight Watchers meeting."

"Okay," Dana conceded. "Fine, but have a Valium on hand, will you? I may need it."

Later that night, in the privacy of her apartment, under the covers of her king-sized bed in the middle of her living room, Lipstick—who'd received two more messages from her mother that day wondering where she was and why she still hadn't contacted her—logged onto her computer and typed in "www.socialstatus.com."

Sure enough, the top picture on the page was of Lipstick at Portia's trunk show with the headline "Lena Lippencrass Outshines Portia's Purses in a Dress by Mysterious New Designer."

Lipstick clicked on the comments. There were fifty-five already. "Jesus, don't these girls have anything better to do than go to this stupid website?" Lipstick asked herself, missing the irony completely.

To her delight, the comments were overwhelmingly positive. But toward the end, things got a little worrisome.

Princessa1 (Ashley's obvious screen name): I don't know who the designer is—Lena is very tight-lipped, but the cut is insane and it's fierce!

Parkavenue79: I agree. So chic. Where can we get this???

PookieBoo: Lena Lippencrass is such a bitch. She probably found it somewhere in the West Village where she lives and wants to keep it a secret so no one can copy her. She doesn't talk to anyone anymore since Thad left her for Bitsy. Not that anyone can blame him. Bitsy is soooo chic.

Princessa1: Lena is not a bitch. She probably got it in Paris with her mother last summer. And Lena talks to me every day—and she couldn't care less about Thad and Bitsy. They deserve each other!

ItsyBitsy: Funny, because I heard she and her mother aren't talking anymore. And that she might not be living in the West Village for much longer. She probably got that dress from a thrift store.

Lena's blood froze. How could Bitsy know what had happened? Her mother would never breathe a word of something that smacked of familial indiscretion.

JimmyChoolover: Do I smell scandal????

Princessa1: IstyBitsy, you are such a jealous witch. Lena is a friend of mine and everything is fine. And wherever she got that fabulous dress, it wasn't from a secondhand store. Lena doesn't do thrift.

Socialslut9: Well, if she did get it from a thrift store, which one? It's hot!

Lipstick sighed, turned off her computer, and went to bed.

9

SCORPIO:

Career cycles start to finally look good as friendships and bonds are formed with coworkers. But in order to succeed, one must pay particular attention to detail—and dress.

Marge wasn't that impressed with Penelope's "Easter Bunnies in Heat" story, but in the end she conceded that the station needed a roving features reporter and there was no one else around who was willing to bow to the job's particular (and particularly odd) demands. Penelope was happy to do anything that allowed her to spend as much time as possible out of the office and enabled her to do actual reporting again—however loosely she could reconcile the definition of reporting with what she'd been doing.

In the five weeks since her "promotion"—a lateral move that came without a pay raise and didn't release Penelope from her occasional gofering or hair-spraying duties—Penelope covered a wide range of stories. There was the "Firesluts: What Pole Won't These Women Slide Down?" story, wherein Penelope had to interview women from the Firemen's Appreciation Club and hear all about the pros and cons of having sex on a parked fire truck as opposed to one in motion. There was the "Celebrities Flying Their Own Planes: A Dangerous New Adrenaline High," in which Marge made Penelope fly with a drunken ex–Air Force pilot who demonstrated what happens when a plane stalls at fifteen thousand feet, with John Denver blaring in the background.

"John Denver died in a glider accident, not a plane," Penelope, still nauseous from the flight, said to Marge after watching the clip air.

"Same thing!" Marge shot back.

And, of course, there was "The Latest Plastic Surgery Craze—You'll Never Guess Where They're Getting Botox Now!" for which Penelope—who suffered from severe needlephobia—received Botox shots to the forehead, brows, armpits, and lip area, on camera. (She put her foot down when the doctor started talking about genital Botox.) A week later she still couldn't move her face properly, but on a brighter note, she didn't sweat either. There was also the "Teddy Bears with Heart" segment, in which Penelope, dressed in Trace's assistant Berry's lime-green blazer and a pink skirt that had been hanging in the makeup room for a decade and deemed a "TV friendly color" by Marge, had gone to the Make-a-Bear factory in Brooklyn looking like a human watermelon to stuff a few plush bears with "real live ticking hearts." During that particular "exclusive," one of the factory workers mimed a blow job behind her back using a literal tongue-in-cheek as Penelope feigned interest—or tried to, considering her face was frozen—as the factory owner described his "fun-filled lifelike love bears!"

Penelope's workday tended to follow one of two trajectories. If it was a bad day, she wasn't assigned a story and had to spend her time milling around the office, playing gofer, and dodging

Trace's wandering hands and eyes. On a not-so-bad day, she was assigned a story in the morning meeting. It was always one of Marge's abnormal ideas, but it was a story nonetheless.

In the latter instance, Penelope would first do groundwork with Thomas, rounding up people to interview and sorting out locations. If the shoot wasn't in the office, she and Thomas would pile into Stew's 1993 Chevy Suburban with Eric and drive to the location of the shoot. While Eric set up the camera, Stew would outfit Penelope with a wireless microphone while Thomas tried to corral subjects and make sure the shoot went as smoothly as possible. It almost never did.

But working in close proximity with a group of people was, to Penelope's surprise, fun. At the *Telegraph* she'd led a mostly solitary existence, doorstepping by herself or with a random photographer. Penelope had never really had work friends.

Eric and Stew were like Jack and Mrs. Spratt. Eric was a short, bearish guy in his early forties, with a permanent five o'clock shadow on his face and a large Jew-fro. He was a doughy man with an easy high-pitched giggle that would transform his face into that of a delighted five-year-old. He wore his press tags around his neck, along with a picture of his wife Marie and infant daughter Sam wrapped tightly in a Mets onesie.

Stew, by contrast, was a towering six foot, four inches, with a bald pate and rimless glasses. He looked almost manorexic, although he ate like a horse ("a metabolism to die for," he joked), lived with his mother in Brooklyn despite being close to fifty, and had a penchant for reading Harlequin romance novels that had their covers ripped off so no one could identify his not-so-masculine reading material. "They're just so addictive," he'd say and shrug when anyone made fun of him.

Then there was Thomas. By now she'd learned he was thirty-three, an NYU graduate who'd spent several years after college living in London and working for Channel 4 as a news producer before traveling in Pakistan as part of a crew filming a documentary series on Islam. He'd returned to the U.S. four years earlier for mysterious reasons—mysterious to Penelope, anyway, as he wouldn't tell her why. He'd gotten a job at NY Access despite a recession and hiring freezes at the major networks. Thomas, who showed up at NY Access every day in a suit, tie, and shirt that was buttoned all the way up, worked hard and didn't talk a lot about other aspects of his life. But he genuinely seemed to like Penelope, who'd developed a raging case of puppy love for him.

The crush was turning out to literally be a crash and had worsened over the past few weeks as Thomas, unlike many other men Penelope had met, including her father, actually took an interest in her life and her history.

"So, what are your parents like?" Thomas asked one afternoon. It had been a slow day and no assignment was given, so Penelope had been relegated to office chores and Thomas was just hanging around waiting to start setting up for the evening news.

"Huh?" Penelope asked, not quite sure if she'd heard the question. She was sitting next to Laura Lopez's desk, collating files for Marge.

"Your parents," Thomas said, leaning over the cubicle divider. "You know, the people who raised you?"

"Oh, right. They're just regular, normal, well, no, that's not quite right," Penelope answered, chewing on a pen and trying to sound relaxed. "Mom's kind of a left-wing Jew from Queens who randomly got stuck in Ohio with my right-wing, born-again Dad. It's a long, bizarre story."

"Ohio? Really?"

"Well, I actually graduated from a convent in Kentucky," Penelope said, leaning back in her office-issued swivel chair.

"Seriously?"

"Yeah—I was the only Jew and virgin in the joint. Nuns included!" Penelope joked, leaning back a little farther in an attempt to look calm, cool, and collected.

"No wonder you have a good sense of humor," Thomas said, resting his elbows on the cubicle top. "A double dose of Jewish and Catholic guilt mixed in with some oddball parents. Nice."

"Yep, that's me," Penelope said, leaning farther back in her chair, as it went almost vertical. "Just one funny, fucked up—" Her chair crashed backward to the ground.

"I should've warned you not to lean too far back on those things," Thomas said as he laughingly helped her up. "They'll get you every time. I fell over twice last week."

Standing up, mortified but trying to pretend like nothing had happened, Penelope said, "Yeah, cool, happens all the time. No big deal. Um, what about you? Your parents?" at which Thomas had checked his watch and said, "Damn. It's news time, gotta go. Talk later," and walked off.

Another crash came the following week. They were on assignment covering "Bat Boy"—a lame name for a stunt derived by a secondhand "magician" who was hanging upside down in Central Park for "sixty straight hours!" despite taking a break every fifteen minutes to stand up and pee. Bat Boy insisted that the only interviews he would do had to be done upside down, so while Stew and Thomas held her upside down, Eric rolled tape. All the blood rushed to Penelope's head and she looked like a giant cherry while asking Bat Boy things like, "So, um, why are you doing this? I mean, what's the point?" "Why do you have to stand up to pee if you have a catheter in?" and "What the heck does this have to do with magic?"

All was going well until Thomas, who'd been taking Zyrtec for his spring-induced allergies, sneezed so violently he dropped Penelope's leg. Thankfully, Stew held on and her NY Access microphone broke her fall, but Thomas was mortified. He'd apologized at least twenty times and the next day brought her the recently rereleased *So 80s* CD, which was a compilation of the decade's biggest hits.

"Oh man," Penelope said, ripping open the CD to look at the album credits. "This is awesome. Thank you. You didn't have to do that . . . and how'd you know I wanted this?"

"Please," Thomas said and smiled. "You bust out singing Journey, Bananarama, and The Bangles at least once a day. Anyway, I really am sorry. I'll never drop you again."

"I do seem to end up on the floor a lot when I'm around you," Penelope said.

"He's a little uptight, but he's just so . . . cute," Penelope said to Lipstick and Dana at yoga that Saturday. "And smart, and nice, and I love working with him. I know this sounds totally unromantic, but he's so efficient. I feel taken care of, like he can get me in and out of a situation pretty much unscathed. Well, except for dropping me that one time, but whatever. Is that retarded?"

"Well," Lipstick said, upon hearing about Thomas's attributes for the nine hundredth time. "Why don't you ask him out?"

"Isn't that what a guy's supposed to do?" Penelope asked. "Besides, I think he has a girlfriend. He's always whispering on the phone and runs home after work. He doesn't seem interested in me that way."

"He sounds okay," Dana said, "even though he makes you do ridiculous stuff."

"Well, that's really Marge's fault. Except for the bunny thing. But he apologized for that dumb idea later," Penelope said.

Meanwhile, Marge forced Penelope to go clothes shopping, which rated very high on Penelope's "top ten things I hate to do list," right after "Teddy Bears with Heart" stories. Marge—remarkably calm due to the refilling of her Good & Plenty bowl courtesy of Dr. Feelgood—explained why Penelope couldn't wear her latest Lipstick-provided dress on air, "Because it's brown. Brown does not pop. Black does not pop. Navy does not pop. Bright colors pop! You got a good wardrobe, toots, but on TV it looks like you're in mourning. Does nothing for the complexion. You're a nice-looking girl after we straighten that hair and slap some makeup on your face, but it's no use if you're still gonna look like a morose blob on camera. If you can't wear anything that looks good on camera, then I'll find something for you to wear!"

Penelope, dreading another garment-based debacle involving anything that Trace's assistant Berry owned, goaded Marge into giving her "an appropriate color guideline." Marge, always happy to create more rules and lists, provided the following

APPROVED COLORS: Hot pink, bright purple, royal or azure blue (but not indigo or navy), teal, kelly green (but not lime or army green), yellow, orange (but not burnt sienna orange), cherry red, fire engine red, or really, any shade of red, just not maroon.

NON-APPROVED COLORS: Black, brown (of any kind), navy, white (unless used under a bright, color-approved sweater), cream, gray, and stripes or other prints ("they confuse the eye on camera—and send epileptics into fits. We can't have that. Numbers show we are very popular in the spastic community," Marge explained).

UP FOR DISCUSSION: Soft pink, light purple—or "any colors you'd see in a Tampon ad."

Basically, if Penelope's outfit was the color of something a child would want to chew on, it was okay. Anything else was prohibited.

"I'm going to look like Rainbow Brite," Penelope said, chewing her lip, before she realized she could still wear Lipstick's muted, classy clothes—just pop a bright shirt or sweater on over them.

As a precaution, Penelope dragged Lipstick to H&M so Lipstick could help her pick out some stylish, appropriate, and cheap clothes.

"Oh, sure, I'll go," Lipstick said when Penelope asked her for some help, "I've never been there before. It'll be an adventure, and I'll tell Jack it's for research!" They arrived at the Midtown H&M on Fifth Avenue and Fifty-first Street, dressed in their best shopping camouflage. Lipstick walked into the discount clothing store in her "undercover consultant" look—a Pucci-print head scarf, oversized sunglasses, and a trench coat. ("Well, it *is* uptown and Cartier *is* across the street—so I have to be careful no one recognizes me," she explained.) Penelope wore a sweatsuit.

An hour and $279 later, Penelope had an arsenal of cheap dresses and brightly colored accessories that would make any outfit Marge-approvable.

SAGITTARIUS:
Your impatience is taking its toll. Not everything has to be done right now, right away—especially at the expense of your health.

While Lipstick and Penelope shopped, Dana made an unexpected discovery.

She was at her desk, working on a brief for MatBank, a small bank that was being sued by the government and shareholders for defaulting on mortgage-related debt, when her secretary buzzed in.

"Mr. Kornberg wants to see you in his office."

"I'll be right there," Dana said, her heart starting to beat fast. She hadn't heard from the law firm's senior partner in two months, ever since she'd put in her application to become a full partner, as opposed to junior partner. It had been a ballsy move. At thirty-two, she was the youngest junior partner in the firm's history, and there had never been a full partner who'd been under forty-five years of age. But Dana, always the straight-A student, the smartest in her law classes, the most aggressive in court, and always having to prove something to herself, wasn't going to let a little thing like age get in the way of her professional ambitions.

But lately, ever since she'd put in for the promotion, she'd started to wonder if perhaps her blind ambition wasn't really hiding something else. She had a constant terror of failure, remarkable even by type-A standards. It was reinforced by having lost a husband and what seemed to be a picture-perfect life. She felt she hadn't lived up to her parents', Noah's, and everybody else's expectations. And sometimes she didn't even know what she wanted anymore—except to lose thirty pounds and not die alone.

"Dana? You coming?" her secretary's voice buzzed through the intercom.

"Right now," Dana said, jolting out of her thoughts and rushing down the hall to Mr. Kornberg's office.

Slade Kornberg was the seventy-six-year-old patrician statesman of the office. He'd started the company with the Struck brothers in 1969, and they'd quickly become known as the most successful white-collar law firm in the city—aggressively and, more often than not, successfully, fighting for their clients. His corner office, which overlooked Central Park and the West Side, was decorated in dark wood, dark leather, and brass, just like his favorite reading room at the New York Athletic Club.

When Dana entered his office, he looked up from the stack of papers he'd been reading at his massive walnut wood desk, but didn't move. The light from the green Tiffany reading lamp cast a shadow on his face, making the wrinkles deeper than they actually were.

"Dana," he said.

"Mr. Kornberg," she answered.

"Have a seat," he said, waving toward the closest leather armchair studded with brass nails.

"I see you want to become a full partner."

"Yes, sir," she said.

"Even though we just made you a junior partner."

"I have the hours and I have the skill," Dana said, getting annoyed. "I do the work anyway, I might as well be recognized for it. And I love the firm and plan on being here my entire career."

"Smart girl." Kornberg cackled. "Just what I like to hear; you know that. I agree. You are a suitable candidate despite your youth—which, I won't lie to you—concerns me."

"But—" Dana said.

"Let me finish," Kornberg said. "I will bring this up with the Struck brothers and the other partners. We'll give you our decision in two months. Until then, I suggest you beef up your billable hours and bring a cot into work. Full partners have no lives."

"Thank you, sir," Dana said, "and may I say—"

"That is all." Kornberg sighed, turning back to his papers. "Dismissed."

Dana didn't breathe until she was safely back in her office. The stress of the meeting had tied her stomach into knots, and she felt her appetite slipping away. She felt something on the back of her head and went to scratch it. When she pulled her hand away, there was a clump of hair in it.

Dana was not only losing control, it seemed, she was now losing her hair.

10

SCORPIO:

What doesn't kill you only makes you stronger. Just watch out for the hands.

The next Wednesday, Penelope—swathed in jeans and a green wrap shirt made in a flattering jersey material she'd picked up on the H&M excursion with Lipstick—was assigned Marge's latest ratings-centered idea: "We're doing an in-house catwalk for National Underwear Day!"

"National Underwear Day?" Penelope, seated at a desk in the newsroom, asked as a feeling of doom overwhelmed her.

"Yeah, yeah, it's some Hanes-sponsored thing. A bunch of models are coming over in their underwear and talking about how it's important to wear it. Very topical, what with Paris, Britney, Lindsay, et al. thinking it's optional these days."

"Oh, okay," Penelope said. "Sure."

"And you're doing the interview in your skivvies," Marge, stuffed into a bright yellow suit, added.

"What?" Penelope squeaked, standing up.

"In your underwear," Marge said. "Don't worry. Hanes—

which, may I remind you, is also a big advertiser on this channel—sent some over. Granny pants and a tank."

"But . . ." Penelope sputtered, "but I didn't shave!"

"Should've thought about that this morning," Marge snapped. She dropped a package from Hanes on a nearby desk, turned on her cherry-red heels, and headed back to her office. "Coffee. Now." she demanded as she passed David's desk.

Penelope sat down at the desk and put her head in her hands.

This is so humiliating, she thought.

She considered calling Dana, who would most likely threaten a lawsuit—why was it that people who worked in the corporate world had no idea what went on in "creative" fields? Dana couldn't understand why everyone didn't wear suits with hose to work and always looked at Penelope after she had once again cursed and, in shock, said, "You talk like that at work?" Instead, Penelope remembered Laura Lopez doing a shoot with the dolphins in the Central Park Zoo in her bikini and thought of Kelly Ripa going into the fish bowl with David Blaine during the magician's supposed "drowning stunt" several years ago at Lincoln Center.

They had it worse. Penelope sighed. She grabbed the Hanes tank top and matching pair of boyshorts—both in a TV friendly shade of orange—and headed to the bathroom to change. At least the outfit looked like something somebody would wear in the summer. If they were fifteen and at the beach.

Half an hour later, as the scantily clad models assembled on the studio's sofa, Penelope emerged from the bathroom, ready to work.

She held her head high and marched over to the IKEA sofa on set, announcing to no one in particular, "I'm ready! Let's do this!"

"Well, hello," Trace, who'd sneaked up behind her, said, leering. Penelope turned toward him. He was staring at her chest, and his just-dyed mustache, which still had remnants of his lunch crumbled in it, was twitching. "A little underdressed, aren't we?"

"Not because I want to be," Penelope snapped, taking a step back.

"Hmmm, what's this?" Trace said, leaning in toward her right breast. Before she could stop him, his hand shot out and with his thumb and forefinger, grabbed a long loose blond hair that was on the undershirt, tweaking her nipple on the way. "Can't have you shedding on air," he said, winking at her.

Penelope, in a state of shock, just stood there, mouth agape, too stunned to do anything.

In her mind she'd already grabbed the offending hand with the hair still in it, leaned toward Trace, and hissed, "I may have to do this shoot, but if you ever—*ever*—touch me again I will call my lawyer Dana Gluck and slap a lawsuit on you so fast your head will spin."

But in reality all she could manage was a meek, "Get off me . . . jerk."

Trace turned a lighter shade of shoe leather under his tanned makeup and said, "Well. That's the thanks I get for trying to help out the freshman!" before walking away.

"Fresh *woman*!" Penelope snarled after him.

Eric, giggling, came over and slapped Penelope on the back. "Nice job, kid. I got it on tape. Now that was good TV!" Stew put a microphone on her and whispered, "Don't worry. We'll get him. I'll spray some mace over his makeup. He'll be out sick for a week with hives."

Thomas, who'd been putting microphones on the models, rushed over.

"You okay?" he asked. "I'll back you up if you want to talk to Marge about that."

"Whatever," Penelope, still blushing furiously, said. "Forget it. I've worked in frat houses before. Let's just do this." She took her seat in the interviewer's chair.

One of the four leggy models, all of whom were dressed in bra tops and string bikini underwear, looked at Penelope's hairy legs and sniffed, "Ew," just as Thomas counted down, "Three . . . Two . . . One . . ."

"Hi, and welcome to New York Access," Penelope chirped to the camera. "But more important, welcome to the Hanes National Underwear Day celebration!"

Ten minutes later the segment was over. Two minutes after that, Penelope was once again wrapped back in her green shirt and jeans and was busy wiping off her makeup in the makeup room when Thomas came in.

"Look, about what happened before," Thomas said. "Trace was completely out of line. That will *not* happen again, I promise."

"It's okay," Penelope said, rubbing a towelette over her face. "Thanks, though."

"On the bright side, I think the shoot went well, and I think Marge is—"

At that moment Marge walked in the room. "Marge is what?"

"Happy?" Thomas squeaked, keeping his eyes diverted. The yellow suit was too bright. It was like looking directly into the sun.

"Damn right I'm happy! Good shoot," she said gruffly. "Genius idea of mine! Amazing!"

"Wow," Thomas said after she left. "I don't think I've ever seen her so satisfied."

"Yeah," Penelope agreed, sitting in one of the makeup chairs. "She looked like a pleased piece of lemon meringue pie."

"But not as tasty." Thomas laughed, putting his arm around the back of Penelope's chair.

"Hey," he said, turning to face her, "would you like to, maybe sometime, um . . ."

"Yeah?" Penelope asked, feeling her stomach tie up in knots and her heart start to pound through her chest.

"Well, I was thinking we could—"

Just then Laura Lopez, back from the junket for the new action flick, *Stargate IV,* starring the buff Danish action star Dane Butch and the newest big screen nymphet Bebe Williams, swooshed in.

Damn you for the interference, Laura Lopez. A pox on Natalie Morales for you! Penelope thought.

Laura flung the latest copy of *Y* at Penelope. "You think you're so great," she snarled. "Well, I've been working here a lot longer than you, sister, and no one—*no one*—does the job better than Laura Lo-PEZ. You better watch it." She stalked out, returned to her cubicle, and pinned a photo of herself sandwiched between Dane and a waifish Bebe to her celebrity wall.

"What the hell is the matter with her?" said Penelope. "What's with the *Y*?"

"You didn't know?" Thomas asked.

"About what?" Penelope said, fidgeting in her chair.

"Turn to page seventy-four," Thomas said. "I figured you'd seen it already. I know you're friends with someone who works there. . . ."

Penelope picked up the magazine and flipped it open to the relevant page. And there it was. On the top of the gossipy "Spy" page.

TACKY CHIC by Lena Lippencrass

> New York City's latest guilty pleasure can be found on none other than its own local cable channel. No, not NY1, the other local cable channel, NY Access. The station's latest endeavor to gain a foothold in the slippery ratings has been to send out its new features reporter Penelope Mercury to do—well, everything you'd never willingly attempt while sober. The cute blond with the frizzy hair will do just about anything—from interviewing fireman fetishists to dressing up in a crotchless bunny suit left over from last year's Comic-Con convention. In outfits that smack of chic—was that a Dolce dress she was wearing last week?—yet are accessorized to add just a touch of crass with neon-bright colors, the former crack reporter for the *New York Telegraph* pops off the screen while attempting the ridiculous. Watch if you want a daily dose of wit, humor, and the bizarre.

"Wow," Penelope said, in a bit of a daze. "I've never been called chic before."

"Watch your back," Thomas said. "Laura and Kandace won't take this lying down. They've been trying to get press on themselves for years."

"Well, it's not my fault—I didn't ask her to do it. I didn't even know about it."

A few minutes later Penelope sneaked to the back of the office by Storm's desk and dialed Lipstick's cell.

"Hey, Lips," she said when Lipstick picked up. "I saw the piece."

"Oh! You did!" Lipstick said. "I was saving it as a surprise.

Normally we close the magazine two months before publication, but I had done a piece on Calvin Klein and his new pet mini-tiger and it was in *Women's Wear Daily* three weeks ago, so I had to fill the space last minute. I hope you don't mind."

"Mind? Nah, not really," Penelope said. "But I think it may have gotten me in trouble with Laura and Kandace. Thomas says they're gunning for me."

"Oh, dang, I'm sorry. I was only trying to help you by raising your profile and showing Marge how fabulous you are. Only a month into the job and people are paying attention! And, okay, kind of an 'eff you' to the *Telegraph*."

"Yeah, that made me laugh," Penelope agreed.

"Seriously, though, the stuff Marge has you doing lately is the funniest thing on TV right now, and Jack loved the piece. We could probably do a profile in a couple months if it works out."

"Ack," Penelope said, feeling her gag reflex starting to kick in. "Um, not sure about that. But thanks. I appreciate the support. Nobody'll notice anyway, I'm sure. You coming to yoga tonight?"

"Of course!" Lipstick said. "But I'm a little nervous. I have to register the designer for my table at the Met today. I'm dying. What if everyone finds out?'

"Who cares?" Penelope shot back. "You make great stuff. I bet they're all just jealous they don't have one of your dresses."

"Well, I have had a few queries asking where people can buy them."

"See? Now, what are you calling it?"

"Dauphin."

"Dolphin?"

"No, Dauphin. It's the French word for successor."

"Niiiiice. Take that, Bitsy Farklestein!"

"Farmdale."

"Whatever."

"Also," Lipstick's voice dropped to a whisper, "Something weird is going on. I think someone is following me."

"Oh, come on, Lips." Penelope laughed. "That's retarded. I love you, but you do tend to be a tad bit dramatic."

"No, really. For the past week, I swear some weird lady with a wig cut just like Anna Wintour's bob with big black sunglasses and a brown overcoat has been popping up everywhere. And every time I look directly at her, she runs away. She was there this morning when I left for work. Last night when I left the bar with Zach—"

"Zach?" Penelope cut her off. "Who's Zach?"

"Oh, um, that guy who, ah, lives on the third floor—remember the one I told you about who helped me move in? The artist?"

"Yeeeeah . . ."

"Well, I finally got around to thanking him—I knocked on every door on the third floor. So embarrassing."

LIBRA:

No need to feel paranoid. If it seems like you're being watched, you are.

And it had been. Lipstick, always one to send a handwritten thank-you note immediately after every event and flowers if it was a sit-down dinner, had been so busy, she'd let her manners lapse over the last month or two. The night before, she was trudging up the stairs after covering another society party following a full day of work and thinking of yet another dress to create, when she spotted paint splotches on the linoleum floor on the third floor landing.

That looks familiar, she thought, as she remembered the Moving Day from Hell. *That guy Zach must think I'm incredibly rude. I should thank him. And he was so cute.*

After she'd tossed her Dior bag into her apartment and

applied some lip gloss—ever since the car incident that earned her her nickname, Lipstick never actually wore lipstick—she marched down to the third floor in her black Louboutin heels, Dior skirt, and a cowl-necked top of her own creation.

Hmm, which one would he be? she thought, looking at the four apartment doors: A, B, C, and D. She knocked on the nearest entrance. Nothing. So she moved on to the next apartment, knocked, and heard a man's voice say, "Coming, coming. Hold your horses." Two seconds later a grizzled man in his sixties wearing only a stained pair of tighty-but-not-so-whiteys and clutching a Coors Light opened the door.

"Yeah?" He belched, scratching his distended, hairy belly. "Whadda you want?"

"Oh, sorry," Lipstick said, not entirely sure where to look, "I'm looking for Zach. Does he, um, live here?"

"I live here. Alone!" the man barked. "I'm not gay!"

"No, no, of course not. I didn't mean to imply that. Not that there's anything wrong with being gay—"

"Says who?" He grimaced.

"Well, perhaps that's a conversation for another time," Lipstick said. "Do you know where Zach lives? He's an artist?"

"I live over here," said a familiar voice.

Lipstick turned around and saw him. He was hotter than she'd even remembered. And wet. He looked like he'd just had a shower. His hair was messily towel-dried and he was wearing a bathrobe and smelled like Ivory soap—or what Lipstick assumed Ivory would smell like if she'd ever used it—with a hint of turpentine. Lipstick, trying not to be too nosy, attempted to get a glimpse of his apartment behind him, but all she could see was a sink and an easel.

Zach seemed to know exactly what she was doing and smiled.

"Mr. Boravsky, I can take it from here, thanks," he said, as

Mr. Boravsky pulled his sagging yellowed underpants up, gave Lipstick another once-over, and slammed the door.

Leaning against the doorframe and looking right at Lipstick, Zach said, "How can I help, princess?"

"You know that . . . man?"

"Mr. Boravsky? Sure, he's been here forever. I think he only pays like three hundred dollars in rent. He's a little nuts, but a fixture—and I gotta respect that. Besides, he takes in packages for me if I'm not home."

"That makes sense," Lipstick said, shrugging.

"So, to what do I owe this visit?"

"Oh, that," Lipstick said, turning red and scratching her head. *Stop that,* she told herself, *it's bad physical etiquette.* "I just, um, wanted to say thank you for helping me when I moved in the other month. I feel really bad that I didn't do this earlier."

"Why don't you do it properly by buying me a beer?"

"Okay, sure. When?"

"Now's fine."

"Wow, you move fast." Now? She didn't have any makeup on or anything.

"Do you have somewhere else to be other than standing outside my door? I already heard you tromp up the stairs from your night out."

"No, no. It's fine. A beer it is." Tromp? That made her sound like a moose. She should work on that.

"Good. Gimme a minute, then," Zach said, shutting the door on Lipstick. He emerged five minutes later dressed in a pair of jeans, an old KISS T-shirt, and Converse sneakers. "Let's go."

They ended up at The Room, a watering hole two doors down from their building. The Room was the perfect place for two reasons: First, it was dimly lit—which pleased the makeup-free Lipstick, whose motto in life was "It's all about timing and lighting." Second, it served only wine and beer. "That way we can't get too crazy," Zach smiled.

"Huh? Crazy?" Lipstick said. "I'm not that kind of girl. I mean, I wish I was, but I'm not!"

"Relax, princess, it was just a joke," Zach said.

"Stop calling me princess," Lipstick said, chewing the inside of her cheek. "The name is Lena."

"Sorry. I didn't mean to offend you or sound patronizing," Zach said. "You just look like a princess. Now what'll you have?"

"A cabernet, please," Lipstick said, blushing again.

After Zach got her wine and himself a bottle of Heineken, they sat in the front booth that looked out onto Sullivan Street.

"So, where are you from?" Lipstick asked, trying to start a conversation.

"Lexington—horse country," Zach said, taking a swig from his beer. "I've been here almost ten years, mostly as an artist, but I've been known to wait a few tables to pay the bills."

"Do you ride?" Lipstick inquired, sipping her wine. "I've been riding since I was five. My mother made me. I've never really liked it all that much."

"I used to—my family bred thoroughbreds," Zach said. "But if you don't like it, you shouldn't do it. Although you strike me as a woman who does a lot of things you don't want to do."

"Not so much anymore," Lipstick said defiantly, looking down at her gloved hands.

"All right!" Zach said, clinking her wineglass with his bottle. "Now that I support."

"So, what'd you do before moving to New York?" Lipstick asked.

"Well, I left home when I was seventeen, went to the Savannah College of Art and Design, and then traveled for a few years to India, Mali, and Cambodia—which was a little scary as the Khmer Rouge was still active so I had to be careful."

"Oh." Lipstick sighed. "That sounds so exciting. I've only ever been to the usual places."

"The usual?" Zach asked, raising an eyebrow.

"Yeah, you know, Saint Barths, Saint-Tropez, Paris, Milan, Rome, and sometimes Mother would mix it up a bit over New Year's and make us go to Cabo. But then it became too commercial and annoying for her. So we stopped. I did spend a summer in Andalusia during college. That was fun."

"Andalusia is supposed to be beautiful," Zach said.

"It was," Lipstick agreed. "It was nice to get out of New York too. That summer and right now are the only times I've ever really been away from my mom and dad."

"Do they live in town?"

"Yeah, but we're not talking right now," Lipstick said, drinking her wine. "They really jerked me around."

"How long are you going to not communicate with them?" Zach asked.

"I don't know," Lipstick said. "My friends keep asking me that too. I'm just really busy and mad."

"Well I can see you're busy, but I don't know what you're so mad about," Zach said, taking a swig of his beer. "And I'm not gonna pry, but I will say, don't let it go on too long. No matter what, they're still your family and they love you. Even if you think they have a fucked-up way of showing it."

"How would you know?" Lipstick snapped, momentarily irritated.

"I didn't talk to my family for a long time." Zach shrugged. "Dad was real pissed when I told him I wasn't going into the family horse-breeding business and wanted to be an artist instead. They cut me off and wouldn't speak to me for years."

"Oh, I'm sorry," Lipstick said quietly. "What brought you back together?"

"I had my first big show at the Milk Gallery in Chelsea six years ago and sent them an invite," Zach said. "I didn't think they'd come, but they did. And it was . . . great. Just really great. Even better than the show." He was quiet for a moment and then said, "Listen, the point is, being angry is a waste of energy and time. You can have a relationship with anyone—you just have to be strong enough to set your boundaries."

"Yeah, I guess so," Lipstick said. "I don't know if I am yet, though."

"Oh, I don't know," Zach said, winking at her. "I think you could be."

"Well, I moved all the way to Soho to get away from them."

"Buckaroo Banzai, princess," Zach said, smiling.

"What's that mean?" Lipstick asked, confused.

"Wherever you go, there you are."

After polishing off their drinks an hour later, Lipstick and Zach left The Room on their way home. But just as they were about to enter their apartment building, out of the corner of her eye, Lipstick saw something odd. Four cars away she spotted what she first thought was a brown rat on top of a white Mazda. Squinting her eyes for a better look and walking toward the car, the "rat" turned out to be the woman in a brown bobbed wig with what looked like a camera aimed right at Lipstick and Zach. When the woman saw Lipstick advance toward her, she scurried off.

"Hey!" Lipstick yelled as the woman ran down Sullivan and rounded the corner onto Houston. "Get back here! Who are you?"

"What is going on?" Zach, grabbing her arm, asked.

Shaken, Lipstick said, "I don't know. It's so weird. You're going to think I'm crazy. . . ."

"I already do." Zach laughed, holding the front door open for her.

"Okay, well, for the past few weeks that woman has just been showing up everywhere. Like she's stalking me."

"Do you know her?"

"I don't think so. I don't know—everytime I try to talk to her she runs away."

"Why would someone try to follow you? I mean, who are you? Mafia? CIA?"

"I'm not that interesting, believe me," Lipstick said as they climbed the stairs. "It's probably nothing. Maybe my parents. They tend to be overly dramatic, especially in times of noncommunication."

"All right, now I have to know—why don't your parents know where you are?" Zach asked, rounding the stairs and coming to a stop in front of his door.

"It's a long story, but believe me, a very boring one. I'm kind of on the run from the Upper East Side."

"Ha. Who isn't?"

"I moved here after I got cut off and am trying to make do. But it's really tiring. I can't let anyone know about my current situation, and so I'm up all night sewing dresses and making up lies about why no one can offer me a ride home or why they can't have a dinner party in my apartment."

"You still seem to care a lot about what those people think," Zach said. "It's your life and you're living it, as far as I can tell. And it's far better to earn your way in the world than to just have it handed to you. I admire that."

"Thanks," Lipstick said, leaning against Zach's door.

"We should do this again sometime. It was fun," Zach said, leaning in toward Lipstick, which made her very nervous.

"Yeah, totally cool, man . . ." Lipstick said, trying to be downtown artsy—whatever that was.

Laughing, Zach said, "Okay, princess, let's talk later." He opened his door and stepped into his apartment. "Have a good night."

"You too." And, disappointed, a kiss-less Lipstick went home.

"Zach is so cute!" Lipstick gushed into her phone to Penelope. "I can't believe you haven't noticed him before—you've lived there for, like, years!"

"Yeah," Penelope said, "but I always kept weird hours at the *Telegraph* and was always so busy I just used my apartment to sleep. I only really noticed Dana because of Karl. I either tripped on him or he'd try to bite my leg."

Lipstick logged on to Socialstatus.com while they were talking. Then she saw it. There, on the top of the page, was a grainy photo of her and Zach from the night before entering their building with the headline: "Lena Lippencrass Sluts It Up in Soho."

"Oh God," Lipstick whispered. "Oh my God. Penelope, are you near a computer?"

"Sure, what's up? You okay?"

"Check out Socialstatus.com," Lipstick hissed. "Oh, Jesus."

Two seconds later Penelope groaned, "Wow. You were right. You are being followed. Creepy. Who the fuck would do that?"

As the two were discussing the photo, Christina Mecklenberg, the sausage heiress and Jack's assistant/enforcer, walked by in her latest S&M-inspired Gaultier outfit and rapped her knuckles on Lipstick's desk.

"Jack wants to see you in his office. Now," Christina said, raising her eyebrows at Lipstick on the phone. "Unless, of course, your current conversation is more important." And with that, she walked off.

"No, No," Lipstick called to Christina's rigid back, "I'll be right in!"

"Darn, I have to go," she whispered into the phone. "Jack wants to see me. Hopefully he hasn't seen this Socialstatus thing."

But the second Lipstick walked into Jack's gleaming office, she knew he had.

Seated behind his Biedermeier desk, in a dark gray pinstriped suit, a pink shirt, and a cravat, Jack motioned for Lipstick to take her place on the down-filled linen sofa. Whenever someone was in trouble, he sat them there. It was incredibly plush, and there was no way an employee could sit down on it and not sink all the way in, making him or her look like a six-year-old awaiting punishment. The only way to avoid being swallowed by the couch was to perch on the very edge, holding most of your weight in your thighs, which is what Lipstick (a seasoned veteran of the couch talks) did.

There was an uncomfortable silence as Jack stared at Lipstick through his black-framed Elvis Costello glasses (*Y*, May 2008 issue), for a full three minutes before he began.

"A post on that"—Jack paused to wrinkle his nose—"*website* has been brought to my attention. They're calling you a slut. A lowlife."

"I can explai—"

"We can't have that," Jack (who ironically once held an orgy on David Geffen's yacht off the coast of Cannes that was captured in *¡Hola!* magazine) retorted. "*Y* women are above reproach—socially, morally, and financially. Is there something you need to tell me?"

"No, of course not," Lipstick said. "I was visiting a friend of mine in the building and that man let me in. That's all."

"Fine. Just make sure this doesn't come back to bite me or the magazine in the ass or you will be sorry. Now, let's discuss these other photos," Jack said, reaching into a drawer and pulling out a sheaf of photographs, before he spread them out over his desk. They were shots of Lipstick at Portia's, at the Alzheimer gala, at the Red March ball, and several other events—all dressed in her own designs.

"Yes?" Lipstick asked, starting to glisten. Again.

"You seem to be not only the muse but the sole customer for this mysterious designer."

"She likes to keep to herself," Lipstick said.

"The clothes are . . ."

"Yes?"

"Vivid. Very well made. A little sophomoric, perhaps, but I suppose that can't be helped when dealing with a new designer."

"I'll tell her, thank you. She'll be pleased," Lipstick said, her heart racing.

"I'd like to tell her myself."

"Oh, of course. Well, she will be at the Met Gala," Lipstick said.

"What is this mysterious woman's name? What is the name of the clothing line?"

"Dauphin."

"Witty. What is her name?"

"I'll let her tell you," Lipstick said.

"Is this some sort of PR stunt?" Jack said, a hint of annoyance creeping into his voice. "Because if it is, I am not amused. And I will really not be amused if I see her in the pages of *Vogue* or *W* before *Y*."

"You won't, don't worry," Lipstick said, "I just promised her I wouldn't say anything until she was prepared to go public. And she will be ready by the Met."

"Wonderful. I look forward to being introduced to this

mystery woman," Jack answered, peering at Lipstick closely. "I thought I had you all figured out, Lena Lippencrass, but it seems you are full of surprises. And I don't like surprises. They rarely work in my favor." He grabbed his cape from the coatrack, whooshed it around his shoulders, and stalked out.

Lipstick allowed herself to slump into the deep couch's cushions and, looking at the ceiling, moaned, "I am in hell."

"No, you are in Jack's office," said Christina, who had silently glided into the room after Jack had left. "Are you planning on staying here all day? Should I order you lunch?"

"No, no, I'm leaving," Lipstick said and headed back to her desk.

After work Lipstick, who was feeling slightly paranoid, decided to mix up her route. Instead of taking the F train, she walked a few blocks east and took the 6 train to Bleecker Street. But, on the corner of Bleecker and Houston, she turned around and once again caught sight of the brown-wigged spy coming out of the train station and walking her way.

"I had to duck into the bathroom at the BP station on Lafayette to get rid of her," Lipstick told Dana and Penelope that night at yoga.

"Ew, public toilets." Penelope shuddered. Penelope had a lifelong loathing of public toilets, which had been instilled in her at the tender age of five, by, naturally, her mother.

"Rule number 44: Never—*ever*—sit directly on a public toilet seat," Susan had snapped at Penelope after catching her youngest daughter clambering down from her porcelain perch in the local Cincinnati IHOP bathroom. "Squat over it. Not on it! Do you know how many diseases you can get from sitting on that?"

Among the maladies one could inflict on oneself by putting one's bare unprotected ass directly on a public porcelain, according to Susan Rosenzweig Mercury, were: herpes, crabs, the clap, syphilis, hookworm, warts, tetanus, gout, rotgut, yeast infections, and teen pregnancy—which was viewed as the worst because, as Susan said, "look at what happened to Karen Klinger from down the street. She got pregnant, dropped out of school, and now works at (shudder) *White Castle.*" Which meant, to Penelope's young fertile mind, sitting on a public toilet was a direct road to ending up pregnant, broke, living in a trailer, and on welfare while working for a fast-food chain.

"Well, it's not like I wanted to go in that darn bathroom," Lipstick said. "But I had to do something to lose that woman."

"Hey, I almost forgot, we can't do yoga next Saturday," Dana said, coming out of her lunge.

"Why not?" Lipstick asked. "Is something wrong?"

"No, it's Passover," Dana answered, twisting her arms and legs around each other, trying to match Sally's squatting eagle pose. "I'm going to Cleveland tomorrow for the holidays. I'll be back Monday."

"It is?" Penelope asked. "And how do you do that damn pose? I always fall on my face."

"Concentration, Penelope, something you seem to lack," Sally murmured.

"You should know it's Passover—aren't you Jewish?" Dana asked.

"Well, not really. I'm Jew-*ish,*" Penelope said. "My mom's a Jew, but Dad's born-again. I'm not really anything."

"You're mom's a Jew, you're a Jew," Dana said, exhaling and standing upright.

"Yeah, but she's not particularly religious. She celebrates Passover, but every year she'll say, 'Services start at six so we'll get there at eight, 'cause that's when they eat!' It's always weird. She drags Dad along, and he tends to antagonize everyone by wearing a 'What Would Jesus Do' T-shirt. Mom always uses the same excuses to get out of services like, 'The dog died,' 'Jim was incontinent,' or 'The car broke down.' Shit like that. Their imaginary dog has died like five times, and Grandma has been resurrected twice. Thank God I don't live in the same city as them anymore. I couldn't handle the stress."

"Yeah, well," Dana said, sighing as she sat down on her mat, "I know what you mean. The prospect of going home and having my mother grill me about Noah and giving her grandkids has kept me up for the past five nights. Between that, my weight, and work—which is killing me right now—I've kind of started to, um . . ."

"Yeeees?" Lipstick prompted her.

"Lose my hair," Dana replied.

"What?" Penelope said, "I don't see anything. Your hair looks fine to me."

"Check this out," Dana said, lifting up the back of her bob. Sure enough, underneath, near the bottom of her hairline by the nape of her neck was a bald patch the size of a silver dollar. Sally and Lipstick stopped their poses and came over to look.

"Hmm, well," Lipstick said unconvincingly, "it's not that bad."

"You can barely tell," Sally said, elbowing Lipstick.

"Does this happen a lot?" Penelope asked.

"Oh, not really," Dana said. "It happened in law school during finals, during the Bar exam, and after the divorce. My doctor says it's stress-induced alopecia. My hair usually grows back when I calm down."

"Oooh, so chic," Lipstick said. "Princess Caroline of Monaco had alopecia. She went full-on bald after her father died and her sister Stephanie ran off with that guy in the circus."

"Hopefully I won't be going full-on bald,'" Dana snapped, letting her hair drop and smoothing it down with her hands.

"It'll get better," Lipstick said, rubbing Dana's back. "Do

you think it will grow back in three weeks? We have the Met Gala, you know."

"Well, if it doesn't, then I'm not going," Dana said.

"Please," Lipstick pleaded, "we can always work around a bald patch. Have a Valium. Spray some Rogaine. Anything—I've been working on our dresses for weeks now."

"And I can steal you some of Trace's spray-on hair!" Penelope offered.

"Does that stuff really work?" Dana asked.

"As long as it's not raining," Penelope said.

"Fine," Dana said.

"Oh, thank God," Lipstick exhaled and gave Dana a big hug. "I promise, it will be fine. And now, I gotta go back to work on those dresses if they're going to be done in time." Lipstick blew Penelope a kiss and went back to her apartment and her sewing machine.

Later that night, after three more hours of sewing, Lipstick checked her voice mail. There were two messages from her mother.

"*First message,*" the machine's digital voice crooned. "Lena, darling, where are you?" her mother's voice wailed. "I'm in fits. Please, please call me or your father. He's very upset. He has had to take three Zantacs with every dinner for the past month. This is getting ridiculous."

"*Second message.*"

"Oh my good Lord in Heaven. I just logged on to Socialstatus .com and it says you are a *whore* in *Soho*? Darling! Please! Come back to us. We don't care what you've done or how you are paying the bills. Daddy will pay off your pimp. Just come home!"

She's lost her mind, Lipstick thought as she sat down at her sewing table, ready for two more hours of work before she called it a night. *I'll call her tomorrow and set everything straight.*

LIBRA:

Indecision is an obstacle to your future, but the creative gods have blessed you. Retrograde impacted your finances, which had a direct correlation on the way you see yourself and how others see you. But that is changing.

At two in the morning, one week later, Lipstick was fading. Her back hurt from sitting in her kitchen chair and stooping over the sewing machine for the past four hours while she slaved away in her own personal sweatshop on the Met Gala gowns she was making for herself and Dana. She stopped sewing and, stretching her back, yawned.

It had been a long day. She'd put in a full day of work at *Y* and gotten yelled at by Jack for not covering Fabiola Winchester's Tea for Tots soiree at the Ritz-Carlton several weeks earlier. It was an oversight, Lipstick admitted. But she'd been so tired lately from her double life that she'd simply forgotten.

But it had not gone unnoticed, especially after the party was missing from the pages of *Y*, but not from *WWD* and

Socialstatus.com. Jack was even more peeved after Fabiola had called his assistant Christina, her best friend, to complain about Lipstick's lack of attendance.

"You're slipping," Jack had hissed at the afternoon meeting. "I don't care how many events there are to cover, or what new fabulous designer you're courting, these people are what make this magazine run. They are the air we breathe and the ink we type. They are the reason *Y is*. And, may I add, the reason you get *paid* (*barely,* thought Lipstick). Don't let it happen again. And what's with those gloves you're wearing lately? Have you suddenly become a germaphobe? And for God's sake, Lena, get some sleep. You look atrociously Goth, which, as we all know, was two seasons ago. Christina has some Ambien if you need it or put some makeup on, but those bags under your eyes are unacceptable."

To make matters worse, Lipstick had had to lie to get out of covering SueAnne's cocktail party celebrating Dolce & Gabbana's latest scent, Torture, that evening. She'd told Jack she was meeting the Dauphin designer at a secret locale to persuade the designer to debut at the Met. In reality she'd had to go shopping.

But it wasn't at her old haunt, Bergdorf. Instead, Lipstick had used the last of her old allowance to go to the fabric stores on Seventh Avenue. The Met Gala's theme this year was feathers, and she had to be creative. There were no feathers in her closet. But at least the bill for several yards of black and green organza and two huge bags full of feathers had come to a little over three hundred dollars, as opposed to three thousand, the typical bill for her pre-exile-to-Soho shopping trips.

Back at her apartment, Lena started the sewing machine up again. The feathers she'd bought were everywhere. On the floor, on her clothes, even in her hair. It looked like she'd stepped into a ring with seven multicolored chickens. And lost. She was so tired she was seeing double, but she had to get the dresses done by the following week, so she continued sewing.

But her mind was on what happened on the way home from the fabric store. Loaded down with four oversized bags, Lipstick had taken the 1 local train down to Houston. On her walk home, she spotted the stalker.

The woman with the Anna Wintour wig was standing behind some scaffolding on the corner of Sixth and Houston. And she was taking pictures again. Three blocks later, as Lipstick turned onto Sullivan Street, she was still behind her, half a block away. Lipstick picked up her pace and ran inside her building.

Why is she doing this? Lipstick thought, sewing feather after feather onto the dress she was making for Dana. *What does she want from me? It's so creepy. And weird.*

Penelope had tried to look on the bright side. "Well, you know you've made it when you have a stalker!" But that hadn't made Lipstick feel any better or made her life any easier at work. Jack was appalled by the posts on Socialstatus.com of Lipstick looking like a commoner—getting off the subway, walking into what looked like a dilapidated tenement building, and hanging out with people (Penelope, Dana, and Zach) who certainly weren't on the social register as far as he knew. And, of course, she was still broke. She'd kept Jack's probing and criticisms at bay, but she wasn't sure how much longer she could hold out for.

And who stalked someone? It was just so odd and unsettling. It infuriated Lipstick. At least the photos of Lipstick on Socialstatus.com—at parties in her creations and on the street—had run up traffic. She was getting more press on the site than anyone ever had before. People had become obsessed with her. The comments section was full of chatter like, "Lena is so cool. She's so urban fabulous." And that week she was ranked number two on the site—just below Bitsy Farmdale, who'd incidentally suddenly taken to wearing little gloves, just like Lipstick.

She'd never been so popular on the circuit before. And much to her own surprise, she'd never cared less.

Her life was so busy that she rarely had the time to check the site anymore and obsess over her ranking. She'd look at it casually at work, but it didn't seem to matter. All of the people who she'd been "friends" with for years just seemed to want something from her. They wanted Lipstick to put them in *Y,* or cover their gala, or be photographed with them as, now that Lipstick was so popular on Socialstatus.com, they knew a picture with Lipstick would ensure that their visage was posted onto the website alongside hers.

It was tiresome. All Lipstick wanted to do was go home and sew more, to do something she felt so passionate about, and create a tangible product. She loved darting dresses and hemming shirts. She adored creating confections out of her own clothes and fitting them to her—or Penelope's or Dana's—body. And when a dress or shirt was done, there was the satisfaction of wearing it, or seeing it posted on the website and then being praised by people who had no idea where the clothes had come from. It was the purest form of flattery, with no strings attached, because no one could figure out who the designer was; they just wanted the clothes.

The few hours of spare time she had were spent with Penelope and Dana, who didn't care what her father did for a living or where she shopped. They were just fun. And for the first time in her life, Lipstick felt accepted for who she was, not what she was—or who her parents were.

Lipstick even began to miss her parents. At the completion of every dress, she would think, *Mother would love this.* When she rode the subway instead of wasting money on a taxi she'd think, *Daddy would* die. *He always said I'd be eaten alive down here.* And every day she'd think, *I'll call them tomorrow.* But she never got around to it.

Lipstick was so lost in her thoughts that she wasn't paying attention and her forefinger ran under the sewing needle.

"Oh! OW!" she cried as blood dripped from her fingertip onto the black dress she was making. "Oh no!" she yelled as she went to the sink and ran her hand under cold water. At least the stain wouldn't show on the dark fabric. She bandaged her finger and just as she was about to call it a night, she heard a knock on the door.

Lipstick, wearing only a white tank top with no bra underneath and a pair of running shorts, opened the door and blushed. It was Zach, holding an open Heineken in his hand.

"Hey," he said, "I figured you might be working late and thought you'd need one of these."

"Oh, thanks," Lipstick said, taking a beer.

"What happened to your finger, and what's with the feathers everywhere?" Zach asked. "You okay? You need some help?"

"No, no," Lipstick said, "I'm okay. Just a bad run-in with the sewing machine. Wasn't paying attention."

Reaching out for her hurt hand, Zach rubbed it against his cheek and said, "You should be more careful. These are precious fingers."

Lipstick gasped. She could feel the jolt from where her hand hit his cheek in her thighs. "Oh, yes. Right," she said.

Kissing her hand, Zach said, "Well, I gotta go. I have an early-morning meeting with some potential clients. But stop by tomorrow if you want. I'd love to see you."

"You . . . you don't want to stay?" Lipstick asked.

"No can do, not tonight, anyways."

"Okay . . . see you later then. And thanks for the beer."

"Good night."

"'Night."

12

SAGITTARIUS:

You're a professional perfectionist and control freak. But now is a good time to let go.

"Sit still," said Penelope, gripping a Can-O-Hair.

She and Dana were in the living room area of Dana's loft, and Dana was sitting on an expandable folding chair, which the two had rescued from the street, that was placed on a plastic tarp, covering Dana's floors and protecting her white furniture. Karl was hiding under the couch, growling at any movement. Penelope, in a sweatsuit with her frazzled tresses piled on top of her head, was wearing a face mask and plastic gloves to avoid touching or inhaling Can-O-Hair.

"Okay, but be careful," Dana said, holding up her hair and exposing her ever-growing bald spot. "My apartment is white. All the furniture is white. This could cause some serious damage. That stuff probably doesn't come out so easily."

"Please, trust me. After four months of spraying this crap on Trace's head, I'm a pro," Penelope said before pressing the can and letting it rip.

Whooosh! The dark brown viscous material erupted out of the can like Montezuma's Silly String, fusing to Dana's scalp.

"Argh!" Dana said, jumping out of her seat, "It's freezing."

"Chill out," Penelope said. She grabbed a beautician's sponge she'd swiped from Trace's drawer. "Now here's where the artistry comes in."

It was the night of the Met Gala and three weeks since Dana had last promised Lipstick she'd show up as her date, bald spot or not. And in those three weeks, the patch had grown from the size of a silver dollar to the approximate size of a baseball card. The growth was roughly proportional to Dana's increase in stress-induced anxiety.

Two weeks ago she'd gone home to Cleveland for an ill-fated Passover service where her mother—who'd run into Noah's mother again in the supermarket—had informed Dana, "She's having a girl. That could have been your baby, you know. I'll never be a grandmother at this rate. You aren't even dating, are you?"

It had gone downhill from there. The Lubovitch side of the family had flown in from Miami and ignored Dana, refusing to acknowledge anyone who'd gone through a divorce. Her father, always the strong, silent type, was even stronger and more silent than usual thanks to a prostate infection. Dana, not wanting details, spent much of the time hiding in the bathroom from her mother, who desperately tried to share them.

Thankfully her weight had stabilized, but only because she was under a lot of pressure. After the meeting with Mr. Kornberg, her usual workload had been boosted up to an almost inhuman one-hundred-hour workweek, forcing her into her office on Saturdays and Sundays. Due to time constraints, she'd stopped going to Weight Watchers meetings altogether, and skipped out of work only to sleep and to host the twice-weekly yoga group.

As a result, her alopecia was threatening to take over the back of her head.

"I can't believe I agreed to go to this damn thing with Lipstick," Dana said as Penelope continued honing her skill with the spray-on hair and sponge. "How come you can't go?" she asked Penelope.

"I already told you," Penelope said, patting down more faux hair on Dana's scalp before removing her face mask. "It's sweeps week for cable stations. And Marge got it in her crazy head to do something called the 'Call Girl Coffee Klatch.' She's had me calling prostitutes all week."

> **SCORPIO:**
> Your hard work will be appreciated—but not everyone will be on your side. Watch out for jealous coworkers.

That Monday, during the morning assignment meeting, Marge had come up with her "most brilliant sweeps idea ever," she said. "We'll get a bunch of hookers to give us sex tips. We'll call it 'inside the seedy underbelly of the sex industry'!" By the end of the meeting, Marge's idea had been toned down to the "Call Girl Coffee Klatch."

After the meeting, Penelope and Thomas sat in the back of the newsroom and began phoning all of the escort services in the back of *New York* magazine and the *Village Voice*. But trying to get girls to agree to go on camera and talk about their profession wasn't easy.

"You want me to do what?" said one woman from Discreet Indiscretions when Penelope asked her to "come on air and just talk about your job. You know, the highlights—the good, the bad, the STDs. Kind of like an informational interview." The woman responded, "And have the cops on my ass? Get the fuck outta here."

A woman from Eastern Massage was more concise. "You no good. You bad!" she said before hanging up on Penelope.

Finally, Penelope had an idea. As Thomas kept plugging away at the ads in the back of the *Village Voice,* she called her old pal Olga from her *Telegraph* days.

"Olga?" Penelope asked when a woman with no discernible Russian accent answered the phone.

"Yes, this is Olga Kain speaking."

"Oh, I'm sorry," Penelope said. "I'm looking for an Olga Khrushcheksvy."

"Who may I ask is calling, please?"

"Penelope Mercury. I used to know her when I worked at the Telegraph."

"Penelope, dahling!" the voice said—now in the Russian accent Penelope knew and loved. "It's me, Olga. I am now vorking on my own. I finally got rid of Stanislas, but he still calls. So I have to disguise my voice vhen I answer the phone. I am my own secretary now."

"Oh, good to hear," Penelope said. "Does that mean you are still, um, working . . . ?"

"Yes, of course. Better than ever now. Such demands for beautiful Russian vomen these days. Thanks to God I fit the bill!"

"Well, I'm now working at New York Access, that local cable channel—and I need some prostitutes to come on and talk about their profession."

"Anything for you, dah-ling, but remember. I prefer the term 'escort.' So does your IRS!"

"So, I have to film that tonight," Penelope said to Dana.

"Why tonight? Why didn't you shoot it today?" Dana asked.

"Eh, Marge was so excited that she started doing promos for it and some people complained about it possibly airing in the afterschool time slot—who knew we had afterschool viewers? So we had to move the Klatch to the 'adult swim hours.' It's taping tonight at nine. So, after a full day of work and being tortured by Trace Feelyhands, Kandace Karllsen, *and* Laura Lopez, I get to go back for more."

And it was torture. Ever since the *Y* article appeared, the claws had come out.

At first Kandace had been supportive of Penelope's odd segments if only because she was grateful Marge hadn't made her do it.

"I (hands swooshing inward toward her heaving chest that was shoved inside a blue strapless dress two sizes too small) am so proud of you (swoosh toward Penelope)," Kandace gushed to Penelope after her "promotion." On days that Kandace was feeling generous, she would introduce Penelope to everyone as "my protégé."

"I (swoosh in) was asked to do the segments but told Marge (swoosh out) *you* were the gal for the job! Besides, my dance card is so full I am afraid it would cause a *riot* of jealousy."

But lately Kandace's largesse was diminishing.

Thanks to the *Y* item, Penelope—or rather, her segments—had been reviewed by the *New York Post* ("Atrociously appalling—you won't believe what they make this poor girl do"—Linda Stasi) and the *Daily News* ("An addictive train wreck. Like *Cosmo* on crack"—Micah Stark), further raising Kandace's ire.

"What is wrong with you?" Kandace hissed that morning after sending Penelope on a coffee run (which Penelope was still obliged to do), "I am a *senior* anchor here. I used to work at CNN. And when I ask for a venti mocha skim latte I want a frickin' *venti* mocha skim latte—not a *grande* mocha skim latte!"

"I'm sorry," Penelope said, in what she hoped was a soothing voice. "I forgot—you usually like *grandes,* remember? You said anything larger gives you gas?"

"I said venti—I want venti! It's not rocket scientry!"

"Rocket scientry?" Penelope asked.

"Yes! Rocket scientry! Are you deaf?" Kandace screeched.

"No, but I think you mean 'rocket science.' 'Scientry' isn't a word."

"Riiiight," Kandace said, eying Penelope suspiciously.

"No, really, it's not."

"Irregardlessy," Kandace said, her hands swishing outward.

Penelope stifled a giggle as Kandace stomped away.

While Kandace was openly hostile, Laura seemed to view Penelope—or, rather, Penelope's unwanted press—as a challenge.

Later that same day Penelope was having a smoke break on the fire escape with David when Laura waltzed outside and announced in a hushed stage whisper, "If you hear anything about me and Jimmy Smits on a boat in Sag Harbor, you know nothing! I'll tell you all later, but for now, it's best you're in the dark. But if Richard Johnson from Page Six or George Rush from Rush & Molloy call, say 'no comment' and hang up!" At that last directive, Laura, stuffed into a bright-red sundress that matched her sunburned chest, turned on her heel and stalked off.

Two hours later, after Penelope finished taping a segment on "Bling Bling Baby Baskets—All the Latest Rage," Laura slunk over to her and, again in a hushed stage whisper, her eyes darting around, said, " Did anyone call about . . . you know . . ."

"Not that I am aware of," Penelope said, "but—"

"Shhh!" Laura said. She put her finger to her lips and scanned the room for eavesdroppers. "It's for the best! Now remember. If they do call—and they will—about me and one Jimmy Smits. You. Know. Nothing!"

After Laura slunk away, David walked over and whispered to Penelope, "Your press is killing her. I just caught her dialing Richard Johnson in Marge's office. She's apparently been ringing him, George Rush, and every other gossip columnist in town all morning."

Laura, deciding to take press matters into her own hands, had sneaked into Marge's office several times during one of Marge's many patrols around the newsroom—which almost always coincided with David's cigarette or bathroom breaks. Disguising her voice, she had rung up the city's gossip columnists and left them messages. "I kan't tell you who theees ees," she whispered into the phone, "but you vould like to know New York Access entertainment voman, thees beeyoutiful Laura Lo-PEZ, she vas spotted on a boat in Sag Harbor with the hot hot hot Latino acter JEEMMY SMITS!"

On her last dash into the office David had followed her and, afterward, as she was tiptoeing down the hall, yelled at her, "JEEMY! JEEMY! I luv yoooouuuu!"

"Kandace and Laura are seriously driving me nuts, and Trace grabbed my ass twice last week. I don't know how much more I can handle," Penelope told Dana, giving Dana's scalp one last pat with the sponge. "There. All done. Keep holding your hair up though; it has to dry properly."

"Why don't you sue that creep for sexual harassment?" Dana asked indignantly. "That's illegal behavior, and you don't have to put up with it."

"It's not that easy," Penelope said. "It's kind of what he does. And I can't be unemployed again. *And* if I sue, I'll have to leave and then it will be publicized and no one will ever hire me again. *And* it's not like I'll get a million-dollar payout. Hell, I don't even think they'd have a million, if that's what I was awarded."

"Do you want me to call your boss and have a chat with her as your lawyer?" Dana asked.

"No, I'm okay. I'll handle it, Mom," Penelope said. "Thanks, though."

There was a knock at the door, and Lipstick's voice from outside came floating through: "Helloooo, Dana? Darling? I've got the dresses . . ."

Karl emerged from under the sofa and hit the ground running, a snarling, barking, frothing mess.

"Your dog is bazonkers," Penelope said as Dana struggled to get up. "Sit. That stuff needs to dry some more. I'll get it."

Penelope opened the door to greet Lipstick, who was dressed in jeans and a T-shirt and carrying two explosions of feathers—one black, one green.

"Whoa!" Penelope said, taking a step back. "What the hell is going on? You look like you got into a pillow fight with a peacock and lost."

"The Met, that's what," Lipstick puffed, out of breath from climbing the flight of stairs with the heavy feathery creations.

Penelope took off her rubber gloves and tossed them on the plastic tarp. "Let me help you with one of those birds," she said, grabbing the bigger dress. Lipstick and Penelope walked to the sofa, with Karl snapping at their heels the entire way, and laid the dresses down.

"Okay," Lipstick said, taking a deep breath and pulling a few stray feathers from her hair. "I had to work for three weeks straight, but here we go . . . " She lifted up the first dress. It was a black strapless dress with a ruched bust and a floor-length silk-organza feathered skirt.

"This one is yours, Dana," Lipstick said to Penelope and Dana. "The green one's mine. Well, what do you think? Do you guys like them? Hate them? Please tell me something . . . anything!"

"It's . . . " Dana gulped. "It's . . ."

"Yes?" Lipstick asked, twirling her hair and chewing on a nail.

"Beautiful. I've never seen anything like it."

"They're amazing," Penelope agreed.

"Oh, thank God." Lipstick heaved a sigh of relief and placed the dress back on the sofa. "I was so worried you wouldn't like it." Turning to Dana, she asked, "How's the hair coming?"

"Okay, I guess. I haven't seen it yet."

Penelope swatted Dana on the shoulder and pulled out a compact from her purse. She angled the mirror toward her head. "It's fine. See? You can hardly tell. And when it's fully dry and she lets her hair down, no one will know!"

Dana asked, "If I might be so bold, I love the dresses, but why so many feathers, Lips?"

"Well," Lipstick said, sitting on the sofa next to the dresses. "Every year there is a theme to the Gala. Anna Wintour is in charge, and for some reason this year she picked 'Feathers, Flight, and Fancy.' It was a nightmare. I had to go to three fabric stores on Seventh Avenue last week to find the right kind and amount of feathers. I looked like a freaky feather-obsessed bag lady on the subway home. And yesterday, when I ran out to replace a zipper, that stalker got another picture of me and posted it. I didn't even see her. She's getting good."

"That's so creepy," Penelope said. "I've been checking that horrible social website and they've been going nuts on you. But on the bright side, everyone likes the dresses you're wearing in the posts, and no one seems to know about what happened with you and your parents."

"Yeah." Lipstick sighed. "Not yet, at least. And I'm ranked ahead of Bitsy. For the first time in my life I made number-one socialite."

"Congratulations," Dana said.

"Thanks," Lipstick said with a wry smile. "But it's not as great as I thought it would be. My life is the same. It's just that a bunch of mean girls voted for me. And it's exhausting leading a double life. I'm just waiting for Jack to corner me tonight."

"If Anna Wintour is in charge of the Gala, then why does Jack get a table?" Penelope asked. "Don't they hate each other?"

"Well," Lipstick said, "I don't think Anna hates Jack. And I'd say he's probably more jealous of her than anything. It's her revenge—invite Jack along to show him she's still the reigning queen of the fashion universe. I get a table anyway because mummy's a very big couture client and on the board of the Met."

"Is your mom going to be there?" Dana asked. "Have you spoken to her?"

"No and no," Lipstick said, absently plucking at a random feather on the green dress and not looking at either of the other girls. "She's allergic to feathers so she can't—and my dad always refuses to attend those things anyway, so I'm in the clear."

"But you still haven't called them?" Penelope asked incredulously. "My mother would have hunted me down by now, if only to tell me my father was threatening to crucify himself."

"Yeah, I guess. But I just haven't had time. I meant to last week. But then I just didn't know what to say. The longer I wait, the harder it gets. I'll do it, though. Eventually."

"When do you guys have to be there?" Penelope asked.

"It starts at seven thirty so we'll get there at eight thirty. By then all the eager beavers will have arrived, and we can run down the red carpet, get our photo taken—"

"What?" Dana cried, "Photos? I didn't sign up for that!"

"Everyone gets their photo taken at the Met." Lipstick sighed. "It's—"

"Lipstick, I'm going to murder you. This is basically my first night out since my fucking divorce, and you're throwing me to the wolves." Dana, who was beginning to realize just how big of a deal this event was, started to get upset.

"It'll be okay, I promise. I won't leave your side all night. You can hide behind me in the photos. Please."

"Hey, you two," Penelope cut in. "You'd better get a move

on and get in those dresses. It's already seven thirty and you still have to put on your makeup."

> **LIBRA:**
> Something you've been working hard on for quite some time is about to be realized. Revel in your achievement, and blow off the potholes on the road to success. But you've overlooked something, which could cause you problems down the line. Think hard and rectify the situation or face the ramifications of a flighty instinct.

By 8:10, Lipstick and Dana were ready to go. Lipstick, wearing three coats of antiperspirant to protect her from glistening too much in what she was sure was going to be the most stressful evening of her life, had applied her own makeup first, giving herself a dark, smoky look complemented by small touches of jade eye shadow, and then done Dana's makeup and hair—artfully giving Dana, who usually wore little to no face paint, a "clean, fresh look" and pulling her bobbed 'do back with diamondesque pins that also added volume in the back to help hide the patch of faux hair. When they emerged from the bathroom, Penelope's eyes widened.

"Jesus," she said. "I mean, wow. You two look like a fairy tale come to life."

And they did. Lipstick, with her hair cascading over her shoulders and in her feathered green dress, looked positively Botticelli-esque, and Dana, well, Dana was a different person altogether.

She was obviously nervous—her upper lip had disappeared into her teeth—but transformed. Penelope had never seen her in a dress—always in yoga gear or a suit—and while Dana always complained about being overweight, she didn't look fat at all.

Instead, she looked voluptuous in the strapless black gown. Her milky white skin was perfectly smooth and, with her hair and makeup tastefully done, she almost resembled a fuller version of Dita von Teese—if Dita von Teese weren't a stripper and had a Can-O-Hair–covered bald patch.

"Really?" Dana asked, "It's okay?"

"Of course it's okay," Lipstick said, trying to hide her nerves. "I made it! Jack got me a car for the evening and it should be here by now, so we should leave. But remember, Dana, no talking in the car. All of Jack's drivers are his spies. Everything we say will be reported back to him. He'll already want to know why we were picked up here instead of at my old place, so not a word, okay?"

"You got it, boss," Dana said.

Lipstick found her little black leather gloves and put them on to hide her red sewing-scarred hands. She took a deep breath and exhaled. "Let's go, then!"

"I'll walk you down to make sure you don't get stuck on anything or molt all over the place," Penelope said.

The girls piled out of Dana's apartment after securing Karl, still snarling, in the bathroom ("He gets angry when I go out," Dana explained. "He pees all over the place"). On the second-floor landing they ran into Zach, who looked like he'd just gotten up.

"Wow," Zach said, looking only at Lipstick. "Princess, you are a vision."

Lipstick turned three shades of red while Penelope nudged Dana and whispered, "That's him. The guy that Lips, you know . . ."

"Where are you ladies off to?" Zach asked.

"The Met," Lipstick said, "and we're late—talk later!"

"Well, have a great time," Zach said, continuing up the stairs to his floor. "And stop by after if you want; it's going to be a late work night for me, so I'll be up."

As the girls rushed down the stairs, Penelope joked, "Oh, I'll bet he'll be up, heh."

"Oh, stop, nothing is going on!" Lipstick said. "We're friends. That's it."

"Well, he looks like he wants to be more than just friends," Dana said.

They got out the front door and Penelope giggled. "Me too! Let's all share! I'll throw in my crush, Thomas."

"You guys are crazy." Lipstick laughed, climbing into the waiting Town Car.

"All right," Penelope said, stuffing Dana in after Lipstick. "I gotta go get ready for the hookers—have fun!"

It took twenty-five minutes (spent in total silence) to drive uptown to the Met and for Jack's driver to jockey into position in front of the red carpet entrance at the bottom of the steps leading into the museum. The photographers were lined up four feet deep behind metal barriers, all the way up the white, marble stairs to the entrance.

They were over an hour late and there were only a few stragglers making their way in, but the flashbulbs were still popping.

Dana's face was blank in fear. Lipstick grabbed her hand and squeezed it. "You ready?"

Dana nodded.

"Then let's go!" Lipstick pulled Dana out of the car and into the spotlight.

As they walked up the red-carpeted steps, flashbulbs exploded and photographers yelled, "Lena, over here!" "Lena, this way!" "Lena, to your left!" "Lena, to your right!"

"I had no idea you were famous," Dana said, temporarily blinded by the flashes but smiling and trying not to let her lips move.

"I'm not. People in the fashion and society world know me because of *Y* and my family—and this is the socials' biggest event of the year," Lipstick said, guiding Dana slowly up the stairs as they walked and posed, Dana mimicking Lipstick with one hand on her hip, head tilted slightly to one side, and knees together.

"Lena, who're you with?" one photographer called out.

"Lena, who're you wearing?" yelled another.

"I'm dressed in Dauphin," Lena said with her arm linked in Dana's, loud enough for several photographers to hear. "And this is Dana Gluck."

"Dana! Dana! Who are you?" the shouting continued.

"Okay, that's enough," Lipstick said and steered a terrified Dana inside the museum, right from the frying pan into the feathery fire.

"Oh my God," Dana said, looking around, "What's going on in here?"

The huge entrance hall had been decked out in gold. Gold fabric lined the walls, gold tables, gold candelabras, everything was gold but the guests—and the animals. To add a physical feathery presence to the Great Hall of the Met, there were three indentured ostriches roaming through the crowd, with harnesses and trainers in tow. Several live eagles and hawks hung from gilded cages in the corners of the room and looked hungrily down at the multicolored peacocks wandering in between tables set with plumes and guests adorned in the feathers of their dead relatives. Every so often the peacocks were prodded by their handlers—not enough to hurt, but enough to scare—so they would fan out their tails and become the living art they were hired to be. They were in the middle of the largest gilded cage ever.

"It's a zoo," Dana whispered to Lipstick, "literally."

"Shhh!" Lipstick said, guiding Dana toward the receiving line. "We have to go through the receiving line and pay our respects before we can mingle."

The line consisted of Angelina Jolie, Natalie Portman, John Galliano, and Anna Wintour—all in downy Galliano-designed Christian Dior creations.

"Don't say anything," Lipstick warned Dana. "Just follow my lead and smile."

After Angelina and Natalie shook the girls' hands and murmured, "Thank you for coming," they were stopped from moving on. The line slowed behind the Count and Countess of Albedonne, who were talking with Anna Wintour and John Galliano.

The designer's eye wandered over to Lipstick and Dana, where it stopped at their dresses. As the line finally moved forward, Lipstick saw Anna's "seeing eye dog" Nu whisper, "Lena Lippencrass and guest" into the editor's ear. (Nu was always by Anna's side, identifying people as they approached so Anna would never be embarrassed by not knowing who someone was.)

"Beautiful," Galliano said to Lipstick and Dana, still looking only at the dresses.

"Th-thank you," said Lipstick.

"These are who?" Galliano asked, waving his hands over her dress.

Lipstick was silent.

"Dauphin—a new designer," Dana answered for her as Lipstick's nails dug into her arm through her gloves.

"Thank you for coming," Wintour said icily. The girls were then sent on their way, descending into the bowels of the party.

"God, that was close," Lipstick said as they walked away. Then a hand grabbed her arm.

It was Nu.

"Anna wants to know about this Dauphin," Nu said. "She wants to meet her. Now."

Dana was starting to drift off toward the bar, and Lipstick said, "Well, she's not with me right now, she went to get a drink."

"Here is my card. Please call in the morning with the information," Nu said, walking back to her post just behind the receiving line.

Lipstick caught up to Dana, who was trying to work her way to the bar. "I'm in trouble," she said. "I think I may have accidentally given people the impression that you are—"

But Dana wasn't paying attention. "Look at this place," she said. "Look at all these people! It's like your magazine come to life!"

In the crowd were fashion icons Donatella Versace, Giorgio Armani, Ralph Lauren, Marc Jacobs, Miuccia Prada—and those were just the ones Dana could identify. The designers were only outshined by the stars they had dressed. In the line for the bar alone was Julia Roberts (in Armani), Halle Berry (in Versace), Will Smith (in a tux), and Matthew McConaughey (in board shorts, a black jacket, and nothing else). Elsewhere mingling in the crowd were Sarah Jessica Parker, Jennifer Lopez, Renée Zellweger, and Sandra Bullock. Not that you could hear a word anyone was saying. The acoustics in the Grand Hall were not suited for this many people and noise from the crowd was approaching a dull roar, which helped to disguise Jack's stealthy approach. He was with Bitsy Farmdale, who was dolled up in a white bell-shaped minidress covered in silvery feathers and dragging a miserable-looking Thad Newton III behind her like last year's Fendi bag.

"Lena!" Jack said loudly.

The girls turned to see Lipstick's boss arm-in-arm with her nemesis.

"Bitsy informs me that not only did you introduce Dauphin to Anna Wintour before me but you're planning on a meeting with Anna as well."

"N-no, no," Lipstick stammered. "We just went through the reception line."

"I saw Nu give you her card. What was that about, then?" Bitsy asked.

"Anna did ask to meet, but of course my loyalty is to you, Jack, I was going to—"

Jack, eyeing Dana, interrupted Lipstick and said, "Aren't you going to introduce me to your guest?"

"Of course," Lipstick said, looking away. "This is Dana Gluck. Dana, this is Jack Marshall and Bitsy Farmdale. And Thad Newton."

"The third," Thad added, staring at Lipstick.

"Shut up, Thad!" Bitsy hissed. "You're embarrassing me!"

Lipstick cringed, half out of embarrassment for him and half out of rage. This was the first time she'd seen him since they'd dated. She'd even broken up with him on the phone. He looked as handsome as ever. But something about him was different. Pathetically different.

Did I ever love him? Or was I with him because my parents liked the match and my society approved? It seems so . . . long ago.

"Hello," Dana said and shook their hands. Except for Thad's. She ignored him—she knew who he was and how he'd treated Lipstick.

Thad didn't acknowledge Dana's slight but just nodded his head and murmured, "My pleasure." And it was those two words that made Lipstick almost gag with pity for her ex-boyfriend.

In the two years they had dated, Thad had always tried to ameliorate any situation, even if it was to his detriment.

When, after two months of dating, Lipstick had asked if they were officially going steady and not dating other people, Thad had said, "Of course, my love," to her delight.

One time, after Lipstick insensitively laughed at Thad's patchwork madras pants, he'd said, "My fault." And in bed, after he'd finished (once again) too early, Thad would mumble, "So sorry."

Even when he contradicted Lipstick, Thad would stay true to form. Early in their relationship, Lipstick had tried to get him to go see a cool new band playing at Cake Shop, a bar on the Lower East Side—an area he deemed "unsafe" and "dirty." When Lipstick had begged, Thad said simply, "Absolutely not." It wasn't that he didn't want to go—it was that he couldn't. He physically couldn't disobey his social standards or (even more so) his mother Tabitha, who'd always warned him, "Our kind just don't go to certain places. Once you soil your hands, you may as well roll in the filth with the rest of the pigs."

It had taken her a while, but right there in the middle of the Met Gala, Lipstick finally realized what Thad really was: a good-looking, socially acceptable, bland doormat.

"I must say, I'm quite impressed," Jack said to Dana.

"As am I," Dana answered, not quite understanding the misunderstanding that was taking place. "This is an amazing gala."

"And so modest!" Jack gasped. "Lena, you have discovered an important talent."

Dana looked quizzically at Lena, who had found a particularly interesting spot on the floor at which to stare. Thad Newton III was trying to catch her eye while Bitsy clutched his hand and stroked Jack's arm possessively with her other.

The trumpeters blasted the dinner announcement from the top of the stairs. Jack took Dana's arm. "You, my dear, will sit with me at my table as my guest," he said, guiding her away from a slack-jawed Lipstick.

Dana looked panicked, her eyes were as wide as saucers, and she twisted back to look at her friend. "What is going on?" she mouthed to Lipstick. But there was nothing Lipstick could do. To defy Jack would mean an instant firing and a public scene. She looked at Dana helplessly.

"Sorry for ruining your moment," Bitsy hissed. "Guess you'll just have to sit at your table by yourself, without your big, fat, fabulous designer. Or perhaps you can call your Soho bum to hold her place?"

"Oh, grow up, Bitsy," Lipstick said, with an uncustomary viciousness. "She's not fat, and you don't know what you're talking about."

"I think I do," Bitsy said before walking off, leaving Thad standing there, still gawking at Lipstick.

"You . . . you look beautiful," Thad said to Lipstick. "I've never seen you look like this."

"Thanks, Thad," Lipstick snapped, furious that her body was betraying her by blushing. "But maybe you should tell your girlfriend that."

"About that. God, I'm so sorry. I . . . I miss you," Thad stammered. "I really do. I—"

"Thad!" Bitsy's voice cut through the crowd. "Get over here. *Now.*"

Thad winced, his head bowed. "Must go, but can I call you?" he asked Lipstick.

"No, you'd better not," she said and walked off to find her table, leaving Thad standing there, looking miserable.

Lipstick felt triumphant, almost vindicated—and something else. For all those months she'd felt humiliated by Thad cheating on her with Bitsy, she'd always wondered what she'd say to him when she finally saw him again. And now she didn't need to wonder anymore. Bitsy treated him like a servant. She almost felt bad for him. Almost. And for a moment Lipstick forgot what deep trouble she was in, having not lied but unwittingly misled Jack into thinking Dana was Dauphin.

Thankfully, Lipstick's table was within spying distance of Jack and Dana, who were seated at the periphery of Anna's inner sanctum of ten tables.

Even though Lipstick's mother Lana was on the board of the Met, that didn't mean she—or anyone who attended the gala, for that matter—got to pick their seats. People often weren't seated with their dates if the dates were deemed inappropriate. In 2007 Christina Ricci had walked out when she found her boyfriend was not seated at her table. She clearly had never been to an Anna gala—where Wintour personally assigned everyone their rung on the social ladder and seated them accordingly.

Lipstick's table was considered a good one. It was just outside of Wintour's inner circle, but not as close as Jack's table, where he was forced to watch his rival all evening. Lipstick was placed in a position of social prominence—and, she was happy to note, Bitsy and Thad were on the other side of the room, insultingly placed behind the marble statue of Venus. At Lipstick's table, there was Helena Hoff, a *Vogue* contributing editor (and also the daughter of a Texas oilman); Marcus Semple, a prominent investment banker (who, despite being only thirty-five, was rumored to have taken home $150 million the year before); Jacques and Mario, a French performance art duo; and Arthur Winksdale, Ashley's husband, who'd been randomly seated at Jack's table but mercifully dispatched to sit in the seat that was formerly Dana's (Ashley was seated at Bitsy's table and looked like she wanted to slit her wrists with her butter knife). To the left of Lipstick was Kitty Foil, a seventeen-year-old actress who'd been raised in the Disney farm leagues but was just breaking out into superstardom, transitioning from tween to hot, sexy teen, thanks to a risqué photo shoot by Annie Leibovitz in *Vanity Fair.* On Lipstick's right was Jann Elder, an attractive but self-absorbed writer/director type who was examining his reflection in the side of the large gold vase in the middle of the table.

Everyone had finally taken their seats. Doing her best to stick to her deeply ingrained societal rules and therefore engage in some sort of conversation no matter how odious the prospect was, Lipstick turned to Jann on her right and said, "So, what brings you here? Are you a huge fashion or feather aficionado?"

"My movie won the grand prize at the Sundance Film Festival," the director said. He already looked bored.

"That's wonderful; what was it?" Lipstick asked, gesturing to the waiter to fill her glass of white wine while trying to keep an eye on Dana at the next table.

"*Meat,*" the director said, closing his eyes in anticipation of the squeal that usually followed his proclamation.

"Oh, no thank you," Lipstick said, "I preordered the fish."

"No," he said impatiently, "my *movie* was called *Meat.* Didn't you see it? Meryl Streep was in it and, I don't like to brag, but I think it was the best performance of her career."

"Really?" Lipstick said, slightly taken aback. She took a sip of her wine. "Better than *Silkwood* or *Sophie's Choice*? Better than *Kramer vs. Kramer*?"

"Please." The director exhaled, rolling his eyes. "I mean, how hard is it to play a woman in anguish? Really. In all those roles all she did was cry, cry, cry, and yell. Typical female roles, which can be played by any woman. Isn't that just what women do anyway? In my film—which you'd know if you'd seen it—Meryl played a psychologist and really explored the depths of human emotions. It was just so . . . subtle."

This is going to be a long night, Lipstick thought as the white-gloved waiters in tuxedos served the asparagus appetizer.

SAGITTARIUS:

The stars are saying you will find love tonight, in the oddest of places, and an act of chivalry will win your heart.

At Dana's table, things were only marginally better.

After Jack had stolen her away from Lipstick, he escorted her to his table and presented her to the six others already seated as, "Dauphin!" before ushering her to her seat beside his.

"Yes, I am wearing Dauphin," Dana said, confused by Jack's excitement, thinking, *If he loves the dress so much, why doesn't he sit with Lipstick? She made it. . . .*

Dana had no clue who her tablemates were, except that they all seemed impossibly glamorous and haughty. The one exception was the skinny man with a potbelly who looked to be in his forties, sitting to her immediate right. He looked as out of place as she felt.

"I'm Gerard Applebaum," the man said to Dana as she took her seat. Like everyone else, he was dressed in a tuxedo, but he was wearing a pair of beat-up Converse sneakers instead of high-gloss shoes. His thick glasses rested on a prominent Roman nose below his shiny bald pate.

"I'm Dana Gluck," Dana said, placing her napkin on her lap.

"She's a *genius,*" Jack interjected, putting his arm around the back of Dana's chair. "An absolute ingenue who is destined to grace the cover of *Y.*"

"Wow," Gerard said, "and what may I ask did you do to herald such an introduction?"

"I'm not quite sure. . . ." Dana said, flustered, as she started to blush.

"She's shy!" squealed Jack. "So rare these days. Dana, this is Gerard Applebaum, a very famous producer who has many Oscars."

"All in my bathroom medicine cabinet collecting dust," Gerard said. "Nothing to brag about, really. In my business you're only as good as your next movie, which, for me, is next year. So until then, I'm nobody. And frankly, enjoying it."

"You don't seem like nobody to me," Dana said. "But, then again, I'm just a corporate litigator, so what do I know?"

"A what?" Jack asked.

"A corporate liti—" Dana said before Jack turned away, his eye caught by the sparkle of the twenty-carat diamond ring on the guest to his left, Ann DeBeers.

"Oh my," Jack said in an awed tone, "the famous DeBeers diamond. However did you manage to get that out of the family vault, Ann? Has your mother-in-law started speaking to you again?"

"He seems a bit flighty," Gerard said to Dana sotto voce. "How do you know him?"

"I don't," Dana said.

"Really?"

"Really. He's my friend's boss. I think there's been some confusion as to who I am and what I do."

"And why is that?" Gerard asked with a twinkle in his eye.

"I'm not sure, but I think he thinks I'm a fashion designer, which is pretty far-fetched. I do enjoy expensive clothes but thanks to my job, most of them are expensive suits."

"Ah, yes. I have a similar problem," Gerard said. "When most people see me on the streets they assume I'm a bum. Little do they know I am a *designer* bum! It costs a lot to look so nonchalant."

"I went through the Marc Jacobs phase as well," Dana said with a laugh. She was surprised to find that she was actually having a good time.

"Well, I don't care who you are or what you really do," Gerard said, "I'm just glad you're here."

"You are?"

"Please. Have you seen the blue-haired ladies at this table? Before you sat down, I was about to fake a stomach virus and bolt."

"So why did you come?" Dana asked.

"It's complicated, but basically, because of my Oscars I'm invited every year. I used to come with my wife, who loved this kind of shindig."

"Oh, you're married," Dana said, trying to disguise the disappointment in her voice.

"Divorced," Gerard answered. "As of March."

"Me too," Dana said, perking up. "Well, actually, as of last year."

"Was it as bad as mine?" Gerard asked.

"Probably worse," Dana said. "Unless your ex-wife left you for a Victoria's Secret model as well."

"Does my secretary count?" Gerard asked. "She *was* pretty hot."

"Seriously? Your secretary?"

"Seriously."

"Wow."

"Yep, they moved to a collective community in Marfa, Texas, to 'explore their relationship through art'—I know, don't roll your eyes—and so now it's just me and my eleven-year-old son, Michael. Two guys taking on the city together."

"Where's Michael tonight?" Dana asked.

"With the babysitter. I hired his old nanny to start babysitting three nights a week so I can try and have a life. Tonight's my first night out."

"Mine too," Dana said. "But why'd you come here for your inaugural night?"

"I came because I haven't really been going out much and thought I would get back on the bull and ride it."

"Nice analogy," Dana said.

"Thanks. I'm having a great ride with you," he said. Dana flushed a deep, dark red.

"So, has she told you all of her design secrets?" Jack cut in, turning back to Dana and Gerard, having had enough of the DeBeers diamond for the moment. "Darling, where in France do you come from?"

"She's French?" Ann DeBeers asked her partner loudly. "I thought French women don't get fat?"

Dana's mouth hung open in shock. She clutched her dinner fork so hard her knuckles turned white.

"She's not fat," Gerard said, wadding up his napkin in anger and throwing it in Ann DeBeers's direction. "She's gorgeous!"

Dana thought, *Thankyouthankyouthankyou for that.*

Shooting the DeBeers heiress a withering glance, Jack changed the subject. "Lena said she got her dresses while in Paris. Are you from there or did you just school there?"

Back at Lipstick's table, dinner plates were being cleared, several bottles of wine had been emptied, and things were taking an odd turn.

Kitty Foil, the pixie-esque teen actress who'd clearly made the most of cocktail hour and the table's wine, was hiccuping. She seemed okay at first, even charming, but as the wineglasses were emptied and she made more and more frequent trips to the bathroom to "powder her nose," she'd resorted to the annoying habit that many actresses adopt when they're not the center of attention—doing funny, quirky things to corral the attention back to her.

Throughout appetizers and dinner she talked about being devirginized at the age of fourteen "in the back of a tour bus in Cannes by Jagger," informed everyone of her equal hatred of underwear and papparazzi, tried to appear intelligent by claiming (dubiously) that she'd been accepted to Harvard a full two years early, and shrieked at an assistant who was hiding behind a hawk cage that "my fucking cell phone won't work in here and Johnny Depp is trying to get ahold of me about that Darfur benefit! Do something—now!"

After dinner was served and waiters interrupted her impersonation of Nicole Steele, her *Teen Deathmaster 4* costar, Kitty became annoyed that the other guests at the table used the arrival of food as an excuse to talk to each other—and not to her. So she tried to start a food fight with the vegetables on her plate. (There were no rolls; Anna Wintour was on the Atkins diet and had banned bread and all other carbohydrates from the gala.)

When nobody seemed interested in reciprocating, Kitty, with white powder lining her nostrils, sat sullenly for a moment before tugging on Lipstick's arm. "Do you (hic) do yoga?" she asked.

Grateful for the interruption of yet another thirty-minute monologue on Jann's inner genius, Lipstick gushed, "Yes! Actually, I love it. I have a group of girls I do it with twice a w—"

"My Rollerblades are heeeeere," trilled Kitty, interrupting Lipstick with what seemed like another non sequitur.

"Huh?" Lipstick said.

"My Rollerblades," Kitty said, rolling her eyes as a frightened-looking assistant dropped off a gym bag at Kitty's feet and scampered away. "I'm bored and (hic) you're box blocking me with Jann Elder."

"Box blocking?"

"It's like cock blocking but with girls," Kitty said, kicking off her Jimmy Choos and putting her Rollerblades on her bare feet. "I've been trying to talk to him (hic) all night, and you keep butting in."

"You want him?" Lipstick whispered. "You can have him—want to change seats?"

But Kitty wasn't listening anymore and had gotten up from the table in her white, tiny minidress with feathery fringe and mini angel wings attached to the back and, before swilling down the last of the wine in her glass, announced, "Look! I can do (hic) yoga in Rollerblades!" Before anyone could stop her, she grabbed the back of her chair with one hand and with the other pulled one Rollerbladed foot over her head, exposing her crotch. "Seeee? Rollerblading yooooga!" she said.

"Man, that is so cool," said Jann, to Kitty's delight. A security guard advanced toward the table. As the guard got within grabbing distance, Kitty dropped her leg and said, "Byeee!" and zoomed off. The guard whispered something in his walkie-talkie and took off after Kitty, who was zipping around the tables like a wheeled elf on ecstasy, or to be more precise, five lines of cocaine.

Several more guards joined the pursuit, but Kitty eluded them for a good fifteen minutes as amused party guests watched, assuming Kitty was part of the evening's entertainment.

"She's pretty good," Lipstick said to no one in particular.

"She's so hot," Jann said. "I want her for my next movie."

And then, Lipstick, as if in a trance, saw Kitty heading for Dana and Jack's table, on a direct collision course with a peacock and a white-gloved waiter carrying a tray of wine and water carafes.

"Nooo!" Lipstick cried. She stood up as the trio of disaster convened toward Dana's back. "Stop!"

But it was too late. The peacock, which had been resting behind Dana's chair, spotted Kitty coming right at him. He let out a raucous caw and spread his tail feathers, confusing the waiter, who stumbled into Kitty's path. Kitty hit the waiter at full speed, dumping his tray of water and wine carafes all over Dana, just as she, for the third and final time, told Jack, "No. I'm not French. I'm from Cleveland. I do not *design* Dauphin. I'm *wearing* Dauphin. I'm a *lawyer*. I practice the law."

The icy water and white and red wine cascaded over Dana's head, down her shoulders, and onto her dress as Jack, also doused, shrieked, "A common lawyer? From *Cleveland*?"

The cavernous hall became silent as guests watched in horror. Dana put a hand up to the back of her head, which took a direct hit from a glass carafe. When she pulled it away, it was covered in brown Can-O-Hair.

"Oh my God," she whispered, her eyes tearing up.

"Is that blood?" Gerard asked before yelling, "Call a doctor!"

"Blood?" Jack squealed and fainted, falling off his chair.

Dana tried her best to keep it together and smile through the tears that were mixing with the liquids already dripping on her face. She looked at Gerard and said, "It's not blood," she said, "I'm fine. Excuse me, I have to go to the bathroom." She ran as fast as she could in her soggy feathered dress to the ladies' room.

As Dana ran off, Kitty pulled herself to her feet, flung her hands in the air, and, giving her audience a ten-thousand-megawatt smile, screamed, "Ta DAAAA!" before slipping and falling over Jack's prone body.

"Well, there goes Kitty's chance at getting in *Vogue*—ever," Helena Hoff smirked to Jann Elder as Lipstick excused herself to follow Dana to the bathroom.

• • •

Lipstick ran into the bathroom and found Dana in the handicapped stall, hyperventilating.

Lipstick grabbed as many paper towels as she could and, drying her friend off, whispered, "It's okay, it's okay. We'll get out of here. Shhh, it's okay." She wiped the brown trail of Can-O-Hair off Dana's back and kissed her forehead as Dana silently cried in mortification.

"I'm so sorry," Lipstick said softly, starting to cry as well. "I'm so, so sorry. Please forgive me."

"You should've warned me that *I* was supposed to be Dauphin," Dana said, sniffling.

"I know," Lipstick said. "But I guess I thought I could pull it off without anyone knowing. I thought I could just allude to it. And we could get our pictures taken, eat dinner, and leave. I just didn't plan on Bitsy and Jack."

"Or a coked-up idiot running into a waiter and dumping water and wine on my head," Dana said. She laughed hysterically. "Look at me! All my hair washed off. I mean, what happened? Did the clock strike twelve and I turned back into a pumpkin?"

"I'm so sorry," Lipstick repeated.

"It's okay." Dana sighed. "You couldn't have known. And up until that crazy girl went nuts and Jack started flipping out, I was actually having a decent time. Despite that horrid old biddy calling me fat."

Lipstick gasped. "Who called you fat?"

"That DeBeers woman."

"I'll kill her," Lipstick snarled. "She'll never be in the magazine again."

"Thanks," Dana said, wiping her eyes. "What do you say we get outta here? I need some air."

"Done," Lipstick said, grabbing her purse from the bathroom floor and helping a soggy Dana up from the toilet.

Dana linked arms with Lipstick, and they paused to look at themselves in the bathroom mirror. Dana's hair was wet and her makeup was half washed off her face. She had brown stains running down her shoulders, while Lipstick's mascara had smudged, leaving her looking like a raccoon-eyed plebian. "Look at us—gorgeous!" Lipstick said, and they both started to laugh.

"Let's make a discreet exit out the side door—follow me," Lipstick said. She pushed open the bathroom door, just in time to catch Bitsy Farmdale, in a crouching position, with her ear to the entrance, as if she'd been listening the entire time.

Bitsy stood up, her silvery feather dress swinging back and forth like a bell.

"Oh hello, Bitsy," Lipstick said.

"I heard you," Bitsy said.

"So?' Lipstick asked.

"So. I heard everything."

"Again," Lipstick said, smiling. "So?'

"So . . . this will ruin you on Socialstatus.com."

"Bitsy." Lipstick sighed. "You're pathetic and I don't care. Oh, and by the way—Thad asked if he could call me. I said no. You two deserve each other." Lipstick and Dana brushed past Bitsy and walked out the side entrance.

On Fifth Avenue, Dana looked at Lipstick and said, "Wow."

"Yeah, wow," Lipstick said.

"You okay?"

"Yeah," Lipstick said and laughed. "Actually I am. Do you know that's the first time I ever stood up for myself with Bitsy? I'll probably be fired tomorrow from *Y* and ruined socially, but right now I feel pretty good."

"You should," Dana said, squeezing Lipstick's hand. "Let's walk for a bit. It's a nice night, and I need to dry off some more."

But as the girls started to walk down Fifth, someone yelled after them.

"Dana!" a man's voice said. "Dana, wait up!"

They turned around to see Gerard Applebaum running after them. The blood rushed to Dana's face. He was adorable. In a red, puffy way.

When he caught up to the girls, Gerard bent over his burgeoning belly, with his hands on his knees, trying to catch his breath. His face was red, and he was sweating in the warm spring night.

"Phew!" he said after a minute of huffing and puffing. "I know you'll be shocked by looking at my fabulously fit physique, but I'm not used to running. Good thing I wore my Converse, eh?"

"Good thing," Dana agreed, smiling. "This is Lips—sorry, Lena Lippencrass. Lena, Gerard Applebaum."

"Nice to meet you," Lipstick said, shaking his hand.

"You too," Gerard said. Turning back to Dana, he shook his head, "I can't believe you were going to leave without saying good-bye."

"Well, it seemed the best thing to do," Dana said. "My design mystique was ruined, and my hair got washed away."

"Your hair?"

"Yes," Dana said, turning around and lifting up the back of her hair to show him her bald spot, "it wasn't blood on my hands. It was my fake hair."

"So?"

"So. I have stress-induced alopecia. I'm going bald."

"Ah well," Gerard countered, rubbing his shiny head, "I don't mean to point out the glaringly obvious, but I beat you on the hairless front years ago."

Lipstick, sensing she was becoming a third wheel, hailed a taxi. Before Dana could say anything, she hopped in and yelled from the open window, "Don't feel so well. Have to go, see you tomorrow, byeee!"

Which left Dana and Gerard on the corner of Eightieth and Fifth. Alone.

"My driver's right over there," Gerard said, pointing out a bicycle rickshaw in the sea of limousines. "Can I offer you a ride?"

"Thanks," Dana said, "but I'd like to walk a bit."

"Can I keep you company?"

"I'd love it."

Which is how Dana Gluck ended up walking eighty blocks home to Soho in four-inch heels, talking and laughing the whole way with Gerard Applebaum.

13

SCORPIO:

While Mercury officially went out of retrograde two months ago, it will feel like it's back for a special encore tonight. But don't worry. Nothing catastrophic will happen this time.

Penelope's night didn't begin much better than Dana's had.

After Penelope helped Lipstick and Dana into the car taking them to the Met Gala, she hoofed it back up the stairs to her apartment to get ready for work.

What does one wear to a call-girl coffee klatch? she wondered, frantically rooting through her closet and several piles of clothes that had somehow found their way onto the living room sofa.

Penelope finally settled on a black pencil skirt, black pumps ("The librarian look is good for authority"), and a teal short-sleeved sweater topped with a strand of fake pearls.

To complete the outfit, Penelope swept her hair up into a bun and added a faux pair of black glasses. *Nice,* she thought, looking in the mirror behind the shower door. *But Lipstick would probably say it was 'too*-too.' She took the glasses off, grabbed her purse, and ran out the door at precisely 8:23, thirty-seven minutes before airtime.

By the time she made it to NY Access, all the women she and Thomas had secured were there already, crammed into the makeup room. "Putting on their faces," Eric cracked.

There was Randi, an outspoken twenty-five-year-old brunette "party specialist" from VIP Luxury Concierge Service, dressed in a black backless jersey floor-length gown (Thomas found a bright pink scarf to tie around her neck so Marge wouldn't have a fit), and Tania, an African-American "thirty-something" foot fetishist expert from Feet Me, dressed in jeans, a Yale sweatshirt, and five-inch Lucite heels that showed off her perfectly pedicured toes. Representing the geriatric segment of the population was Bernadette, from the Grandma Party Hotline, in what looked like a hundred-year-old red lace and satin nightie with matching robe and four-inch heels. And finally there was Penelope's old pal Olga, in a light gray business suit and a pink button-down.

"Makeup room is full—you'll have to do yours in the bathroom," Marge said, striding by Penelope on her way to her office.

"Why is Marge still here?" Penelope asked Thomas, who was setting up the studio.

"It's sweeps. She lives here," he said, laughing.

"Ah, of course," Penelope said, putting on her microphone. "So, what's the deal?"

"The deal is, tonight is live—not taped. And we have fifteen full minutes to fill before our first break. Marge wants sex, drugs, money, and scandal. But be careful, Penelope, don't let them name names. The lawyers will be on our ass, and then we'll all be screwed."

"English, please."

"Don't get us sued."

"Oh, right. Okay!"

David, on hand as Marge was still in the office, walked up to the two in the studio and said, "Penelope, hurry up and get your makeup done; we're on in like seven minutes. Thomas—go away!" David marched Penelope over to the bathroom and pushed her through the swinging door.

Six and a half minutes later, David barged into the ladies' room, grabbed Penelope as she was putting on the final pat of powder, and yodeled, "Shoooow tiiiime!" before guiding her back out to the studio and plopping her in the "interviewer" chair from IKEA, next to the four women, all lined up sitting cross-legged on the couch.

"Three, two, one," Thomas counted down, "and go!"

Penelope read from the teleprompter: "THANK YOU FOR JOINING US. WE'RE HERE WITH FOUR NEW YORK WOMEN WHO MAY LOOK LIKE YOUR AVERAGE SUBWAY RIDERS, BUT BY NIGHT THEY RIDE THE SHEETS." *Who wrote this crap?* Penelope thought. *Ride the sheets? Seriously?*

"They're prostitutes." She turned to the women. "How did you all get into this line of work?"

BERNADETTE: I always wanted to be a hooker. But I prefer to be called a courtesan.

RANDI: Me too. I love sex and I love money.

TANIA: I just let people play with my feet and suck on my toes for money. There's a difference.

BERNADETTE: Not really.

TANIA: Whatever. No actual genital contact . . . unless, of course, I say so. And it usually involves a stiletto heel and someone else's genitalia.

Penelope looked nervously at Thomas, whose eyes had widened. "Right, okay," she said. "Next question! Ladies, do you guys have boyfriends? And do they know what you do?"

OLGA: I got rid of Stanislas. He vas my boyfriend, but he vas also my pimp. He took too much money and played dominoes vith the old men in Brighton Beach vhile I paid all the bills. I prefer customers to boyfriends. They have fun and don't punch you . . . most of the time.

BERNADETTE: I've been married thirty-five years. My husband is an engineer. I think he gets off on what I do. And it keeps me from cheating with someone I'd get emotionally involved with.

TANIA: I met my boyfriend through the business. He loves feet.

RANDI: I stick to clients.

BERNADETTE: It's hard for some women to be in the business and have boyfriends. People's feelings get hurt when sex is involved. But going to a hooker is better than fooling around with, say, a coworker. Nobody gets hurt. Office romances ruin everything and people get fired, I know. I worked in an office in the seventies.

Penelope sneaked a peek at Thomas, who had a *what the hell did we get ourselves into?* look on his face. "Well, let's um . . ." she wanted to change the subject but wasn't sure how. "Aren't you worried about health concerns?"

TANIA: Please. It's like going through a McDonald's drive-thru—but you won't get fat, you'll get exercise. And we're better looking than anything that was ever served or worked in McDonald's.

RANDI: What's the big deal? I love my job. I'm my own boss, and I make a lot of money. Just set up an online escort service—and you can get a background check on any john these days in five minutes or less for free.

OLGA: It is true. Very chic. But I vould suggest to vomen starting out to not get pimp. That is where I ran into problems, Penelope, you remember Stanislas . . .

Penelope wasn't sure NY Access should be giving people tips on how to be a prostitute. She wanted to change the subject again but Randi interrupted.

RANDI: I don't know why everybody's got to be so judgmental about us. Shit. George Clooney picks up a waitress in Vegas, flies her out to his house in Italy, and pays her bills, and then everybody was like 'Oh, she's so great.' What's so great about her? She's okay looking, but he didn't move her ass in 'cause she's so nice and pretty and all. He did it 'cause she fucked him—and good. She's no different than us. She just got lucky.

PENELOPE: Did you just call George Clooney's ex-girlfriend a hooker? I don't know if we can say that, even on local cable—

BERNADETTE: It's true—I've been around forever and it goes on all the time. It's called socially acceptable prostitution. The girls put out; the men pay. Maybe not up-front cash, but believe me, they pay.

Thomas was dragging his index finger across his throat and looking vaguely ill.

PENELOPE: George was probably just bored and, you know, she was fun. And why not go to Italy with George Clooney? They were, like, full on in love.

RANDI: Oh, I get it. Now they were in *love* and all, so it's okay. She was his *girlfriend*. How do you think she got all those nice dresses? How did she afford the pretty diamonds? How did she pay her rent?

OLGA: (*to Randi*) Dah-ling, you don't get it, do you? Vile she may be hees Pretty Voman—the difference betveen George Clooney's ex-girlfriend and prostitutes ees seemple—men pay us to leave.

TANIA: I could've been Quentin Tarantino's "girlfriend." He loved my feet. Met him at a club and my toes were like tractor beams, suckin' him in. Wouldn't leave 'em alone all night—kept trying to touch 'em and even wanted to kiss 'em. I was like, "Bitch, I charge for that!" He's a big foot guy—just got to keep 'em pedicured and in five-inch heels and he'll do anything you want.

Penelope was sweating now. "Okay! Time for a break. Thank you, ladies, it's been informative, and thanks to everyone who's been watching. We'll be back in two minutes!"

The second the cameras stopped rolling, the phones started ringing.

"What's going on?" Penelope asked Thomas, who, after loosening his tie, was trying to undo the top three buttons of his shirt. *Yum,* Penelope thought, catching a glimpse of some chest hair.

"What did I tell you?" he gasped, looking faint.

"It was live?"

"And no names!" he said.

"Oh, God. Oops." Penelope gave him a wan smile.

"Yeah. Nice touch, getting them to call Clooney's chick a whore and outing Tarantino as a foot fetishist. Oh my god, we're both fired. I should've stayed in Pakistan doing documentaries. At least there you could hear the bombs before they dropped."

"Penelope!" Marge roared over the din of the phones. "You're back on in two seconds. What're you doing chatting up Thomas? And someone shut off those damn phones! We're live here!"

Penelope took her place back in the interviewer's chair but before she could admonish the women for naming names, she heard Thomas's voice, "Three . . . two . . . one . . ."

PENELOPE: (*reading the teleprompter*) Good evening and welcome back to the "Call Girl Coffee Klatch." I'm Penelope Mercury, and tonight I'm joined by Randi, a party specialist. Randi, thanks for being here.

RANDI: (*smiling as the camera pans to her*) You bet!

PENELOPE: On her right is Bernadette, who's been in the business for over thirty years. Tania, a foot specialist.

TANIA: I prefer fetishist.

PENELOPE: And Olga. Ladies, thank you for coming.

OLGA: Our pleasure, dah-ling.

PENELOPE: Being a prostitute is, you know, technically illegal—have you been arrested?

OLGA: Dah-ling. Ve simply provide company. Dates, as you call them. If the dates get romantic—well, that is not our fault. The men don't pay for sex, they pay for the dinner and company.

TANIA: I ain't no prostitute or escort. I provide a much-needed service to the foot fetishist community.

RANDI: I'm with Olga. I'm just good company.

PENELOPE: What kind of men use your services?

OLGA: Oh, all types, dah-ling.

TANIA: Rich, poor—well, not that poor, they got to pay the rates, but you know—white, black, Asian, Caucasian, whatever. They're ain't no type when it comes to men wanting good . . . company.

BERNADETTE: Believe me, she's right. Over thirty years in this business, I've seen it all. There was this Hollywood manager who'd only use washcloths to wipe his ass. Can you believe that?

RANDI: Mmmm . . . I bet I know who it is.

PENELOPE: No names!

RANDI: Please. He used to try on these dresses. It was like stuffing Rosie O'Donnell into Jessica Alba's prom gown. Not pretty.

BERNADETTE: That's him.

OLGA: Some of them just vant to talk. Vee are like psychologists, sex therapists, and anthropologists all rolled into one. You know trouble vhen it valks in the door. I can spot a bad man a mile avay now.

PENELOPE: Like what?

OLGA: I had thees one actor. He's very big, very popular. So he comes to see me and starts talking about hees mother as hee's getting naked and calls her a fucking whore. I took offense. She vas not actually a hooker.

BERNADETTE: You gotta watch out for the ones that hate their mothers. They're the serial killers.

OLGA: Mostly, they are just old boring men who need a thrill.

RANDI: Oooh, that's the truth. I had a guy last night. He's the head of a news network, and the entire time all he did was re-enact a Geico commercial. For two hours. I was doing my shopping list in my head.

PENELOPE: Well, at least he didn't just sit there and quack like the Aflac duck.

RANDI: True, true. I don't get off on bestiality.

PENELOPE: Any major dislikes?

BERNADETTE: Oh, I do hate a hypocrite. Take our mayor, for example.

PENELOPE: Huh?

BERNADETTE: Mayor Ed Swallows cracks down on prostitutes, escorts, art shows, and anything he sees as immoral, but Swallows is no saint.

RANDI: Oh, he swallows all right. He made me do a threesome with this basketball player for the Knicks once. Naaaasty.

TANIA: I'd heard he swang both ways from my friend, but he's not into feet so he never called me.

RANDI: Girl, you have no idea. We were all going at it, then he just leaves me in the dust. Like I was just there as an excuse so he could get off with that guy. Then he tried to stiff me. Cheapskate.

OLGA: Yes, he's living, how you say? On the DL.

PENELOPE: Wait, what? The MAYOR is on the down low?

OLGA: Yes, everybody knows thees. I too have been vith him. By myself, but he inseests on doing eet from behind. But I always get my money upfront.

TANIA: You're lucky he didn't donkey punch you.

PENELOPE: (*realizing things may be once again spiraling out of her control*) Donkey punch? He's into animals too?

BERNADETTE: No, no. It's a sexual term. Like a fish eye or Dirty Sanchez.

PENELOPE: (*putting her hand to her head*) I think I'm going to throw up.

BERNADETTE: Don't be so puritanical.

Penelope looked up and saw Thomas, sheet white, hoarsely whispering, "Wrap it up! Wrap it up!" Next to him was Marge, who was gagging after attempting to dry swallow a Blue and a Green, and David, who was trying hard not to laugh.

PENELOPE: (*with a crazed smile plastered on her face*) Right, well, ladies! Thank you all very much. We've loved having you and hope to see you all again soon. This is Penelope Mercury for New York Access. Have a great night, everyone!

The next ten minutes were a blur. Between the women leaving, Marge choking on her pills, David trying to hand her a glass of water and tripping over the camera wires, accidentally dousing her with it, Penelope wasn't quite sure what to do.

She was snapped out of her trance by Thomas, who took her arm and said, "Let's get out of here. Now." And he dragged her to the elevator. But before they could get on the elevator, Trace, there to do the late-night news, appeared. Drunk.

"Hello, gorgeoush," he slurred to Penelope.

"Ew, get away from me, you nutbag," she said.

"Kish me," Trace slurred and lunged at Penelope.

Thomas stepped in, pushed Trace, and said in a low voice, "Don't go near her."

Penelope had had enough. Irate and sick of Trace's constant lechery, she looked at Thomas and said, "I got this." Just as the elevator doors opened, she cocked her fist back and punched the soused anchor full in the face, knocking him to the floor.

As she heard Marge scream in the background, "What the hell . . . ?" Thomas grabbed Penelope's arm, pulled her into the elevator with him, and escorted her outside.

"You know there's a high likelihood that we'll both be out of a job by tomorrow," Thomas said as they lingered outside of the NY Access building.

"Yep," Penelope said. "Figured as much."

"So."

"So."

"Should we go, maybe do something to celebrate?"

"Yeah, okay," Penelope said, surprised—it was, after all, the first time he'd ever asked her to do anything outside of work. "Wanna, um, have a drink by my house?" she asked.

"Sure," Thomas said, grinning. "Where?"

"There's this great bar, The Room. Just beer and wine and stuff," Penelope said, trying to be nonchalant.

"Sounds good."

They walked away just as news trucks from NBC, FOX, and ABC local affiliates were pulling up outside NY Access. Penelope could hear one ABC producer yell, "Yeah! Yeah, they just put on the air that the mayor had an affair. With a dude and a bunch of hookers! We're on it!"

They hopped on the subway, got off at the West Fourth Street station, and started walking south on Sixth Avenue.

"We've worked together every day for months now, and this is our first after-work drink," Penelope said. "Why is that? Why do you always have to rush home after work? Do you have a separation of church and state thing going on?" she asked. "Or do you have a secret wife and kids to take care of?"

"No," Thomas said, looking away, "nothing like that."

"So what is it, then?"

"My mom's been sick," Thomas said as they turned east onto Houston.

"Oh. I'm sorry," Penelope said, embarrassed.

"It's okay. That's why I work at New York Access in the first place. I was doing documentaries in Pakistan for the BBC when she was diagnosed with a pretty aggressive case of multiple sclerosis. I had to come home and take care of her."

"What about your dad?"

"He died when I was a kid."

"Oh. Right."

"Yeah, my life for the past couple of years has basically been work and my mom. Last month she finally got approved by Medicaid to go to a decent hospice in Queens, but it's been . . . hard."

"Wow. I had no idea," Penelope said. She felt ridiculous. His tale of woe and selflessness had somehow turned her on even more than she already was. She wondered if that were wrong.

"Well, shit happens," Thomas said. "And I can start having a life again, I guess. I'm glad to be out tonight with you."

"Thanks, me with you too," Penelope said, blushing.

"And whatever happens with New York Access because of tonight, Trace, and that stupid Coffee Klatch, I'm glad I met you."

Just as Penelope was starting to think all was right with the world, despite her possible once-again imminent joblessness, she spotted something odd.

As they were turning onto Sullivan Street, Penelope saw a woman in a brown bobbed wig and what looked like a silvery feather duster crouched down between two cars, clutching a camera and looking at the entrance to her apartment building.

"Hey," Penelope whispered to Thomas, grabbing his arm. "Stop."

"What's up?" Thomas said.

"I think my neighbor's stalker is here."

"Your neighbor has a stalker?"

"Shhhh!" Penelope hissed, pulling Thomas into a nearby doorway.

"What is going on?" Thomas whispered.

"Just wait for a sec. See that woman with the bob hiding by the cars?"

"Yes."

"She's been following my friend."

Sure enough, three minutes later a taxi pulled up. Lipstick, in her beautiful green dress, emerged from the backseat. The woman with the wig started taking pictures with her camera.

"Lipstick!" Penelope yelled, "she's here—your stalker!"

As Lipstick turned toward Penelope, the woman, caught in between them, stopped taking pictures and tried to run off. But she was blocked by Penelope, who grabbed her arm and ripped off her wig, exposing her blond hair tucked up underneath.

Lipstick gasped.

"Who are you?" Penelope demanded from the struggling woman. "And why are you following my friend?"

"It's all right, Penelope," Lipstick said, "I know her."

"Huh?" Penelope asked. "You do? Who is she?" Turning to the woman, Penelope shook her and demanded, "Name!"

"It's Bitsy Farmdale," Lipstick said. "You can let her go." Bitsy'd seen Lipstick leave the Met and, while Lipstick and Dana had strolled for a block outside, had taken a cab back to Sullivan Street to get there ahead of her.

"Really?" Penelope asked. "That chick who's always so mean to you?"

"Yes," Lipstick said.

"I can rough her up a bit, if you want. I'm from Cincinnati. Jerry Springer used to be the mayor there, you know."

"Let her go." Lipstick sighed.

"Fine," Penelope said and released Bitsy with a shove.

"If I have one bruise, you'll be hearing from my lawyer," Bitsy snarled at Penelope, rubbing her arm.

"No, she won't," Lipstick said, standing up straight. "You won't be calling anyone, Bitsy."

"Really? You think so?" Bitsy said with a mean laugh. "Just wait till I'm done with you. You humiliated Jack tonight by bringing some random person—and not that designer—to the ball and now you're clearly shacking up with some bum in this . . . tenement. He'll be so pissed."

"Why is anything I do your business?" Lipstick asked.

"Because it is!" Bitsy said, stamping her foot. "You think you can just have my spotlight after all these years I've spent cultivating my seat at the top of society? You were always trying to steal my thunder at the debutante balls and in cotillion. You were always the center of attention, and finally I worked my way onto the right committees and into the right luncheons and was considered *the* young socialite. I even stole my boyfriend back after you took him."

"What?" Lipstick said, aghast. "I didn't take Thad away from you."

"Liar!" Bitsy cried. "We'd gotten back together for three months before you two started dating."

"I had no idea, Bitsy," Lipstick said. "He told me you two were just friends. And it's not like you and I talk to each other."

"I was going to be Mrs. Thad Newton III until he broke up with me tonight."

"He broke up with you?" Lipstick gasped.

"You know he did, you bitch. I don't know what you told him, but whatever it was—he left me."

"I don't think it was anything I said," Lipstick said, confused. "I think it had more to do with you treating him like a dog. And you should be thankful. He's a liar and a cheat."

"How dare you?" Bitsy snarled. "Even so. Even if you didn't say anything, you're still a fraud, living down here in this cesspool, and your mysterious designer is a lawyer! Wait till everyone finds out."

"Please. Everyone finding out?" Lipstick laughed. "About what? About me actually working for a living and paying my own bills in an apartment my salary can afford? And *I* made those dresses. So what! They're great and everybody loves them."

"*You* made them?" Bitsy asked, looking genuinely shocked. "That's not possible."

"Remember all those stupid etiquette classes we had to take from Mrs. Frampton?" Lipstick asked. "While you and your friends shunned me and skipped class to go have lattes, not to mention locked me out on balconies, I stayed there and had to learn how to sew. All these clothes I've been wearing are just deconstructions of my old closet."

"They'll eat you alive on Socialstatus.com." Bitsy sniffed.

"Please. What if I told people you were so obsessed with me that you've been dressing up in wigs and spending your time following me? And that you're the one behind all the nasty posts on Socialstatus.com? I'll sue you for stalking and harassment and you'll never get over the shame!"

Bitsy turned sheet white. "You wouldn't." She gasped.

"This is getting good," Thomas said.

"Are you on drugs? Should we call a doctor?" Penelope asked Bitsy delicately, not wanting to further enrage a woman she was convinced had probably snorted her fair share of lines that evening.

"This is ridiculous!" Lipstick said. "Bitsy, go home and don't bother me ever again. I'll shut my mouth if you shut yours. Permanently."

"I hate you," Bitsy spat out, stalking off to the corner of Sullivan and Houston to hail a cab.

"Wow," Penelope said as Bitsy got into a taxi. "That was . . . interesting."

Lipstick was silent.

"I've never seen you angry before. I've never even seen you raise your voice," Penelope said in awe. "You totally took command of that situation. That was awesome."

"Socialites are so fucked up," Thomas said.

"Tell me about it," Lipstick said. "And who are you?"

"Thomas, this is my neighbor and friend Lena," Penelope said. "Lena, this is my producer, Thomas."

"Oh yeah," Lipstick said. "I've heard about you."

"It's all lies, I assure you," Thomas said.

"How 'bout a drink?" Penelope asked. "I think we could all use one."

"No, you two go ahead; I just want to go to bed," Lipstick said. "I'm exhausted."

But as she was climbing the stairs to her apartment, Lipstick reconsidered. The night had been such a mess. Except for in the very beginning, with Penelope and Dana. And she thought back to Zach and how he'd looked at her. Like he'd never seen anything or anyone so beautiful. Lipstick smiled. Even though she'd been through hell, remembering Zach made her feel like a princess.

Feeling empowered, she stopped on the third floor and, taking a deep breath, knocked on Zach's door. When he opened up, Lipstick said defiantly, "You said to stop by for a drink. I've had a hell of a night." Before she could say anything else, he leaned in, put his arm around her waist, and kissed her.

"Wanna come in?" Zach asked when they finally came up for air.

"Yes," Lipstick said, and the door shut behind her.

14

LIBRA:

The last retrograde was a tough one, but it forced you to expand your worldview and seek out your own strength. You have become a force to reckon with.

The next morning was the start of a gorgeous late spring day. The birds chirped from the small trees dotting the Soho streets. The sun shone between the buildings as a few bankers who had to be at their trading desks by eight a.m. brushed by the last of the bums waking from their slumber on the steps of Saint Anthony's Church, as they went on their way to the coffee shops and subway stations. Over at 198 Sullivan Street, Lipstick, Dana, and Penelope were just waking up. And one of them was not in her own bed.

Lipstick opened her eyes and scanned the room that was darkened by heavy drapery. She was in a small room in a smallish bed that didn't smell like her or even remotely feel like her thousand-count Pratesi sheets. An electric alarm clock, which certainly wasn't hers, blinked 7:02.

Where the heck was she? Her eyes eventually focused on Zach, snoring softly next to her. She slapped her forehead.

She was an idiot. Who sleeps with a guy on the first date? Actually, it wasn't even a first date. God, he was cute. And nice.

And then she remembered the previous night's non-Zach events. Lipstick pulled the covers up over her head and sighed. Zach mumbled in his sleep and flung an arm across her.

What am I going to tell Jack? she thought, feeling overwhelmed and panicky. *What is Bitsy going to do? What will be on Socialstatus.com? What am I going to tell my mother? She will be furious. I have to get out of here.*

She silently lifted Zach's arm and slipped out of the bed, careful not to wake him. She found her underwear that had been flung onto his dresser during the night's activities, stepped into them, and tiptoed out of the room. In Zach's living room she found her feathered dress lying atop his easel with its edges dipped into some oil paint, her purse on the floor by his fridge, and her heels stuffed into the cushions of the leather sofa.

I can't squish myself back into this, Lipstick thought, looking balefully at the dress. *And half the feathers have fallen off anyway.*

Lipstick bit her lip for a moment and then—rationalizing that as she lived only one floor away and no one in the building roamed the halls before eight a.m.—grabbed her paint-spattered dress, purse, and shoes, clutched them to her chest, and, clad in just her underwear, bolted up one flight to the safety of her own apartment.

SCORPIO:

The last few months hurt, but they were worth it. You are now on the precipice of a whole new globe of opportunities.

• • •

Five minutes later and one floor up, Penelope woke to her CD alarm clock blaring Journey's "Wheel in the Sky."

She yawned, stretched her arms, and, in doing so, accidentally punched Thomas in the face, waking him.

"Ow!" He cringed, covering his nose with his hand.

"Oh, sorry," Penelope said, more than a little hungover from the night before—which aided in her momentarily forgetting she had a houseguest. "You're here." Looking under the covers, she added, "And we're naked."

"Yep," he said.

"Right," Penelope answered.

"Awkward," Thomas said.

"More like odd."

"Why's that?"

"I've never even seen you with your jacket and tie off, much less your underwear."

"Am I that uptight?"

"Kind of. In a nice, nerdy way."

Thomas turned toward her, grinned, and murmured, "I promise to never wear a jacket and tie again if you promise to go out with me again"—which lead to Penelope slamming down the sleep button on her alarm clock.

Half an hour later they finally got out of bed.

"I can't believe I belted Trace," Penelope said.

"That was brilliant." Thomas chuckled.

"He's going to kill me."

"Not if I kill him first."

"Oh. And the hookers . . . and the mayor!"

"That was also brilliant, in a totally different we-might-not-have-a-job way."

After they'd both showered, Penelope asked, "Should I call in to work and see if we're fired?"

"No, let's just show up and see what happens. It's more fun that way," Thomas answered, buttoning up his shirt.

Penelope and Thomas walked out of 198 Sullivan and into the eye of the storm.

At the newsstand on West Third and Bleecker, by the train station, they caught a glimpse of the day's papers.

The *Telegraph*'s headline read, "Swallows Is Spitting Mad Over Call Girl Klatch."

The *Post* had "Swallows Chokes: Gets Kinky with Knicks" on its front page.

The *Daily News,* a champion of the mayor's, blared, "Swallows: I Won't Take This Lying Down!"

Even the *New York Times* got in on the fracas, albeit with a more subdued headline in the Metro section that read, "Prostitutes Tell Local News Station They've Slept with Mayor and Unnamed Knick."

"Wow," Penelope said, grabbing Thomas's hand, which, she noted, fit perfectly into hers. It had been a long time since she'd felt that way about anyone, and she savored the moment. "I guess I didn't really realize what we did. Or what happened. I can't believe it's on all the front pages."

"Yeah," Thomas said, "Let's just hope those hookers don't recant and say we drugged them."

Penelope's looked at her cell phone. She'd forgotten to put the ringer back on after turning it off before filming the night before. It registered six messages. All from that morning.

"Uh-oh," she said. "Six messages before nine a.m. is never good news."

She turned the ringer back on just as the phone rang.

It was Marge.

"Where the hell are you?" Marge hollered. "Get here now!

We got the biggest story in town, and the woman who broke it—my reporter, *you*—are nowhere to be found!"

"I'm on my way!" Penelope said, "but I'm actually early."

"And where's Thomas?" Marge asked.

"Thomas?" Penelope giggled, looking at her rumpled crush.

"Yes, Thomas! The producer who was seen slinking off with you last night. He's not answering his phone!"

"How would I know? He's probably on the train."

"He'd better be! We got more news to break. Every outlet in the city is dying to get ahold of you. The girls have gone underground, can't get ahold of 'em, so we're under siege. Every news truck ever made is outside, so come in the back way."

"So I'm not fired?"

"Fired? Why the hell would you be fired? You've put us on the map! The mayor is pissed and threatening to shut us down, but who cares? We're on the front page of every paper! All the morning shows are on the horn. Every station I ever worked for is begging me for an interview with you. I got calls from a station in China this morning! Everyone wants to talk to you, but they'll have to go through me first."

"Okay," Penelope said, swallowing hard, "I'm on my way."

"Now!"

"Now."

"But Marge," Penelope said before her boss could hang up.

"Yes?" Marge snapped.

"About Trace—"

"That's been taken care of," Marge said curtly.

"What do you mean?"

"We'll discuss it when I see you," Marge said and hung up.

Penelope looked at Thomas. "We gotta go. She's ramped up. But good news. We still have a job, and she actually sounds pleased. It was odd. Almost uncomfortable."

Just before she and Thomas descended into the subway station, Penelope checked her messages.

MESSAGE 1: "Penelope Fleming, this is Marge Gelb Green. We need you at the station now. Wake the fuck up already."

MESSAGE 2: "Penelope Fleming, this is Marge Gelb Green. Your boss. Where the hell are you? Call me back. Now."

MESSAGE 3: "Honey, it's David. Where aaaaaare yoooou? Please call me back. Soon. Marge is about to blow up and I can't find her blues—and she's run out of the greens."

MESSAGE 4: "Darling, it's David again. Please tell me you haven't been shot on the mayor's orders and dumped off the Brooklyn Bridge. We need you in the station. Now. It's a little nuts here. I've staved Marge off with a couple of pinks I found in the crevice of her chair cushion but they won't last long. Get here, ASAP."

MESSAGE 5: "Penelope, it's your mother. What is going on? You didn't tell me you were going to be on *Good Morning America* and the *Today* show! But there I was this morning, fixing your father his holy hash and on comes a clip of you and some hookers. Your father got so upset he locked himself in your old bedroom with his Jesus doll. But what's this about the mayor and the hookers? You said you were only on local cable. Call me. I'm very confused."

MESSAGE 6: "Penelope, it's your mother again. Kelsie Browsmith from down the street called. She's so jealous. Her daughter's never been on TV."

SAGITTARIUS:
You have finally awoken from a deep sleep to find your heart is finally alive again. The courage to change has sparked a desire to live your life in a more productive and awake state.

As for Dana, she woke late at 8:15 a.m. with a smile on her face and swollen feet. She checked her messages. Gerard had already called.

"Dana, it's Gerard. I don't know when I've had such a nice night. Can we do it again tomorrow? I have the babysitter for Michael, so I'm free until ten. But this time no walking."

Dana was elated. She couldn't remember having a nicer night either, or at least a nicer walk home, despite the drama and the catty comments from the DeBeers woman. And the Can-O-Hair stain was still on her back and her pillowcase. As she lay in bed, Dana gave Karl a kiss and stroked his stomach. She'd love to go out with Gerard. But tomorrow night she had to be at the office late. Again. Actually, she had to be at the office late every night for the next month. As she thought of her grueling work schedule, her smile faded, her stomach started to cramp, and she unwittingly put her hand to the back of her head, pulling out yet another small clump of hair.

Work was killing her. If she didn't do the hours, she wouldn't make full partner. But why did she want to make full partner so badly? The rent was paid for ten years, thanks to Noah. She already made a decent six-figure salary. Why did she need it so badly?

"*What do you mean?*" she heard her mother's voice in her head. "*You need to be the best! If you're not first, you're last.*"

"*Listen to your mother,*" she heard her dad say. "*I don't want to get involved.*"

"You are the smartest person I know," she heard Penelope's voice try to break in.

"My sister and her Lubovitchers are horrified. There's never been a divorce in our family," her mother's voice rang out. *"You failed at marriage and failed at having children. Where will the failures end?"*

"You're my idol," Lipstick whispered. *"And you don't have to prove anything to anyone."*

"God, you're such a fat loser," Noah chimed in. *"You can't do anything right. You can't even have a baby."*

"Enough!" Dana shouted, pounding a fist into her pillow and scaring Karl under the bed.

Taking a deep breath, she got out of bed. Before stepping into the shower, she called her assistant and said, "Please tell Mr. Kornberg I'd like to have an eleven a.m. meeting with him. I'll be in by nine."

Lipstick arrived at the offices of *Y* at 9:30, dressed in a green sleeveless top of her own design and dark, skinny jeans—which she felt was a bit of an oxymoron. No one looked skinny in skinny jeans except anorexics. The waistband cut into her knot-filled stomach as she sat down at her desk. She popped the top button on her jeans and relaxed. A bit.

She took a deep breath and turned her computer on. The second she logged in, an instant message popped up.

"See me. Jack."

He couldn't possibly be here this early, Lipstick thought, chewing on the inside of her lip. She started to perspire, and her eyes darted around the empty office.

It was the day after the Met Gala, after all, and historically no one came in until at least noon.

"He must have sent that yesterday," Lipstick rationalized.

But two minutes later, another message appeared.

"See. Me. Now."

Her phone rang. It was Jack's assistant, Christina.

"Good morning, Lena," Christina's voice clipped through the line. "Jack will see you now."

"Okay, I'll be right—" Lipstick said, to a dial tone.

Lipstick stood up, rebuttoned her jeans, smoothed down her shirt, and walked around the corner to Jack's office. She was thirty feet away from the glassed-in enclosure when she saw two other people in there with him. They had their backs to the entrance, sitting on Jack's plush "punishment" sofa.

He must have called human resources. You couldn't fire someone without human resources there. Lipstick stopped, took a deep breath, and began the death march down to the office.

As she passed Christina's desk, the impeccably dressed blond assistant looked up. "Well, there you are; I thought you'd never get here—" she snipped as Lipstick brushed by, ignoring her.

She pushed the glass door to the office open, walked in without turning to look at the HR people on the couch, looked only at Jack, who was dressed in a Ralph Lauren Purple Label dark gray pinstriped suit over a starched white shirt and light blue tie. His face was accented with a black eye, a leftover from Kitty slamming into him on her way down to the floor.

"Lena," Jack said with a nod.

"Jack," Lena said in a cool voice, belying her nerves.

Looking past Lipstick, toward the couch, Jack said, "And I believe you know my guests?"

Lipstick followed Jack's gaze to the couch and saw her parents perched uncomfortably on the edge. Martin had bags under his eyes and looked like he hadn't slept in a month, while Lana looked like she had taken at *least* two Klonopin that morning.

"Mom!" Lipstick said in shock, "Dad!" Her mother rushed over, enveloped her daughter in a hug, and started crying.

"I missed you," Lana babbled, glass-eyed. "You never called back. You just disappeared. You . . . *left* me."

"I'm sorry," Lipstick said, "I meant to call. I did. I was so angry, though. And then I just got so busy."

"Doing what, exactly?" Martin asked gruffly.

"Moving, for one," Lipstick said softly, looking at the floor.

"And?" Martin asked, with an eyebrow raised. "We've been worried about you. Your mother showed me that damn website that had those pictures of you in a slum! And Bitsy told us you were—"

"Wait," Lipstick said. "Bitsy?"

"Well, yes," Lana said. "We ran into her several months ago and mentioned that we hadn't spoken to you. Of course, we didn't say what had happened, but she was so sweet. She offered to keep tabs on you for us."

"You had Bitsy follow me?" Lipstick asked.

"No, of course not," Martin said, rubbing his head. "Don't be absurd. We just . . . well, yes. But it was the only way we could find out what you were doing. And she offered—"

"Why didn't you just ask me?" Lipstick said.

"We tried, darling, but you didn't call us back." Lana sighed.

"May I interrupt this family reunion for one moment?" Jack asked. "Lana and Martin, please take a seat. Lena, I called your parents here because I was worried about you. You've been very secretive these past months, and rumors have been flying over that website that you were shacking up in Soho, that you are broke, that you are a fraud. And then last night. Well, *that* was an unmitigated disaster. That woman you brought is a lawyer—not the Dauphin designer. And Kitty's mess and my fainting spell were reported in the *Post,* the *News,* the *Telegraph,* and *Women's Wear Daily,*" Jack said, throwing the papers onto his desk. "I am humiliated. I was lied to. And I thought we needed to clear the air, with everyone involved."

At that moment Christina's voice buzzed in, "Bitsy Farmdale to see you."

Lipstick's heart froze as Bitsy, with her trademark corkscrew curls, wearing a lavender Tory Burch shirtdress with matching flats, strolled in.

Penelope and Thomas knew something odd was going on the second they hit NY Access's lobby. The big NY ACCESS NEWS banner with a picture of Trace and Kandace had been ripped in half, and Gladys looked like she'd been through a war zone. The ancient receptionist's hair was out of place, her Coke-bottle glasses were hanging at an odd angle on her face, and her watery eyes were glazed.

"PAMELA AND THOMAS HERE TO SEE MARGE!" she shrieked into the phone as they breezed past her.

Inside, Penelope almost keeled over from shock when Laura Lopez walked up to her, gave her a kiss on each cheek, and said, "So good to see you! Congratulations!"

"What the hell is going on?" Penelope said to Thomas, feeling ill at ease. "She's never been that nice."

"I have no idea," Thomas said as David ran toward them.

"I don't trust it," Penelope grumbled. "She'd only be happy if I was getting fired."

"There you are," David said, flushed. "I thought you'd never get here. Marge wants to see you two. Now."

"What's going on?" Penelope asked David.

"Marge will fill you in," he said, ushering Penelope and Thomas toward Marge's office. "But you missed some pretty spectacular fireworks this morning."

David shoved them into the office and shut the door. Marge was at her desk, drinking coffee, and dressed in a bright turquoise suit.

"Where have you two been?" she demanded.

"I, uh, but we're early," Penelope gushed as Thomas scratched his head and simultaneously said, "Home, sleeping."

"Never mind," Marge said, "Thomas, you can wait outside. I want to talk to Penelope alone."

As Thomas left, Penelope cringed.

"There've been some changes," Marge said.

Penelope started chewing the cuticles on her left hand and began preparing her résumé in her head.

Back in Jack's office, Lipstick and Bitsy stared at the ground, avoiding eye contact while Lana and Martin, chastened, took their places back on Jack's couch.

"Just what is going on here?" Jack demanded. "Last night I show up to the Met Gala expecting to meet Dauphin, and instead I meet a lawyer. I'm getting frantic calls from Martin and Lana asking me if their daughter is a crack whore, and Bitsy, you, frankly, have been instigating quite a lot of this."

"Oh, Jack, it's nothing," Bitsy said, trying to laugh.

"It's *not* nothing when I have to read on that website every day how a valued member of my staff is slumming it, and bizarre photos, which you apparently have taken, are showing up."

"I can explain," Bitsy said, fidgeting with her Fendi bag, "Lana and Martin—"

"Certainly didn't ask you to embarrass them or their daughter," Jack snapped. "They just wanted to know how she was doing."

"I—"

"Don't interrupt," Jack said, leaning back in his chair. "I have always thought fondly of you, Bitsy. And the magazine has been very generous to you. We have promoted you from day one and been very supportive of your social quest. But now you are attacking a member of the magazine and thus, the magazine itself."

"I never meant to upset you," Bitsy said quietly. "I'm sorry."

"It's not just me you need to apologize to," Jack said.

"I'm sorry, Lena," Bitsy said, more quietly.

Lipstick's mouth was agape. It was, admittedly, a bit much to take in all at once.

"And Lena," Jack said.

"Yes?" Lipstick asked.

"You're not off the hook. Why did you lie to me and say Dauphin was coming last night?"

"She didn't lie," Bitsy interrupted.

"What?" Jack asked, slamming a hand on his desk. "I met that woman. She was wearing Dauphin—she wasn't Dauphin."

"Dauphin was there," Lipstick said. "I am Dauphin."

All heads turned. Lana gasped. "But darling, how?"

Martin harrumphed. "Huh?"

"It's true," Bitsy said. "Lena made all those clothes."

"Not possible," Jack mumbled.

"I did," Lipstick said. "My parents cut me off five months ago, and I couldn't afford the gowns and clothes for all the galas and parties. So I reconstructed my old ones and bought cheap fabric—or feathers, for the Met—and made my own."

"Genius!" Jack whispered. "This is a genius story. Those clothes are amazing. You're the next Dior . . . and you are my employee!"

"*Vogue* wants Dauphin too," Bitsy said.

"Shut up, Bitsy," Lipstick hissed.

"I'm helping you, stupid," Bitsy hissed back.

"*Vogue*?" Jack said breathlessly. "*Vogue*? No. Never! You're mine! I want you on the cover and a spread of your designs . . ."

"I don't have time to do that and be the social editor," Lipstick said, truly worried about never getting any more sleep, ever.

"Then you'll be a contributor," Jack said. "The clothes are

more important. Fashion always is. And now I, for once, can say I truly found and broke a designer. Anna Wintour will choke on her watercress soup."

Penelope was still sitting quietly in Marge's office, contemplating unemployment, when Marge interrupted her thoughts. "Penelope, you're the new entertainment reporter."

"What?" Penelope squeaked. "What about Laura?"

"She's the new evening coanchor with Kandace."

"But what about Trace?" Penelope asked.

"Trace is no longer with the station."

"Huh?"

"I'm not stupid," Marge said. "I know what's been going on. We've had complaints for years about him."

"But why fire him now?"

"You have your crew to thank for that," Marge snapped. "Eric and Stew showed me the outtakes they've been shooting of him harassing you. And I saw him last night. You may think I'm just an old warhorse, but I've been around the block plenty of times. I had to climb my way up the all-male ladder for years, fighting tooth and nail for everything along the way. I know what these guys think they can get away with. But not anymore. Besides, Thomas informed me last night that your best friend is a lawyer, and frankly, I'm not interested in a lawsuit. Especially when it involves the reporter who broke the biggest story in the city."

"Okay—" Penelope said.

Marge wasn't finished. "I have some interviews for you lined up. You are going on *Today, Good Morning America,* and *Dateline* to talk about this mayoral mess. David has the details."

"But—"

"David! More coffee!"

• • •

At that moment, in the hallways of Struck, Struck & Kornberg, Dana was headed to the office of Mr. Kornberg. She'd made up her mind. She knew what she had to do—for her sanity, for her life, and, if for nothing else, her hair.

As Lipstick walked her parents out of the pink-limestone-and-glass building, she grabbed her mother's hand. "I love you," she said. "I missed you."

Lana let out a primal moan like a wounded bear and hugged Lipstick more tightly than she'd ever hugged her before and began crying. Martin put his arm around his wife and daughter and harrumphed for attention. They looked at him.

"I'm impressed," Martin said. "I never thought you could or would do it. Living on your own, making your own way. Why, you even could start your own business. My daughter. A fashion magnate."

"You're getting ahead of yourself, Daddy," Lipstick said.

"Nonsense," Martin shot back, rubbing his chin. "You heard Jack. He wants you on the cover and a spread of your clothes. Everyone will want those clothes. Bitsy, even."

"I need to think about it. It's going to take a lot of money, and Jack didn't say how much contributors make."

"I've decided to resume our old arrangement," Martin said. "Tomorrow you'll have your credit cards and allowance reinstated, and you can move back into your apartment whenever you like. Max, that playboy, never even came back from Africa, so it's just as you left it."

"But Daddy," Lipstick said, sighing, "it's not my apartment. It's yours. It always was."

"Not anymore," Martin said, producing a piece of paper.

It was a letter from his business manager, informing Lipstick that the deed to the West Twelfth Street apartment had been signed over to her.

"Thanks, Daddy," Lipstick said quietly. "But I can't go back to how it was."

As Dana walked out of Mr. Kornberg's office, she texted Gerard: "Tomorrow's great. Dinner at Cafe Cluny?"

Later that evening the girls congregated in Dana's apartment, joined by Neal—who'd just returned from Thailand researching his latest Zen client's apartment—and David, who'd officially decided to become a "monogamous gay couple—so scandalous!"—for a drink and the day's recap.

"So, I'm going to have some free time," Dana announced as Neal popped the cork on the Dom Pérignon. They were all seated around Dana's coffee table on the couch and settee.

"Did you quit or something?" Penelope asked, reaching for a glass.

"No, of course not," Dana said, rolling her eyes.

"Well, what happened?" Lipstick asked.

"I rescinded my application for full partnership," Dana said, sipping her champagne.

"Cheers to that," David said, holding his glass up.

"Why?" Penelope asked. "You wanted it so badly, and you do the work of a full partner."

"Not anymore. I'm trimming my hours," Dana said. "I feel like in order for me to move forward, I may have to take a step back. And now I can go on that date with Gerard."

"You gave up partnership for a guy you just met?" Penelope asked.

"No, not for a guy I just met," Dana snapped, "do you think I'm that crazy?"

"No, but . . ." Penelope mumbled.

"Let her explain, doll," Neal said as David refilled his glass.

"I turned it down because I want to be more than Dana

Gluck, robo-lawyer. You guys said it last month—I don't do anything outside of work except for yoga. Well, I used to go to Weight Watchers, but whatever. I haven't been on a date since Noah, I haven't moved on since the divorce, and financially I'm set. I think I needed the validation of being the youngest superwoman in the firm's history for reasons that had nothing to do with me. Or at least the real me. I'm not even sure what that is anymore, but I'd like to find out."

Penelope nodded her head, finally understanding.

"Amen," Lipstick said. "I'm right there with you. I feel like I spent my whole life trying to live up to my parents' ideals. Always trying to be the perfect society girl, with the right look, the right job, the right friends."

"Yeah—Bitsy looked like she was going to gnaw your head off last night." Penelope snorted.

"She's not my friend," Lipstick shot back, taking a sip of champagne.

"Well, you put up with her for long enough—and even hung out with her and her friends," Penelope said.

"Darling, society is different," Neal cut in. "Even if you don't like someone, you still have to be friends with them."

"And still. She may be useful," Lipstick said.

"What?" Dana asked.

"Did you just say she 'may be useful'?" Penelope yelled.

"Oh, my ears," David said, snuggling up to Neal. "This is just like a Marge meeting."

"I have an idea," Lipstick said. "About my dress line. And Bitsy."

"Do tell," Neal said.

"I'm going to lay down the bridge of détente and ask her to be the ambassador for Dauphin. I'll give her clothes in exchange for publicity."

"Why the fuck would you want to do that?" Penelope asked. "I want to kill her, and I'm not the one she was stalking."

"It's like Anna and Jack at the Met Gala," Lipstick explained. "Keep your friends close and your enemies closer. Besides, all the socials look to her for what to wear and do. And she loves the limelight. Our making peace would get her ink in all the Upper East Side magazines. Besides, now that I won't be able to go out as much—and I'm never looking at Socialstatus.com again—she would be the perfect person to display my clothes on. Socialites are sheep. They'll do whatever she does."

"Ah yes," Neal sighed. "The Park Avenue march of the ovines continues apace."

"I underestimated you," Dana said. "That's an amazing plan."

"Besides," Lipstick said. "I feel . . . bad for her. She's just living up to the role her parents and everyone set for her. Just like I was. And no one should have to be involved with a creep like Thad. He embarrassed her too, you know."

"I'm so proud of you, darling," Neal said, blowing Lipstick a kiss. "I don't know when I've ever heard you sound so grown up. Not Carcrash-like at all, really."

"That is pretty big of you," Penelope agreed, chewing on her thumbnail. "So you're gonna make dresses full-time?"

"No," Lipstick said. "I'm keeping my job at Y. Kind of. I'm going to be a contributor, which will give me some free time to do my dresses."

"That's great," Dana said. "But you're going to be able to run a business from your apartment?"

"Weeell . . ." Lipstick said.

"Yes?" Dana prompted her, as everyone stopped drinking and looked at Lipstick.

"My parents kind of showed up at work today."

"What?" Penelope said. "And I thought my day was fucked up!"

"I hadn't talked to them since I moved out, and I think they wanted to make sure I was still alive and breathing."

"What happened?" Neal asked.

"This is getting good," David said.

Lipstick filled them in on her parents' subsequent offer.

"What're you gonna do, Lips?" Penelope asked.

"Darling, please tell me you did not turn down the apartment. Please," Neal begged.

"I told them no on the credit cards, but yes on the apartment. And I'm meeting with my father to discuss funding for my new company on Monday. I may be standing on my own two feet, but I'm not stupid!"

"We'll miss you," Dana said softly.

"Why?" Lipstick asked, topping off her glass of Dom. "I'm only ten blocks away, and we're still doing yoga on Saturdays and Wednesdays, right?"

"Right!" Dana said.

"You bet!" Penelope agreed.

"Wow," Lipstick said. "If you'd told me a year ago that I would have been kicked out of my apartment, by my own parents, no less, and cut off—*and* that it was the best thing that ever happened to me, I'd have thought you were crazy."

"Yeah," Penelope said. "Same here. I couldn't even imagine a life beyond the *Telegraph*. And now, here I am, the entertainment reporter for New York Access. And I'm banging my hot producer."

"Penelope, my love, must you be so crass?" Neal sighed.

"The point is, all good things came from my being fired."

"And all good things came from you two being in my life," Dana said.

"Aw, stop," Penelope said. "You'll make me blush."

"Back at you," Lipstick said.

"You know girls, all this started back in January when Mercury went into retrograde," Neal said.

"Well," Penelope said insolently, "my life needed that kick in the ass."

"Oh, good," Neal said. "I'm glad you see it that way, because it's going back in retrograde next month."

"No!" Lipstick cried.

"I'm staying home sick," Penelope said.

"For three weeks straight?" Dana asked.

"For as long as it takes, just to be sure." Penelope laughed.

15

Over the next few weeks, the call girls of the famed Coffee Klatch—Olga, Bernadette, Randi, and Tania—were all questioned by the police and IRS. All of them, with the exception of Tania, the foot fetishist, were arrested—and promptly released after announcing they'd made a deal to testify against the mayor.

But the sudden fame was good for their careers. Olga ended up posing seminude with her finger to her lips on the cover of *Maxim,* Bernadette did a piece for *AARP The Magazine* on sex and the aging woman, Randi had a pictorial in *Penthouse,* and Tania appeared in *Us Weekly* on the arm of a well-known action star/foot devotee. All of them signed a deal with VH1 for a reality show called *Celebu-Sex: Kinky Star Secrets,* and collaborated on a book titled *Hook Your Husband for Life: Keep the Man You Love from Straying with Sex Secrets from the Pros.* They all vowed—mostly for legal reasons—that they'd all quit "the business" for good.

• • •

Mayor Ed Swallows, who'd built his reputation as a politician tough on crime and prostitution, didn't fare as well. He stonewalled the press for a week, but once the girls started talking, more women came out of the woodwork to claim he'd paid them for their services. One even had a videotape of her servicing the mayor that was bought by one of the entertainment news shows and aired to huge ratings for more than a week.

Swallows, after consulting lawyers and his real estate magnate father, resigned in disgrace, finally understanding that the only thing people hate more than a criminal is a hypocritical criminal. Happily, his wife—who'd once told *Dateline NBC* that Hillary Clinton was a fool for standing by Bill Clinton after the president had so callously humiliated her by diddling an intern under Hillary's own roof—stood by his side, having realized that while she no longer had the cachet of being the mayor's wife, the ex-mayor was still worth $2.4 billion, which was a lot more than she'd get in a divorce, thanks to the airtight prenup she'd signed seventeen years earlier.

Neal and David moved in together.

As for the girls, well, they were all on a new track.

Penelope became a minicelebrity in New York for a month. The hullabaloo eventually died down, and she settled into becoming the entertainment reporter for NY Access, which, without having to dodge Trace's clammy hands, was actually fun.

Marge still wouldn't give up the idea of the "Call Girl Coffee Klatch"—so instead, Penelope hosted a once-a-week show called *The Klatch,* which was a sort of talk show featuring whatever dregs of society Marge could summon into the studio on a Tuesday night. Penelope's only complaint was that the name of the show sounded like something she'd once caught from a one-night stand in college. But Thomas was producing it, so she was happy.

And every Tuesday night they'd go back to Penelope's place and intimately discuss whatever bedroom techniques they'd learned during the evening's show.

Penelope's parents, Susan and Jim, continued to live unhappily together, calling their daughter thrice weekly to complain that they couldn't see her on air in Cincinnati.

Lipstick started an actual business with her Dauphin designs while dabbling in society journalism. As a contributor to *Y*, she was no longer on social patrol every night, but responsible for two to three articles every month. It was an arrangement that suited all involved. Jack was happy to tell everyone in town and the fashion community that he'd found her and encouraged her the whole time to become the brilliant new talent that she was. Her father, happy that Lipstick had started an actual business, seeded her new company with $150,000. Within a year she paid him back and, working out of her second bedroom, expanded the line from dresses into sportswear and ready-to-wear. Not a month went by when her creations weren't featured or worn by models in *Y, Vogue, Glamour, Elle,* and other fashion magazines. Lipstick no longer had the time to look up Socialstatus .com and, in fact, even blocked it from her computer.

But the best part for her was the sense of self and confidence that came from working hard at what she loved—and reaping the rewards. The change in her was apparent to everyone, even if they couldn't figure out exactly what was different. Was it that she now walked into a room with her back straight and shoulders held high? Was it that she made eye contact and never second-guessed herself? Or her refusal to be drawn into petty society gossip that had been the focus of her world from junior high on? Whatever it was, everyone agreed, Lipstick wore a permanent glow.

In an odd twist, she and Bitsy became friends, of sorts. Bitsy accepted the position of Dauphin's "ambassador." Lipstick threw Bitsy a free dress every month in exchange for Bitsy hosting cocktail parties/trunk shows for the socialites Lipstick no longer had regular contact with, but who paid full price for her clothes and then wore them to galas and got photographed in them.

And while she no longer lived at 198 Sullivan, Lipstick was over at least three times a week—for yoga with the girls and to see Zach, who was not only her strongest supporter, but blew Thad—and the rest of the men she'd ever dated—out of the water in every single way.

Old man Kornberg was disappointed that Dana withdrew her application for full partnership at Struck, Struck & Kornberg but said he understood. "Dana, you're one of the firm's best and brightest," he told her. "When you're ready, we're here." Within a week Dana's hair started growing back.

Dana used her extra time to invest in a good psychotherapist who taught her how to deal with stress, forgive and forget Noah, and finally, to throw out her scale. She even allowed Lipstick and Penelope to drag her out to a social function at least once a week. Meanwhile, she and Gerard went on that date, which led to a second and third—and an actual relationship that wasn't tinged with self-doubt, loathing, or trying to be someone she wasn't.

Acknowledgments

Thanks to the following—without your help I would be a complete and utter mess: my family, the *New York Post,* Richard Johnson, Kate Lee, Elizabeth Spiers, Sloane Crosley, Raina Penchansky, Greer Hendricks, Judith Curr, Sarah Walsh, Elaine Goldsmith-Thomas, Chip Kidd, Hampton Carney, Jeff Klein, Marcy Engelman, and many others I am sure I forgot.